P9-EMJ-889

DISCARDED

Bruce County Public Library
1243 MacKenzie Rd.
Port Elgin, Ontario  N0H 2C6

Books by Adrienne Kress

# THE EXPLORERS

*THE DOOR IN THE ALLEY*

*THE RECKLESS RESCUE*

*THE QUEST FOR THE KID*

# THE EXPLORERS
## THE QUEST FOR THE KID

# ADRIENNE KRESS

Illustrated by Matthew C. Rockefeller

DELACORTE PRESS

This is a work of fiction. Names, characters, places, and incidents either are the product of the author's imagination or are used fictitiously. Any resemblance to actual persons, living or dead, events, or locales is entirely coincidental.

Text copyright © 2019 by Adrienne Kress
Jacket art and interior illustrations copyright © 2019 by Matthew C. Rockefeller

All rights reserved. Published in the United States by Delacorte Press, an imprint of Random House Children's Books, a division of Penguin Random House LLC, New York.

Delacorte Press is a registered trademark and the colophon is a trademark of Penguin Random House LLC.

Visit us on the Web! rhcbooks.com

Educators and librarians, for a variety of teaching tools, visit us at
RHTeachersLibrarians.com

*Library of Congress Cataloging-in-Publication Data*
Names: Kress, Adrienne. | Rockefeller, Matt, illustrator.
Title: The quest for the kid / Adrienne Kress ; illustrated by Matthew C. Rockefeller.
Description: First edition. | New York : Delacorte Press, [2019] |
Series: The explorers; [3] |
Summary: "On the run from nefarious, nameless thugs, Sebastian and Evie must travel the world to reunite the other explorers from the Filipendulous Five if they are to put all their clues together and find Evie's grandfather before it's too late" —Provided by publisher.
Identifiers: LCCN 2018059291 (print) | LCCN 2018061240 (ebook) |
ISBN 0-978-1-101-94015-0 (el) | ISBN 978-1-101-94013-6 (hardback) |
ISBN 978-1-101-94014-3 (glb)
Subjects: | CYAC: Adventure and adventurers—Fiction. | Secret societies—
Fiction. | Missing persons—Fiction. | Voyages and travels—Fiction. |
BISAC: JUVENILE FICTION / Action & Adventure / General. | JUVENILE
FICTION / Social Issues / Friendship. | JUVENILE FICTION /Mysteries &
Detective Stories.
Classification: LCC PZ7.K8838 (ebook) | LCC PZ7.K8838 Que 2019 (print) |
DDC [Fic]—dc23

The text of this book is set in 12-point Sabon.
Interior design by Michelle Gengaro

Printed in the United States of America
10 9 8 7 6 5 4 3 2 1
First Edition

Random House Children's Books supports the First Amendment and celebrates the right to read.

*For Scott*

The best kinds of stories, as we all know, start with pigs in teeny hats. Then they continue and take you to far-off countries and involve great white sharks and K-pop bands. Some stories start in the middle of the sentence and with brand-new characters you've never met. And still others begin suddenly and unexpectedly with a random paragraph for some reason.

And if you're really, really lucky, some stories combine all those things.

And also maybe involve me getting to play the French horn.

No?

No French horn?

You sure?

Okay. No, that's cool. That's . . . cool.

# PART ONE

The Quest for the Kid

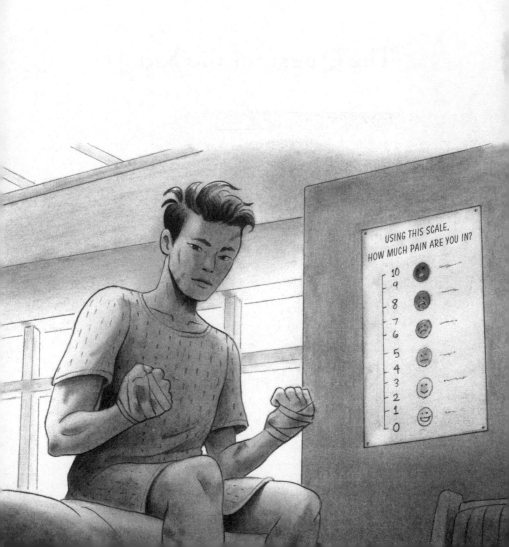

The Kid sat staring at the chart of faces. Little circles showing expressions ranging from very happy to very sad. "Using this scale, how much pain are you in?" read the bubble letters printed on top.

He stared at the palms of his hands. They were wrapped in white gauze. Some red could be seen on the bandage of the right one. He balled his hands into fists. They stung but felt kind of right.

"Dangerous business, stunt driving," the doctor said.

The Kid nodded. But of course, it wasn't. Not really. It was far less dangerous than what he had been through in his former career. This time, though, things had gone wrong. How had the crew not seen the unfinished road?

How could he not have taken it upon himself to check out the set? Time pressures. "Get it all done in one take. We only have the helicopter for one day." Stupid excuses. All of it was so stupid. He'd almost fallen to his death over the side of a cliff. All for what? For a movie? Not even a very good movie, if the script he'd glanced over was anything to go by. Thank goodness for fast-acting second assistant directors coming to save your life.

"Well, you're good to go when you're ready." The doctor smiled at him briefly and then left the room.

The Kid sighed and slipped off the table and onto the floor. Time to put himself back together. He reached for his jeans and slipped them on under the hospital robe before taking it off. Then he put on his shirt. Then he reached into his pants pocket and pulled out a small water-filled vial attached to a thin leather string. He stared at it for a moment.

There was a knock on the door. Quickly he put the vial around his neck and hid it under the shirt. "Yeah," he said.

A man entered. Someone he'd never seen before.

"Charles Wu?" asked the man, with a smooth British accent. If the man hadn't used his stage name, the Kid might have been suspicious. But he was used to Hollywood types showing up out of the blue, and he just sighed inwardly.

"Yeah."

"I have a job offer for you," the man said, getting straight to the point.

The Kid sighed and almost burst out laughing. "Dude, this is so not the time or the place. Talk to my agent."

"Your agent seems to be MIA." That was true. The Kid hadn't been able to get in touch with Annalise for two days, now that he thought about it. "How would you like to work on a project that's low-risk, well paid, and safe? And very easy."

"Never been a fan of any of those things," said the Kid. He tucked in his shirt and grabbed his leather jacket off the back of the chair. He walked past the man to the door.

"Think about it," said the man, reaching into the inside pocket of his tweed blazer. He pulled out a business card and passed it to the Kid. "Call me if you're interested."

The Kid slipped the card into the back pocket of his jeans without looking at it. Then he pulled out his sunglasses and put them on. "See ya," he said, then walked out into the hospital corridor.

He strode with purpose and a little swagger as he made his way to the outside world and took a deep breath of cool nighttime air.

Yes, breathing was a nice thing that he was still able to do. His mind flashed to dangling off the side of the cliff that morning. The memory was so vivid, he could feel the fear rush through his system as if he was still there.

*Low-risk.*

*Safe.*

*Very easy.*

The Kid crossed in front of the taxis and made his way to the parking lot, and eventually reached his bright red BMW 4 Series convertible. He smiled when he saw it. His agent's assistant had brought it for him, knowing full well that there was no way the Kid was taking a taxi home.

After slipping into the driver's seat, he adjusted all the settings. He took in a deep breath and sighed long and hard.

*Low-risk.*

*Safe.*

*Very easy.*

He turned on the engine.

*Good money.*

The Kid peeled out of the parking lot and roared toward the freeway, the wind in his hair, his palms, stinging a little, holding the wheel.

# ➤ CHAPTER 1 ◄

## In which there is a phone.

Sebastian stared at the phone in Benedict's palm, held out toward him, a kind offer. The buzz of the Los Angeles International Airport dimmed as Sebastian focused in on the small black box.

He didn't know what to do.

Well, that is to say, with the phone. He knew in general what he was supposed to do. Or at least, what his friend Evie needed him to do: she needed him to help her find and rescue her grandfather Alistair, leader of the formerly famous exploring team the Filipendulous Five. Alistair was Evie's only living relative. Sebastian knew that they had to put the team back together, then use the information hidden in the letters that Alistair had sent each of them to rescue him. They'd already gotten as far as finding and recruiting two of the four other explorers—animal expert Catherine and cartographer/photographer Benedict. And Sebastian knew that what he had to do was stay away from the scary trio of thugs in black leather jackets who had shown up a week earlier and were also after Alistair. The men wanted a map that the team had that led to a waterfall that was supposedly a fountain of youth. He knew he had to stay away from those men because he had memorized the key to the map before destroying it and was therefore very important to the bad guys, who had tried to kidnap him. Repeatedly.

All this he knew.

What he didn't know was what he should do with a small phone sitting in a cartographer/photographer's palm.

Now, it wasn't about knowing how phones worked. That was obvious. Or why Benedict wanted him to use it—he wanted Sebastian to call his parents.

It was about knowing whether or not he *should*.

The thing was, Sebastian had put off calling his parents for a long time, coming up with explanations that pushed reasonableness boundaries at every opportunity. There was the fact that he and the others simply had to keep running away fast from the men in black who wanted his brain, so that he didn't really have a second or the brain capacity to spare a moment to stop and make a phone call. There was the fact that when he did have a moment, it was while he was accidentally being held hostage by the manager of a K-pop band. The truth was, though, all that was behind him, and Benedict had a phone and Sebastian could have called by now.

But when they'd been in the capital city of Newish Isle and Benedict had been busy forging a passport for Sebastian to get him back home, and they'd had to sit around waiting for that—instead of maybe looking for a phone—Sebastian had decided to focus his mind on the moral question of breaking the law by using a fake passport, taking into consideration the fact that kidnap victims certainly were allowed a little bit of leeway to get back to their home country. To be fair, he had, for a moment, thought that maybe he should get his parents to send him his passport instead. But that would have meant talking to them, and that would have meant he'd have had to make a decision about whether he wanted to call them. So he hadn't bothered making the suggestion of having his parents send him his passport. He had known that he'd be calling them soon enough. And from American soil. And when he was safe and sound. Which he'd thought might freak them out less. Maybe only a hair less, though.

It was interesting that Evie hadn't made the suggestion either.

He'd hoped no one would ever actually say anything to him about the whole parents issue. He, Evie, Catherine, and Benedict had made it to Cairns, Australia, and then to Sydney. But when they'd been waiting for their connecting flight home, Evie had finally broached the topic.

He'd said he didn't want to talk about it.

She hadn't bugged him about it since.

Which was weird, since, of course, she was very good at bugging him about things.

Now they were in LA, ready to seek out the Kid. Not that they knew for sure he was here, but Benedict seemed pretty confident. The Kid had always wanted to be a stunt-car driver, evidently, and Benedict said that he'd once seen the Kid very briefly in a movie when his face had been accidentally visible.[1] So they'd traveled thousands of miles on a hunch. Definitely not something Sebastian would ever have approved of before. Not really something he approved of now.

---

[1] I too have once been seen briefly in a movie where my face was accidentally visible, which is strange because I don't remember filming that movie. . . .

But the hunch voyage had given him time to think. Time was up.

"It's really time, I think," said Benedict, no judgment in his tone of voice, though Sebastian was starting to suspect that regardless of tone Benedict did have opinions and wasn't always mildly ambivalent.

"You're right. . . ." Sebastian glanced around the airport as if looking for a way out, some kind of magical solution to his situation.

That was when he saw it.

"I think I'll use that, though." He pointed at the pay phone on the wall near the restrooms. It looked a little out of place, sad and lonely, unused and unloved. And just what Sebastian needed. Why did he need it? He wasn't sure. Clearly his consciousness wasn't quite up to speed with his problem-solving subconscious.

"How strange," said Benedict, but he withdrew his phone and allowed Sebastian to wander over to the pay one.

"I'll come too!" said Evie, joining him with a bright smile. "For support," she said a little more quietly, so as—he imagined—not to embarrass him in front of the grown-ups.

Sebastian appreciated the gesture, but he'd really wanted to do this alone. With no witnesses.

Witnesses.

As if he was about to commit a crime or something. What a strange thing to think.

They approached the phone and then stared at it for a moment. Sebastian almost felt sorry for it. Nobody used public phones anymore. This one had become kind of a museum piece, but it had not been treated half so respectfully. Someone with Wite-Out had tagged it with a flourish of initials. Others had left behind a couple of stickers peeled off bananas. Still someone else had evidently taken something sharp to it and carved away at the dark plastic, not really creating anything particularly profound, just using the phone as an outlet for some seriously pent-up frustration.

"Are you going to call them?" asked Evie. Sebastian glanced at her. She looked very Evie. Wide-eyed, hopeful, generally excited. But there was something beneath the surface that he couldn't really read exactly. It was weird. He had missed her so much when they'd been apart, while he'd been kidnapped, until she'd come to rescue him, and he had been so happy when they'd finally come together again. But he'd forgotten just how much pressure it was having her around, him not wanting to let her down. His life wasn't just about him and his plans anymore.

He didn't really answer her question. Just kind of shook his head and nodded at the same time. Then he turned back to the phone.

Sebastian picked up the receiver. It felt a little sticky.

"Do you need some change?" Evie's voice sounded far away, small and thin, like it was coming through the speaker of the phone. Sebastian peered at the phone carefully. He noticed a question mark drawn on it, black on black, almost invisible.

"Or . . . should I let you have some space, maybe?"

Sebastian looked at her again, again no idea what to say. They stared at each other for a moment, and then he nodded. She gave him a quick smile and headed back toward Catherine and Benedict.

This was it. This was the moment of truth. He had to make this call. But what did he want to say? What did he really want?

Deep down.

*I think I have to ask them if I can continue to adventure,* Sebastian thought. *I think if maybe I make it sound like extra credit for school or something, they might think it's worth it. Seeing the world. Experiencing different cultures.*

That sort of thing.

It had been the one hope Sebastian had. That his parents would consider such bold exploits a most excellent educational opportunity. But it was a small hope. His parents weren't that interested in alternative forms of education. Even sending Sebastian to a special math-and-science school had made them a little uncomfortable.

The biggest problem really was that his parents were smart people. If there was a convincing argument against Sebastian staying with this adventure, they would make it. And there were plenty of those types of arguments. He knew a ton of reasons himself.

He put the phone to his ear and inserted several coins. He raised his fingers to the key pad and held them there, not pushing down. Instead he ran his fingers over the buttons, feeling the texture of the metal and the bumps of braille indicating to the visually impaired what the numbers were.

*Just do it.*

*Or don't do it.*

*But do something. Even if it is nothing.*

The anxiety of not knowing what to do was probably at this point worse than any bad news his parents might share. He'd never felt like this before.

He felt trapped.

Sebastian hung up the phone and stared at it, mindlessly wiping the stickiness off his right hand and onto his pants.

"Well, what did they say?" asked Evie.

He turned around, shocked. He hadn't heard her come back.

Sebastian felt put on the spot. Which was probably why he said what he did. "They are glad that I'm safe." He gulped quickly before forging on. "And said that they'd tell the school what was going on, and said that as long as I stayed in touch, this seemed like an excellent learning experience." He widened his eyes in shock at his own lie, wondering whether Evie could tell what he'd just done.

But she apparently didn't notice the guilt written all over his face.[2] Or, maybe, chose not to notice. He wasn't sure. Instead she smiled broadly and clapped her hands. "Oh, yay! Oh, I'm so happy! This is so wonderful!"

---

[2] Obviously not literally. That's not a thing that people have written on their faces. Except, that is, for Gerald Haversham, the infamous bank robber, who had a giant tattoo of the word "guilty" on his face and still managed not to be picked out of the police lineup.

And true to form, she launched herself at him. He was used to her hugs by now, and better prepared, but this hug didn't make him feel better the way they usually did. Instead it made him feel even more anxious. She released him and said, "I'm going to go tell Catherine and Benedict! Next stop—find the Kid!" She flew off, leaving Sebastian alone with his thoughts and the sticky phone.

What had he done? It was one thing to lie to bad guys, something he had come to learn was occasionally necessary in a life-and-death situation. Or to lie to managers of famous K-pop bands, which might be a matter of self-preservation. Even, well, to lie to himself if he needed to make himself feel braver. Sometimes, as he was slowly learning, lying wasn't always so bad. But there were certain lines that surely, surely should never be crossed. And lying to a friend? To Evie? That felt like a big no-no.

She waved him over then, still grinning that big toothy grin of hers, and Sebastian's feet felt like they were sunk deep in quick-drying cement.[3]

If he said something now, maybe it wouldn't be a

---

[3] Slow-drying cement, on the other hand, feels pretty much like you're standing in a puddle. Which is totally fine if you get out of it right away. But if you are enjoying the feeling of cool liquid against your ankles, you might still end up stuck about twelve hours later. Trust me on this one.

big deal. If he told her the truth now, he could be forgiven. But then she'd try to convince him to call his parents for real, and then he would have to, and he'd probably get yelled at. He probably would have to go home.

He'd tell Evie later. Maybe after. Or maybe a perfect time would present itself. Conveniently.

Besides, she'd understand. She was the one who'd wanted to go on this whole adventure in the first place. She was the one who had wanted his help. She knew how important all this was. And she'd been the one to teach him how to lie in the first place.

Yes.

Sebastian mentally unstuck his feet from the imaginary cement.

She would totally get it.

She just had to.

## ➤ CHAPTER 2 ◄

# In which . . . Hollywood.

It had taken some effort for them to collect their bags and rent a car and then, despite Benedict's excellent sense of direction as the team's cartographer, for Benedict to drive them out of the maze of streets and parking lots that was the airport itself.[4] Eventually they found themselves on their way to the West Coast operations of the Explorers Society, where they would be staying while they searched for the Kid, on the freeway and predictably stuck in heavy traffic. The inability to do anything about it, the fact that they had to sit there

---

[4] Interesting to note, I'm currently attempting to drive out of an airport at this moment, and it's been three days. I may have to live here now.

and inch along with no possible second option, gave Sebastian a great deal of anxiety.

And this was on top of the anxiety he was already feeling.

"We could play a game!" said Evie, sitting next to him in the backseat.

No one said anything.

Sebastian glanced over at Evie, but she just shrugged and happily stared out the window. He wondered what it was like to be so sure of oneself the way she was. There had been a time when he'd felt that way too. But it felt like ages ago. Everything had changed ever since the pig in the teeny hat. No! Before that. Ever since he'd seen that sign for the Explorers Society in the alley.

It turned out that mulling over his confused feelings and his questions about a sense of self was the perfect car game to pass the time. Despite the mess of traffic they were in and the long journey into the city, Sebastian was quite surprised when he heard Catherine say, "We're here."

Sebastian refocused his gaze out the window as they drove off the freeway and into the side streets. "So, this is Hollywood," he said as they moved onto a wide boulevard with tall palm trees rising up on either side.

"No," said Benedict. "This is Los Angeles. That is Hollywood." He pointed directly ahead as they turned a corner to reveal the green and brown hills in the distance and a very famous white sign perched near the top.

"Oh! The Hollywood sign! That's so cool!" said Evie, leaning as far forward as her seat belt would allow.

Sebastian knew of the sign. He'd seen it in movies and such. But the experience now was a little surreal. It was the first time he'd ever seen the sign when a camera hadn't been up close, or zooming over top of it. When swelling music wasn't being played. When it was kind of just a sign. And small-looking, being far away and high up. He was feeling almost disappointed.

Clearly, though, not Evie. "I've never seen it like this—in the distance, but right in front of me. It's so . . . real."

Sebastian wasn't sure what that meant. So instead of saying anything, he sat back in his seat and rolled down his window. The warm air filled the car, smelling vaguely of citrus.[5] He watched as the storefronts got

---

[5] By which I mean smelling like lemons and oranges and stuff. Not like Vaguely Citrus, the indie band from the early 1990s. That wouldn't be pleasant-smelling at all.

nicer- and nicer-looking, and the people got shinier. One woman he saw wore the largest sunglasses he'd ever seen, and he was pretty sure they were framed with diamonds. The woman's tiny dog appeared to have its own diamond collar.

The street they were on opened up onto an even wider boulevard, and the palm trees now ran along either side at regular intervals. Sebastian arched his neck to look at them.

"Such strange things when you think about it," said Evie, doing the same on her side of the car. "Long sticks with leaves way at the top. And coconuts." She squinted, holding her hand to her forehead to shield her eyes from the sun. "Are there coconuts on palm trees in Los Angeles? Do movie stars have a constant fear of them falling on their heads or, more likely, denting the hoods of their expensive cars? Like fish?"

"Like fish?" asked Sebastian.

"Sometimes fish fall on people from the sky," said Evie like it was something perfectly normal.

"They do," agreed Catherine from up front.

"Well, okay then," Sebastian said, not really knowing what else to say.

They continued on their drive, leaving the ritzy neighborhood, and eventually made their way into one that, while it wasn't at all like Sebastian's neighborhood at home, felt a lot more like his neighborhood at home. But the houses weren't as tall, and they had arches and tiled roofs. They were also painted various vibrant colors like blue, pink, and orange. Still, they looked cozy and like houses built for families.

A knot formed in his gut then. The reminder of home. And parents. It was hard to know what the guilt was specifically referring to, though, in this moment. Was it that his parents were probably totally upset with his not coming home or that he'd lied to Evie about them? He didn't want to guess which it was, because either possibility was pretty bad, and feeling one and not the other, regardless of which one, would only make the guilt worse.

"This is nice," said Evie. "Is this where the West Coast Explorers Society is?"

"No," replied Catherine. "That is."

Above the rooftops was a towering black skyscraper wedged between two smaller silver ones. On the flight over, Sebastian had been surprised to learn that there was another Explorers Society building. He had also been surprised he was surprised. Of course, it made perfect sense that there would be, and he'd felt instantly let down by his own logic that hadn't quickly realized that obviously the nature of the job would dictate that there were explorers everywhere, all over the country—all over the world, for that matter. And they needed places, therefore, to meet up or sleep over no matter where they were.

"And you've been banned from it too? From every building that the society has?" Evie had asked Catherine.

"Yes," Catherine had replied softly. "But, like with the East Coast, the West Coast has agreed to help us until we find Alistair. And then . . ." She'd stopped and looked a little sad.

Now as Sebastian stared at the tall black building rising above the houses, he wondered what all this meant. Not for Evie or for him. But for the former members of the Filipendulous Five. To return to a place where you weren't wanted. Somewhere that had once been home.

He threw Evie a glance. She returned it, looking pretty much as he felt.

He turned back. "So that's West Coast operations? That's huge," he said.

"Not the entire building," Benedict explained. "It also contains two acting agencies, one modeling agency, and the place where they determine the expiration dates on food packages." The building vanished from sight behind some trees just as Benedict pulled into a small driveway and slowed to a stop next to a Spanish colonial home. Rolling down the window, he leaned out and pushed a buzzer attached to a small speaker. There was the sound of white noise crackling, and then: "Password."

Benedict glanced at Catherine, who quickly passed him a piece of paper.

He read it: "Marco."

There was a pause. "Polo," answered the scratchy voice from the speaker.

The garage door opened. Sebastian was confused. If they were going to that black skyscraper in the distance, why were they parking at this house?

Unless . . .

"This is going to be another special garage, isn't it?" asked Sebastian.

"Another?" asked Evie.

"Yeah. The K-pop band had a secret entrance to their place too," replied Sebastian as they drove straight into a small single-car garage.

The inside of this one certainly did not look special, but if his experience with the most popular K-pop band in South Korea, the Lost Boys, had taught him anything about secret entrances through garages, Sebastian knew looks could be deceiving. The garbage can in the corner, the kids' bikes lean-

ing against the wall to his side, they all seemed innocent enough. And maybe they were. Then again, so did the shelves along the rear wall they were facing, piled high with tools and Christmas decorations and school projects from years ago.[6] But the shelves began to sink into the earth, and a grinding noise suddenly started to shake the car. A large, bouncy workout ball tumbled off the very top shelf and rolled by Evie's door, as if to say, *What the heck is going on? I'm outta here!*

"Whoa," said Evie as the shelves completely vanished into the ground and revealed a steep ramp down into the darkness beyond. "Cool."

Benedict started the car moving again and carefully maneuvered into the tight space in front of them, driving into a long dim tunnel lit at intervals.

"Let's not forget how they feel about us here," said Catherine. "Please be on your best behavior."

Evie made a sound that Sebastian took to mean she'd found that request a little insulting. To be honest, so did he. He and Evie were always on their best behavior. At least whenever possible. At least when they weren't being chased by bad guys. Besides, they

---

[6] My school projects from two years ago are all about Alberta, Canada. And they're all in my parents' garage.

weren't the problem; the Filipendulous Five were. If anything, he and Evie should be keeping an eye on Catherine and Benedict.

But neither of them said anything. Instead they sat in silence as the car traveled on for what felt like forever.

Eventually the tunnel opened up and they discovered they were . . . inside a parking garage again. But this one was much larger, with many levels and many cars. They pulled up to an enthusiastic man in a bright red jacket waving his arms at them. He motioned for Benedict to roll down his window.

"Hello! I'll take the car now," said the enthusiastic man.

Benedict nodded and turned to the others. "I guess they have a valet to park for us. Everyone out!"

They piled out of the car, grabbed their things, and stood as the man jumped happily into the front seat and sped off, leaving them quite alone.

"Now what?" asked Evie.

Sebastian glanced around the cavernous space. Then he noticed something totally out of place. "Uh . . . maybe we follow that?"

Everyone turned to see a red carpet that ran right through the center of the garage and disappeared in the distance.

"Yes, I think we do," said Catherine.

Across the garage, they followed the red carpet wending this way and weaving that way, until it ended eventually at a small wooden desk. Behind the desk sat a man who seemed to have walked straight out of a very fancy magazine ad. He was wearing brown tweed pants, a brown tweed vest, and a creaseless crisp blue shirt.

"Welcome," he said, standing up to his precise six feet and smiling with teeth so white that Sebastian had to blink a few times.[7] "Sign in, please."

They took turns signing their names with a pen-shaped metal stick onto a computer tablet, and then the man with a twinkle perfectly situated at a sixty-seven-degree angle in his right eye led them to a bank of elevator doors that opened directly when they arrived. They stepped inside, and the four of them turned in time to see the man give them a pleasant nod as the elevator doors shut and they were whooshed in the general direction of up.

"That was a very good-looking explorer," said Evie, breaking the silence.

"Oh, well, from what I've been told about West Coast operations, he's not an explorer. He's an actor. He's the Explorers Society concierge between acting gigs," replied Catherine.

---

[7] Even I am blinking right now, and I'm just writing about it.

"An actor!" said Sebastian, more loudly than he probably should have, as they shot out of the dark and were surrounded, on three sides and below, by Los Angeles views.

"Oh!" said Evie. Unlike Sebastian, she made her exclamation at just the correct volume that one would expect in response to such a sight. It was a dizzying experience, looking down at the ground falling far away below them. Around them Los Angeles seemed to smile in greeting in her hazy way. The sun was glinting off the Pacific Ocean in the distance, and the bright glow warmed the faces of the elevator occupants.

They stood in rapt silence for a moment, gazing around them, taking in, Sebastian was pretty sure, not just the view, but the whole experience of being whisked up to the society and what was waiting for them. And suddenly they were surrounded by black again. And then the elevator stopped.

The doors opened to reveal a woman who, if she had been a man, would have been the identical twin of the concierge downstairs. She wore the exact same outfit, and her smile was equally blinding. The only difference was that her eye twinkle was at sixty-eight degrees.

"Welcome to the Explorers Society," she said

as they stepped into a gleaming white marble foyer. "Please follow me. Alejandro would like to see you."

Catherine exchanged a quick glance with Benedict, and then Sebastian traded one of his own with Evie. He obviously couldn't read her mind, but for some reason it felt like she'd been able to read his concern. "Yup," she seemed to say. "Here we go."

Here we go indeed.

# ➤ CHAPTER 3 ◀

## In which we meet a president and a pug.

Evie took a deep breath. She couldn't help but remember the society board members yelling at her and one another when it had been revealed that the person Evie and Sebastian wanted to save was her grandfather Alistair Drake. She knew her last name made explorers kind of freak out, and she wasn't really in the mood to have it happen all over again in LA, especially when they needed to get to the Kid as fast as possible.

She exhaled with determination, and the four of them nervously followed the woman. The woman led them down a white hallway full of natural light, undecorated except for one giant femur bone displayed at the far end on a chrome pedestal. They made a right at the bone and entered an equally gleaming and minimalist white dining room with floor-to-ceiling windows along the far wall. It was full of sounds of clinking, sparkling cutlery on pristine white plates, and murmuring explorers in hushed conversation. Their water glasses shone in the brilliant sun. None of the patrons turned to look at them, but Evie could tell they were still being watched. She held her head high. She would not be intimidated, and she would get her answers.

The woman took them over to a man sitting by himself at a table on a platform raised maybe a foot off the floor in the corner where two walls of windows connected. He had thick black hair, graying at the temples, and a pair of the most exuberant-looking eyebrows Evie had ever seen. In fact she'd never before even considered that eyebrows could look exuberant. The man was wearing a deep red shiny suit with a gray T-shirt beneath and seemed altogether relaxed and content. When they stopped in front of his table, he looked up at them thoughtfully for a moment. Then, after wiping the corners of his mouth with a surprisingly clean napkin, he folded his hands in his lap and spoke with a rich voice tinged with a slight accent.

"Forgive me for not standing, but I only rise for people I respect. Please have a seat."

It was the least-gracious gracious welcome Evie had experienced so far in all the welcomes she'd had during this adventure. And for a moment she didn't know what to do.

And then she noticed that the other three had sat rather awkwardly, so she did too, perching herself on the edge of her pristine white seat.

"Mr. Mendoza, we want to thank you for your hospitality," said Benedict in his indifferent tone of voice. It came across as kind of rude, actually, as if he wasn't thanking the man but rather quite the opposite. Evie thought about it. Benedict's tone rarely reflected his level of interest, passion, or intent. Meanwhile Catherine was downright flummoxed by humans, even more so than Sebastian was, which was saying something. Neither Catherine nor Benedict was really the right person to express the level of gratitude needed to help calm the general level of, well, hate that most society members felt for the team.

Evie realized in that moment that there was only one person here who maybe could express the proper gratitude. She smiled brightly.

"Yes! It's so lovely of you to help," she said quickly, eyes wide. She reached out her hand, and Alejandro, being a polite sort of person just as she'd thought, had no option but to take it and shake. "It's so tricky, I know, and I get that there are complicated feelings, and feelings should be complicated, but it's still super-nice of you to let us stay here and use your resources."

The adults stared at her for a moment. So did Sebastian. She really didn't care. Someone had to take charge of this situation.

"You must be the granddaughter. You have passion, like your grandfather. It got him into trouble. Be wary," said Alejandro, though not unkindly. "But you are most welcome. Your access will be limited. You do understand, of course." He said the last bit turning back to Catherine and Benedict.

"Of course," said Catherine.

"What does 'limited' mean?" asked Sebastian.

For the first time Alejandro made eye contact with the boy. He managed to make a simple look in Sebastian's direction seem somehow elegant. "Limited. Ah, it means—how to say it?—it means 'restricted in size.' 'Small.' 'Less than.'"

Sebastian stared at the man for a moment. "What?" he said. "No. No, I know what the word means. I meant, what does 'limited access' mean in practical terms?"

"Ah." Alejandro leaned back in his chair and tented his fingers together, tapping them thoughtfully against each other. "You will not be allowed to use any of the public spaces—the archives or this dining room, for example—or, quite plainly, leave your suite aside from entering and departing the building. In general you may not wander through the society. Meals will be provided as room service."

"We're not going to do anything bad," said Evie. This all sounded rather unfair. They weren't toddlers stumbling about knocking into things. It was really judgmental of him, quite frankly, to treat them with so much suspicion.

"No one ever thinks they are going to do anything bad. And yet bad things happen, do they not?" He looked pointedly at Benedict and Catherine.

Evie huffed and sank back in her chair, arms folded across her chest.

"Your stay here is not about wants but about needs," continued Alejandro. "We will provide you what you need. Your wants you will have to satisfy elsewhere."

"Yes, thank you, Mr. Mendoza," said Catherine quickly. "We understand. We won't wander. When we're here, we will stick to our rooms and our common area."

"Yes, and of course the pool," added Alejandro.

"Wait, the pool?" asked Evie skeptically. How was that not a public space?

"We may be untrusting, but we aren't uncivilized."

At that, Alejandro made an elegant sweeping motion with his hand, and the woman in brown tweed reappeared, her teeth reflecting brightly in the silverware on the table. "Take them to the East Coast suite."

She gave a nod and extended her arm, and the four of them rose to follow her. Evie looked at Alejandro as they walked away, but he was already deeply immersed in the view outside. She turned and had to rush to catch up to the others.

"Do you think we'll ever meet a not-weird explorer?" she whispered to Sebastian when they'd returned to the bank of elevators.

"Unlikely," replied Sebastian. They both watched as a large, imposing man in the tallest cowboy hat she'd ever seen sauntered past them toward the dining room, the spurs on his boots jangling at every step.

Once more they entered the elevator, and with a similar wave to Alejandro's, the woman disappeared as the doors closed and the group was whisked up yet farther. But only for a moment. The elevator abruptly stopped, causing Evie a tiny moment of weightlessness. The doors opened, and she expected once more to be welcomed by a perfect-looking human in a brown tweed vest. But there wasn't one.

Instead they were greeted by a small pug in a teeny brown tweed vest.

"This is silly," said Sebastian.

The dog seemed to agree, and far from sharing the happy disposition of its human counterparts, it seemed soulfully forlorn as it waited for them all to step out of the elevator.

"Hello," said Catherine, her voice soft and warm. She crouched down and offered her hand for the pug to sniff. It did, and then, though still with the same mournful expression, it rubbed its face against her hand. Then it bit her finger and held on.

"Stop it!" said Evie, immediately rushing over.

"No, Evie. It's fine. It doesn't hurt," replied Catherine quickly. "He seems to want to drag me somewhere." And sure enough, they watched the pug tug on her finger, attempting to pull the over-six-foot-tall animal expert after him.

He released the finger and with head held high began to trot down the hallway. The humans followed obediently and were eventually led to a door with a plaque that read EAST COAST SUITE.

"But how did he know?" asked Evie as Catherine gave the dog a solid pat on the head.

Benedict didn't wait for an answer, probably because he knew the dog couldn't actually explain himself, and pushed through the door. They entered another brightly lit modern room, this one with white walls and Danish minimalist brown teak furniture. Again there was a complete wall of windows, this bank obviously facing east, away from the water. The room had a sitting area, a little desk and computer nook, and a small kitchenette—all set down a few steps, sunken from the door.

"Very nice," said Benedict, casually removing his dark green jacket but keeping his camera on and tilting his head slightly to crack his neck. "Everyone choose a room. And once we're settled, let's meet out here to deal with the next step."

Evie looked around, and sure enough there was a hall to her right, along which were several doors. She picked up her bag and gave Sebastian a smile. He looked a little concerned.

"Are you okay?" she asked as the adults passed them and chose their rooms.

"I don't have a bag," he replied.

"Well. I mean, you were kidnapped, you didn't have time to pack." She laughed a bit, imagining a kidnapper actually giving their victim time to pack and maybe feed the cat, grab a few books. It seemed very silly.

Sebastian didn't laugh.

"I'm an accidental adventurer," he said.

"The best kind!" she replied. But nothing she said seemed to shake him from the strange faraway-ness she'd noticed lingering about him since they'd gotten into the car. Since he'd spoken with his parents.

She probably shouldn't pry. Even though she really wanted to.

"Let's choose our rooms," said Sebastian suddenly. And he turned and walked away before she could say anything else.

She shrugged and followed him and watched as he slipped into a room and closed the door behind him. She made her way to the last door in the hall and went into a small white room with more Danish furniture and more windows. Evie put down her bag, crossed over to the windows, and placed her forehead against the cool glass. Positioned like that she almost seemed as if she was floating in space, above the noisy Los Angeles streets.

The accidental adventurer.

She supposed he was.

But so was she. All of this was just a means to an end—a means to rescuing her grandfather. Her only known living family member. The only person she could call family. He was her home. After that, well . . .

After that maybe they would go on chosen, deliberate adventures together.

That would be nice.

Being on-purpose adventurers together.

That would be nice.

She watched the cars zoom about the streets beneath her and thought of the Kid. So many cars and he might be driving one of them right now. But in a stunt-car way. Maybe with other stunt-car drivers even. Like as part of a club or a . . .

That's when she had the idea.

## ➤ CHAPTER 4 ◄

### In which there is planning,
### both out loud and in loud.

Sebastian didn't much feel like leaving the quiet comfort of his room once he'd chosen it. Interacting with people was difficult enough on a day-to-day basis. But interacting with people when you were so conflicted on the inside, when you didn't even know what you wanted, when you had lied to the person closest to you . . . that was the opposite of easy. One could even call it hard.[8]

But he knew he'd hear a knock on his door soon,

---

[8] Me, I'd call it "not easy" just to make sure everyone totally understood what I was going for, but I get that not everyone is me. That would be weird. If they were.

someone wanting to know where he was, what he was doing, why he wasn't with them. The anticipation of the knock was probably worse than the knock itself, and so he stood and wandered over to the door, and opened it before anyone could get there first. Just as Evie had her hand hovering before it.

"Oh!" She laughed. "I was just about to knock."

Sebastian nodded. "Yeah."

They returned to the sitting room, where the adults were waiting for them. Sebastian pulled out one of the kitchen chairs and dropped into in. A little too hard. It hurt. But he didn't say anything because it was embarrassing.

"Okay. So the next step in finding the Kid—" started Benedict, getting down to business.

"Yes!" interrupted Evie with a great deal of enthusiasm. "I've been thinking about it. Since we don't necessarily have access to the resources we'd hoped for, but we are where we are, and I was wondering if there was a society or something, kind of like this one, but for cars. Like a stunt racing association or society . . . for cars . . . ?"

"You mean the SRAC?" asked Benedict.

"Okay," replied Evie.

"The Stunt Racing Association of Car-drivers. Yes.

I was thinking that too. I think you're right. That's our first stop," said Benedict with a soft nod. Then he blinked for a moment, thinking. He leaned forward and added, "I would like to say that I hope I'm right that the Kid is actually a stunt-car driver, and that I'm sorry if I'm not."

"Oh, I think you're right," said Evie. "It definitely all makes sense, and you have an eye for pictures, after all. You see things the rest of us don't. If you saw the Kid in a movie, I believe that you saw the Kid in a movie. 'Trust your gut,' I always say. Or at least I'm saying that now."

Benedict gave her a small smile and then glanced at Sebastian. Sebastian wasn't sure why, so he simply nodded in agreement with everything because, yeah, it did sound like the best option, of course.

"Great," said Catherine. "Benedict and I will go visit SRAC now, if everyone's on board with the plan."

Sebastian's brain suddenly went from all over the place to a singular focus. Evie.

"What do you mean . . . you and Benedict?" asked Evie slowly, each word sliding out of her mouth as she squinted at Catherine.

Catherine wore an expression that Sebastian could

finally understand. It was a kind of fear—but more like a worry—of letting someone down. Like letting Evie in particular down. Benedict, meanwhile, stood up, started putting on his green jacket.

"It makes the most sense if only a couple of us check it out, now that we have a home base. I'm sure you agree that the journey here was tricky enough, organizing four people—" said Catherine.

"Great, so you and I can go, then," said Evie, once more jumping in.

"Evie, please," said Catherine.

"Come on, Catherine. We should get going," said Benedict. Catherine turned, made her way toward the exit, and joined Benedict at the door.

"You can't just do this," said Evie, standing too. "Sebastian, say something!"

"I don't think we have much of a choice," said Sebastian.

"I know you're upset, but trust me that this is better in the long run. It'll be faster this way, and don't you want things to go faster?" asked Catherine.

"I want things to be done right, and you need us. And how do you actually know it'll be faster without us? We have a lot of good ideas and are super-useful." Evie was practically shaking, and Sebastian got it. Not so much the degree of her anger, but the frustration made sense. She made a lot of good points.

"We're wasting time. We'll talk about this when we get back," said Benedict, opening the door. In short order they had passed through and closed it behind them. Leaving the kids alone.

There was a silence. A terrible, tension-filled, waiting-for-the-dam-to-burst silence.

And then: "Are you kidding me?" said Evie, whirling around to Sebastian. "How can they leave us behind? This is *our* adventure, not *theirs*!" She started pacing back and forth so furiously that Sebastian was sure she would dig a groove in the floor.

"It's not really mine either," said Sebastian quietly. Evie kept pacing but looked at him. "Well, it's not! It's yours, and I'm helping, and they're helping, and they should be allowed to help," he said, trying to be helpful. "Isn't the most important thing that we find Alistair as fast as possible?"

Evie sighed hard. "Of course it is. But help is one thing. Taking over, saying we'd make things take longer . . . that's another. I mean, who's to say this will make it faster? And I mean, they knew that they were doing something wrong. Otherwise why would they leave like that? Not respecting us enough to listen?" Her voice was rising in pitch and volume.

"Well, maybe because of—" Sebastian stopped.

Evie also stopped. "Because of what?" she said, standing still and placing her hands on her hips.

"Your reaction." He was now scared of her reaction to that statement.

There was a long pause, and then Evie shook her head. "No. They felt guilty."

"Maybe," replied Sebastian.

"And they think that since they're adults, they know better than us."

That made Sebastian think hard for a moment. It was true that adults often did think they knew what was best. He thought of Suwon, the manager of the Lost Boys, who, in trying to give Sebastian a new family, thinking that was what Sebastian needed to feel better, despite his protests, had essentially held him prisoner.

Evie finally sat down on the sofa with a "Harrumph" sound, crossing her arms over her chest.

Sebastian carefully walked over to the couch and sat beside her.

"Come on. Let it go. There's got to be something useful and important we can do while they're gone," he said. Though, as he said it, he really couldn't think of a thing. *Or we could sleep,* his brain suggested. *That would satisfy both too.*

Evie sat frowning, and breathing loudly through her nose. Finally she exhaled a long slow sigh and looked at him. "Like what?"

That, Sebastian didn't have an answer to. "Well, we could maybe just relax a bit, recharge, appreciate being on solid ground and not being chased by those men in black for once," he said. That sounded really good, actually.

"Yeah . . . ," said Evie, but he could already tell she was thinking about something important.

"What's going on?" he asked.

"I need to think for a second, about what you said about the men. Something kind of clicked right then, but . . . I can't exactly figure out what. Let's go to the pool," she said, standing in a thoughtful daze.

"The pool?" Couldn't they just stay here, in the quiet? In the air-conditioning?

"Well, it's the only other place we're allowed to go," she said, and she made her way back toward her room.

Why did they have to go anywhere, thought Sebastian. Wasn't the point of "going" that once in a while you were allowed to stop going? If you never stopped, how would you know you were going in the first place?

"Come on, Sebastian!" said Evie, poking her head around the corner. "They left swimsuits in our rooms. It's a sign!"

Sebastian nodded. It was time to get going again.

# ➤ CHAPTER 5 ◄

## In which we lounge.

*W*ell, *if one has to not think, this is certainly the way to do it,* thought Evie, closing her eyes and enjoying the sun warming her body. Sitting beside a rooftop pool, the gentle breeze blowing and Shirley Temple drinks being brought to her by smiling individuals in brown tweed was everything she never knew she'd been missing.

She didn't want to be disrespectful to the society headquarters on the East Coast, of course. That was her home. And she generally preferred its dark coziness. Besides, nothing could be better than a tree that burst out through the center of a building up through a huge skylight and housed a lovely tea tree house.

That was awesome. But . . . second best might be a rooftop pool with a view of the Hollywood hills.

Evie opened her eyes and glanced down at the little pug sleeping in the shadow of the umbrella they were sharing. He was clearly off duty, no longer in his brown vest but instead in a T-shirt that read PUG LIFE. Though he still managed somehow to look a little melancholy, despite his general contentment. She looked over at Sebastian sitting on the edge of the pool, dangling his feet very reluctantly into the water, gazing down. She couldn't help but smile. If there was one person here who could make lounging by a pool look totally uncomfortable, it had to be him.

She leaned back and closed her eyes again. She needed to think. That's why she'd wanted the change of scenery. Like back in Australia when she'd sat on the beach to contemplate the existence of Steve the shark, there was something about being near water and in the sun that allowed her brain to work its magic.

And there was something about what Sebastian had said that had stirred something inside her. Something about not being chased by the men in black . . .

Should she be on the lookout? Is that what her brain was trying to tell her? Should she be worried the kidnappers would find them? Probably, though they had run away quite successfully. Still, those men were

pretty great at finding people. Who were those guys? What was their deal with chasing them? Why did they act like that?

Of course!

She opened her eyes and sat upright. "Hey! Sebastian!" she called out loudly across the pool. A few heads on fellow lounging swimmers glanced up at the noise, but she didn't really care. She knew she and Sebastian were already disliked, so what did it matter if she annoyed people further? Sebastian looked up. "Come here!" she yelled again.

He pulled his legs out of the water and quickly came over to join her, as fast as he could without running. Evie smiled. Sebastian would never run around a pool's edge. That was against the rules, after all.

"Yes?" he asked, sitting on her lounge chair.

"I realized what I realized!"

"You did?"

"Yes, when you said that thing about the men in black earlier downstairs. It just came to me now. It's so obvious. Finding out who they are would be hugely helpful in finding out why they want the map, why they have my grandfather." She was overcome with excitement.

Sebastian thought about it, and then a small smile crossed his face. "That does make a lot of sense."

"Yes! It might even lead to finding him without having to put the team together. And if we can't find the Kid and Doris, well, it would be good to have a Plan B!"

This was such a good idea. She was seriously proud of herself.

"That's a really smart idea. I'm kind of shocked that this is the first time anyone's actually asked that question," said Sebastian, looking exactly as he'd described himself.

"Well, I think it's that sometimes we get wrapped up in solving what's right in front of us and the bigger picture can get lost." *And sometimes,* she thought secretly, so secretly that she only half allowed herself to think it, *we focus on the now to avoid the bigger picture on purpose.*

Like, what would happen if she didn't find her grandfather? Or worse. What if she was too late in finding her grandfather?

"Okay," she said, shoving the thought aside, "so let's think for a second. What kinds of people are these men?"

Sebastian contemplated. "They are all wounded somehow . . . and they like black leather jackets. . . ."

"Well, a lot of people like black leather jackets."

"Yeah . . ."

"Maybe they're soldiers! Maybe they got injured fighting!" That could totally be a possibility.

"Maybe they're gang members," said Sebastian, sounding not nearly so enthusiastic at that thought. "Gang members also fight and get injured, from what I understand."

That was true. In fact, a lot of people fought, even people who weren't part of organizations. And who was to say that's how the men had gotten injured? Accidents happen. And Mr. M might even have been born with only one eye. Or maybe he actually had two eyes but covered one because he thought it was cool.

"I think we should forget about their looks as a clue," she said.

"Yeah," agreed Sebastian. "We need to think of it another way. We need to ask . . . why."

Evie thought about that. Why. "Why do they want my grandfather and the map?"

"Yes. What kind of people would want access to a waterfall with supposed life-sustaining properties?"

"Yeah . . . what kind of people?" What kind of people indeed. Well, there would be a lot of people who would want something like that. People who made medicine, probably. And people who just wanted to make a lot of money selling something that precious to the highest bidder. Possibly on something like the black market.

"Scientists? Or people who work on the black market?" she said aloud. She didn't know what kinds of people did both and what those jobs would be.

"Possibly," said Sebastian. "The thing is—" He stopped.

"What?"

He looked around the pool, and Evie followed his gaze. They watched the few other explorers on the opposite side tanning themselves, and the one woman scuba diving at the bottom of the pool.

"The Explorers Society is very secretive," said Sebastian. "But the Filipendulous Five were famous. . . ." It almost seemed like Sebastian was talking to himself, but he wasn't, and she heard him and she understood what he was getting at. The question wasn't only about who would be interested in the waterfall but who would also know it even existed in the first place.

"But no one knew about the waterfall except the team, no matter how famous they were," said Evie, thinking it through. "And Myrtle. She was already president of the society at the time, and banned them all for causing the tsunami." Sebastian made eye contact with her once more. "The men had to have known at least one of the Filipendulous Five or her pretty well. To know about the waterfall."

Sebastian sat there for a quiet moment, and then, finally, he smiled. It was small and it was tired, but it was still a smile and it counted. It was so nice to see again. It had been a while, Evie realized.

"They could be explorers," he said.

Evie smiled now too. "They definitely could be."

# ➤ CHAPTER 6 ◄

## In which there is complicated vindication.

"We need to go to the library. We need to find a database of explorers!" said Evie, standing. Sebastian stood a little more slowly, unsure how they would manage to go to the library, considering it was off-limits. But just as he stood, someone sat down hard on the lounge chair next to them, and he turned to see Catherine in her usual Catherine attire: boots, khaki pants, shirt, and whip at her hip, looking more out of place than normal.

"Hello, Catherine," said Evie, sitting back down. Her tone was anything but friendly. She was clearly still holding a grudge from earlier.

"Hi. This looks very refreshing," said Catherine, matter-of-factly indicating the pool.

"Yes. You can borrow a swimsuit if you like. They left some for us in our suite," said Evie. Sebastian shook his head. Even when angry at someone, Evie was still accommodating.

"Maybe," said Catherine in that way that meant, "I'm not interested, thank you."

"What's wrong?" asked Sebastian. He wasn't great at knowing what Catherine (or really all that many people) was thinking, but he had a feeling that something was off. The fact that she had returned so fast from the stunt-car place might have been the biggest hint.

"They were very unhelpful at the SRAC. They wouldn't even let us in. Such a ridiculous reason," said Catherine with a sigh.

"Was it because you have to be a stunt-car driver to be allowed into the stunt-car society?" asked Evie.

"Oh. Yes. How did you know?" asked Catherine, furrowing her eyebrows and looking at Evie with suspicion.

"It seems to me societies have more fun keeping people out than letting them in. You and I both have experience with that," she replied, and Catherine nodded slowly.

"Yes. Yes, I suppose we do."

"Where's Benedict?" asked Sebastian.

"He's having a rest downstairs. What do you think we should do now?" asked Catherine, awkwardly lifting her legs and stretching out on the lounge chair, but she looked so stiff that it almost seemed like she had no knees. The moment she was settled, the pug crawled onto her and happily curled up in her lap.

Sebastian could tell Evie felt conflicted. He could understand why. On the one hand, obviously they needed to figure out a way to be allowed into the SRAC. On the other, she was probably feeling a little more than vindicated that things hadn't worked out as the grown-ups had hoped. Maybe if they had actually invited her and Sebastian along, this wouldn't have happened.

Still.

She wasn't answering the question. He needed to do something.

"Do we know any stunt-car drivers?" he asked, looking to Catherine.

"The Kid was the only one. And we don't even know for sure if he is," replied Catherine.

"Okay. So if we don't know any stunt-car drivers and they already know that you guys aren't, because

I'm assuming you didn't lie . . ." Sebastian trailed off. He really didn't know what else to suggest.

"Then I guess the only thing to do is for either me or Sebastian to pretend we're stunt-car drivers," concluded Evie, speaking up finally.

What? No. That was impossible. "That's impossible," said Sebastian.

"I mean, it's not easy, but I don't think it's impossible," replied Evie.

"No. Sebastian's right. You're what? Eleven and twelve? Both too young to drive—and do either of you even know how to in the first place?" asked Catherine.

"Well . . . I don't." Evie looked at Sebastian.

"Are you kidding me?" asked Sebastian. He was completely aghast. "Do you think that, of all the rules out there, *that's* the one I'd be interested in breaking?"

"Well, we don't have to actually drive," replied Evie. "This is silly. We're getting very . . . Oh, what's the kind of acting that actors do when you pretend to be the character all the time even when you aren't on set, like in your day-to-day life?" Sebastian didn't say anything. No one said anything. They just stared at her. "Okay. Whatever. The point is, we don't need to have any driving skills. We just need to be convincing as drivers. As kid stunt drivers. And I think that that could be a thing. I mean, there's got to be movies

*  61  *

where kids our age have to drive, and so maybe there's a way to convince the association that we are those people."

"This is wacky," said Sebastian, shaking his head. It was too much, even for an Evie suggestion.

"I think if there is any place in the world to be wacky, it's here in Hollywood. Besides, didn't you tell me about how the Lost Boys had those cars and stuff? And they were all underage. Adults even ask kids to drive trucks around on farms, too. So why not in movies?" The more Evie spoke, the more confident she sounded. And the less confident Sebastian felt. "And don't forget, we're kids," she added.

"We're . . . kids?" said Sebastian doubtfully. He didn't understand. That is to say, he understood that they were kids but not what she was getting at.

"Adults find kids confusing, I think. And sometimes cute and funny. And they make up excuses for us. We can get away with more, I think."

"No, Evie. Stop," said Catherine, clearly wanting to stand up but frozen in place by the tiny pug cuddling in her lap.

"No?" Evie asked.

"You can't do that. Let me talk with Benedict. We'll figure something out," said Catherine, scratching the pug's left ear.

"Why can't we figure something out now?" Evie's voice cracked just a little.

"Because you need to let us sort out the details," said Catherine.

"Why?"

Oh no, not again.

"Because we have experience. We're familiar with dealing with uncompromising people. This is what we did together as a team for years. Please, Evie," said Catherine.

"'Please, Evie' what? What? Am I being unreasonable? Are my ideas bad? You thought my ideas were good ones before. You used to be totally about my good ideas. What's going on? Suddenly another adult shows up and . . ." Evie stopped. She took in a deep breath. Something inside her seemed to change then. She had a realization. "And now you don't need me anymore. That's it. You don't need me. Us." She glanced at Sebastian. He didn't know what she wanted from him, and all he could do was return the look with one of desperate discomfort. "Sebastian and I are the reason we're all here today, and now you want to push us aside because you have your old team member. Because we're kids and you're not."

"Evie, we want your help—"

"Only when it's convenient. Otherwise you just

sneak out to do stuff on your own. Even if it means a plan isn't going to work and we waste more time not finding my grandfather." Evie stood in a rush, teetering slightly as she did. When she regained her balance, she said, "Come on, Sebastian."

"Why?"

"Because we're not wanted!"

## ➤ CHAPTER 7 ◄

# In which it's finally time
# to do things right.

Evie stormed toward the door to the building, hoping Sebastian was behind her. She paused at the exit and turned to look.

Sebastian was standing back by the pool chairs, looking really confused, not following her. Fine! She'd storm off on her own. She could do that. She didn't need help with that!

Evie turned in a huff and walked into the cool white foyer that divided the changing rooms. She went through and out into another stark hallway, and suddenly she realized that she hated it. She hated all this white brightness. It wasn't refreshing. It wasn't open. It was cold. It was unfeeling. It had no personality, and while she was at it, maybe the society headquarters where she was supposedly living now had too much personality. Maybe everything was terrible.

And why didn't Sebastian care? What was up with him? Sure, when they'd first met at the beginning of all this, he'd been kind of careful and scared of taking risks, but he'd changed so much since then! And anyway, his participation in this adventure was technically his fault. He was the one who had seen her crying outside the old Explorers Society back home and asked what was wrong. He was the one who'd invited her over. He was the one who'd shown her her grandfather's puzzle box. This was his adventure as much as hers!

But now? Now he was acting weird. Not usual-Sebastian-weird, either. But unsupportive and quiet—not Sebastian quiet but regular-person quiet . . . and . . . and . . .

She climbed into the elevator and pushed the door-close button. She stood for a moment catching her breath, calming her thoughts. *Stop blaming him,* she told herself. *You're mad at Catherine. You're mad that your grandfather is in danger and people are wasting time not listening to you. You're mad at yourself for getting mad. Be mad at the right people. No point in taking it out on everyone.*

Evie pushed the button for her floor and instantly was whooshed down to their suite. She fumed at the sprawling city out the windows and below her. Stupid amazing views with stupid oceans, and why did views matter anyway? They were just things you looked at with your eyeballs.

The doors opened, and standing there was Sebastian, sweaty and out of breath.

"How did you . . . ," asked Evie, stepping out of the elevator as if in slow motion.

"The . . . stairs . . . ," wheezed Sebastian, bending over and placing his hands on his thighs as he caught his breath.

"Why did you . . ."

Sebastian raised his finger to stop her question and continued to pant for a moment. When he'd collected himself and stood upright, he said, "Because you were upset. Because I didn't want you feeling you were alone. I don't know. I didn't really think about it." He didn't seem too happy at that pronouncement.

"Okay." She was still angry, but her shock at seeing him had been a bit of a metaphorical bucket of cold water over her head and had definitely cooled her down.

"And also because I agree with you. Let's do it. Let's pretend to be child stunt-car drivers. Let's pretend that's a thing people do." He said it totally sounding unsure of himself, but Evie didn't care.

She gave him a big hug, and he didn't even flinch that much this time. Then she said, grinning, "Fantastic! Okay, let's figure out exactly how we're going to do this!"

## ➤ CHAPTER 8 ◄

# In which we meet some
# stunt-car drivers.
# And Wheels.

"W here are all the cars?" asked Evie as their driver
pulled into the parking lot.

Sebastian didn't say anything because he assumed
she didn't actually think he knew the answer. She was
just puzzling out loud. But it was a decent question,
considering the location.

The SRAC, short for the Stunt Racing Association
of Car-drivers,[9] was located along the coast, south of
Malibu. It was a large building that looked almost

---

[9] *Not to be mistaken for the Stunt Racing Association of
Cars, which is a totally different thing and has a very different
kind of membership. And even more exclusive . . . stupid four-
wheels policy.*

deserted, sitting beyond a wide empty parking lot. Where the cars belonging to the members were, Sebastian had no idea.

The building itself was nothing much to look at, a large white stuccoed rectangle with a single black door slightly to the left of center. It was in fact altogether possible, Sebastian considered as they approached the door itself, that this was not actually the right place. It was possible that the driver who worked for the Explorers Society and who had been more than happy to bring them here had taken them to the wrong place. There wasn't even a sign. After all, organizations enjoyed signs, did they not? At least, that's what he'd experienced in his short time knowing about them. Maybe it was only explorers who liked signs, though. Perhaps spending your life searching for places made you really want to know what a place was if you had the opportunity.

"That's a big white building with a little black door," said Evie, stating the obvious, as she sometimes did.

Mind you, the door wasn't little. It only looked little in proportion to the vast white walls of the building. Sebastian was about to say as much, but then he realized that it didn't matter logically that the door wasn't little. It looked little. And the building looked big.

"Yeah," he said. He could tell that Evie was looking at him. "What?" he asked.

"I thought you might point out that the door was actually normal-sized," she said.

"I figured you meant it as more in appearance than literally."

"I did."

He looked at her. She was smiling. He shook his head.

"Okay, so let's do this," she said, raising her hand to knock on the door. She took a moment and then, with a nod to herself, she knocked.

They stood.

They waited.

What if this was the wrong place? What if it was an abandoned building? Worse, what if it wasn't abandoned? What if—now he actually shuddered at the thought—what if one of the men in black answered the door?

The door opened.

Staring down at them was a person in a full race-car-driving uniform, all white with a red stripe up the side and a matching helmet, the visor of which was on and tinted a deep black.

Well, it certainly seemed like the right place.

The person said something muffled.

Sebastian and Evie looked at each other, then back at the driver.

Another muffled something.

"I'm sorry, but we can't understand you," said Evie.

There was a heavy muffled sigh from within the helmet, and its owner finally pulled it off, revealing a sheet of perfectly straight long black hair that fell smoothly over the driver's shoulders. Sebastian was impressed. He imagined that his hair would not look nearly so neat and tidy after being smushed up inside a helmet like that.

"I was asking," the person said, "who are you and what you want?"

"We're stunt-car drivers and would like to join the society," replied Evie, her chin tilted upward slightly.

Hearing it said out loud to an actual stunt-car driver . . . well, it seemed an even sillier idea than when they'd first come up with it.

The woman stared at them for a moment.

"You're stunt-car drivers," she said slowly.

"Yes. We haven't worked on much, but there's a new kids' film coming out soon, and we were hired as the stunt-car drivers. Our director said we should join the society before filming begins." Sebastian was seriously worried, but also, he had to admit, impressed.

Clearly Evie had been preparing for this meeting as they'd journeyed across the city.

"What's the name of the film?" asked the woman quickly.

"*The Little Car That Could,*" replied Evie just as quickly.

"Who's the star?"

"Heather Dann."

"What's the story?"

"When a twelve-year-old girl is left behind at a racetrack by her neglectful parents, she has to use all her wiles to prevent a group of burglars from stealing the Golden Gearshift trophy."

The speed with which Evie was answering all these questions astounded Sebastian. The woman looked at him.

"Are you in it too?" she asked.

There was a moment when he tried to think of something as impressive-sounding as what Evie had said. To show his friend that he, too, could think on his feet. That he could be creative and even a little whimsical.

"Yes," he said.

The woman turned back to Evie. "Where are your parents?"

On that one Evie faltered. "Uh . . ."

"We asked them if we could come on our own. We're tired of being chaperoned everywhere," replied Sebastian a little too quickly, trying to help Evie.

There was a long pause now as they were scrutinized by the woman in the white-and-red suit. After what felt like just enough time for her to see through their rather thin story, she finally said, "Okay. You can come in." And she turned around and disappeared inside, leaving the door open for them.

Evie and Sebastian exchanged another look, then followed.

They found themselves in a small foyer. The floors and walls and even ceiling were checkered in black and white squares, and the effect was enough to make everything look like it was spinning slightly. *Yay, optical illusions,* thought Sebastian, blinking hard.

"Have a seat," said the woman as she vanished through a door hidden in one wall.

Evie and Sebastian looked around and then at each other.

"Where?" questioned Evie.

Sebastian agreed. Exactly what were they meant to sit on? The floor, maybe?

"Maybe there's something we can fold out from the wall," suggested Sebastian. And they each made their way to an opposite wall. At almost the exact same moment they both stumbled, banging into something seemingly invisible, and they cried out in pain in unison.

"What was that?" said Evie, wincing.

Sebastian looked down at the empty space before him. Tentatively he reached out until his hands grazed a surface. Was it . . . was it an invisible chair? He leaned in closer. It was then that he realized what was going on. The chair was a totally visible chair, as most chairs are,[10] but painted in the exact same checkered squares as the rest of the room. The chairs were camouflaged.

"That's pretty dangerous," said Evie, realizing it at the same time and taking a seat across from him.

"Yeah," said Sebastian, also sitting. They sat facing each other kind of awkwardly. Evie laughed. "What is it?" he asked.

"You look like you're floating, or like you're holding yourself up in a sitting position," she said.

Sebastian smiled. "Yeah, you do too."

A previously totally invisible door right beside Sebastian suddenly swung open and a man in a bright purple suit jacket and trousers entered the room. He had blond wavy hair, and the angles of his face were

---

[10] Except for the non-visible ones, but no one knows where they are or that they exist, so it's not really a thing.

as severe as his expression. He glared down at the two of them.

There was a small quiet sound of squeaking then. The man didn't avert his hard gaze even as Sebastian felt a need to turn to see where the squeaking was coming from. It slowly got louder and louder until finally he saw the source.

A small red dachshund with a small set of tires supporting his rear legs, as well as goggles covering his eyes, had slowly but purposefully wheeled himself into the room.

Sebastian turned back to the man, not entirely sure what was going on.

"I'm Daniel Dashing," said the severe-looking man finally. He stopped. And waited. When neither Sebastian nor Evie said anything, he tried again. "I'm Daniel Dashing."

"I'm Sebastian," said Sebastian slowly, confused.

"Oh, Mr. Dashing!" said Evie, springing to her feet and extending her hand. "It's so great to meet you in person. We're such big fans."

Sebastian got up too, now racking his brain for where he was supposed to know Mr. Dashing from.

For his part, Mr. Dashing shook Evie's hand with a softened expression. "This is Wheels," he said, introducing the dog.

"Of course," said Evie. "The famous Wheels." She
bent down and gave the dog a small tap on the head
before glancing at Sebastian. That was when he understood. She was pretending to know who the man was
because Mr. Dashing assumed that he (and his dog)
was so famous that they would. Or assumed that, at
the very least, fellow stunt-car drivers would.

"Oh, wow. That's . . . Wheels," said Sebastian, awkwardly standing to pet the dog himself. This did seem to be the right move for both dog and owner, and the man appeared to relax as he sat on a heretofore unseen chaise longue. He stretched out along it, resting his right elbow on its arm, now looking like he was floating on his side. "Thank you," he said as Evie sat. Sebastian followed her lead. So much up and down, and he had no idea why. The dog wheeled itself over to the side of the chaise longue and started to slowly climb up what was evidently a ramp. He then sat next to his owner and stared at them blankly through his dark goggles.

"So, Ms. Velos tells me you are child stunt-car drivers," he said.

"Yes, and we'd like to join the association," replied Evie.

Mr. Dashing thought for a moment. "That can't be legal."

"Oh, I assure you that we work the same hours as child actors, and we always have a tutor on set," replied Evie. Sebastian had no idea how she understood that this was something she should say or even knew such things were rules.

Mr. Dashing shook his head. "No, I meant a person your age driving."

"Oh!" said Evie with a kind of laugh that Sebastian had never heard before. It sounded slightly, well, dismissive. Like she thought the man had said something foolish. Which wasn't exactly polite, and also Sebastian couldn't figure out where the man had said something that wasn't accurate.

"You laugh?" said Mr. Dashing.

"I'm so sorry. Yes, it makes sense that you'd think that. A lot of people do. But no, it is legal." Evie stopped there and continued to smile at the man.

Mr. Dashing furrowed his eyebrows. For his part Sebastian was terribly unconvinced. Just because someone said something was legal didn't make it so. Surely Mr. Dashing would see the flaw in Evie's logic.

"Hmm. Well. Still sounds suspicious to me," he said, sitting upright and stroking Wheels. He examined Evie's determined expression. "Then again, maybe not."

He finally looked over at Sebastian, and Sebastian stared back at him hard. So hard that he forgot to blink. He was totally confused about why his eyeballs were feeling all dry and stinging and how he could solve that problem.

"And do you have any films you can show us as proof?" Mr. Dashing asked Sebastian.

"No," replied Sebastian, his eyes now trying to compensate for his forgetfulness by starting to water.

"What my fellow kid stunt-car driver means is that we don't have any finished films, no," added Evie quickly. When Mr. Dashing turned to look at her, Sebastian suddenly remembered and blinked hard. Or, well, it was more like he closed his eyes for a moment, which is just an intensely long blink, when you think about it.

The door opened then, and Ms. Velos entered and sat down next to Mr. Dashing. In what was evidently a tall wingback chair with high armrests. Or she was sitting on a stool and holding her back very straight and her arms up at ninety-degree angles for some reason.

"Ah, Ms. Velos. I need your help. They have no paperwork and no proof that they are stunt-car drivers. It's all so much, I think we should send them home," said Mr. Dashing, turning to her.

"Hmm," said Ms. Velos, now resting her elbow on the armrest and her chin in her hand. "That is a puzzle."

The two drivers sat considering what to do, and Sebastian took a moment to look at Evie, who rolled her eyes back at him. Sebastian glanced at the drivers, fearful that they'd noticed her disdain, but they were both still thinking.

And thinking.

Sebastian blinked intensely again.

"I have it!" said Ms. Velos. "It's so simple. Let them drive!"

"Let them . . . ," said Sebastian, slowly opening his eyes their widest.

"Not the race car track, obviously," she said. "I don't care what is legal or not. They are children. But the go-kart track. Should be a piece of cake for a real driver." She said it in a way that implied she still didn't fully believe they were on the level. Which they weren't, so Sebastian didn't blame her for thinking it.

There was a pause.

"Sure!" said Evie loudly, jumping to her feet. "But I mean, surely one of us is proof enough, though. Let's not waste time here. I'll do it!" It was a rush of words that did not make Sebastian feel any better. He turned and gaped at her as she smiled a hard smile, her teeth a bit too exposed, almost like she was baring them in a snarl.

Mr. Dashing nodded. "Very well. Let's get you suited up!"

"Great!" said Evie, still smile-grimacing.

*Oh, Evie,* thought Sebastian, rising slowly, *what have you done?*

# CHAPTER 9

## In which we drive!

Evie could hear the sound of her own breathing magnified within the helmet. It sounded very loud. And definitely too fast. She tried to slow it down. She closed her eyes and focused and counted the seconds on her intake of breath. There was a tap on her helmet, and her eyes were wide open again.

It was Sebastian.

"Hey," she said, not sure he could actually hear her.

"Are you okay?" he asked.

"Oh sure," she said, her voice squeaking a little. "This pedal makes it go fast. This one stops it. I steer the kart with this. It's all been adjusted to my height." She was essentially repeating back what the mechanic had said to her earlier as she'd asked for a refresher on how to work a go-kart.

"It's not the same as a regular car, you see," she'd explained as her fake excuse.

The mechanic had nodded and shown her what to do. Then, after a pause, had added, pointing toward the track, "It's a normal oval with four bends." She'd looked at him and realized maybe he didn't quite believe her excuse. But he was still kind enough to help her out. She'd smiled. He'd smiled back.

Now Evie slid into the seat of what to her seemed more like a little open car and less like a kart. "Kart" implied something wooden and homemade. This, she'd been told, was a C5. The fastest go-kart in the world. Which was just dandy, she supposed, but right then she probably would have preferred a nice red wagon or something.

"I can't believe you're doing this," he said, shaking his head.

"Honestly, me neither," she replied.

"I know they said they were timing you, but just remember that safety is the most important thing. Don't try to prove anything," he said.

"Aside from being a stunt-car driver?"

Sebastian nodded and glanced up over the kart toward the stands. Evie turned her head to follow his gaze. Mr. Dashing, with Wheels in his lap, and Ms. Velos were sitting in the otherwise empty stands, waiting. Such a small audience. But the most intimidating audience in the world. Way more than a thousand people sitting up there.

No. No, that would have also been pretty intimidating, actually, thought Evie.

"I had a thought," said Sebastian, leaning down again.

"Yes?" *Please, all the amazing Sebastian thoughts right now would be more than welcome.*

"When you get to the bends in the track, don't follow the curve on the outside edge. Instead drive straight across them."

"Why?"

"Basic geometry. The shortest distance between two spots is a straight line. That's surely got to be the faster way to take a corner. I bet it will make it look like you know what you're doing." He gave a nervous smile, possibly for encouragement, but it was really hard to tell.

Evie nodded, but she didn't think Sebastian could see her do so, considering how the helmet held her head heavy in place.

"Drive slowly going into the curve. You can speed up as you go through it," he added. "And just don't, you know . . . get hurt. The worst thing that happens is they don't believe us and kick us out."

Seemed pretty bad as a worst thing, thought Evie. If Mr. Dashing and Ms. Velos didn't believe that Evie and Sebastian were stunt-car drivers, then the association members wouldn't share with them where the Kid was, which meant they wouldn't be able to find him, which meant then not being able to get his letter, his clue to where her grandfather was, and that meant not finding her grandfather. Unless, of course, she could figure out where these men in black might have come from.

She had to do this. She had to drive this go-kart. Other kids did this all the time. The thing was . . . she had never been one of those kids. She really didn't actually know what she was doing, even though she'd seen enough people drive and stuff. When you've seen so many people do it, you think you can just do it too.

Except there was nothing "just" about any of this.

Sebastian was still standing there, staring at her.

"What?" she asked.

"Good luck."

Once again she nodded. Finally, and seemingly with great reluctance, Sebastian walked away from the kart, and she watched him take his seat next to Ms. Velos in the stands.

Right. Okay. This was easy. Stop and start. That was all there was to it. It wasn't a real car. Kids drove these all the time. Because they're easy.

Easy.

Oh yeah.

So.

Turn on the ignition.

Evie leaned over and pushed the button in the center of the steering wheel.

She screamed. She screamed loudly into her helmet as the kart came to life, rumbling around her like an ancient monster that had been trapped underground for hundreds of years and had now found its freedom and was going to eat her alive.

She sat, her hands shaking, the whole car buzzing around her, the sound engulfing her, the fans to the left and right of her head whirring fast, and she tried once again to breathe.

Nope, breathing wasn't working.

She had to calm down. This wasn't that loud, nothing compared to a real car, she was sure of it. It was just that she was sitting there with no roof and super low to the ground, and she'd expected it to be a lot less noisy and more . . . cute. Certainly the high-pitched scream from the motor was nothing she'd ever heard before. But that didn't make it bad. It was just different. Different could seem scary even if it wasn't.

Okay. Okay, she was breathing now.

Well, she might as well attempt to drive, then.

She wanted to close her eyes as she brought her right foot down on the gas, but she knew that that was a very silly idea, so she squinted them instead, bracing for movement. And pushed. The engine roared even louder, like someone had stepped on the monster's toe, but she didn't go forward. She tried again. Another roar, but again she didn't move forward.

Evie glanced at her audience and gave a wave as if she was doing whatever she was doing on purpose.

Sebastian was the only one to wave back.

*Okay, kart. Why aren't you moving forward?*

Evie looked down. Oh. She had forgotten to take her left foot off the brake pedal. She was pushing down hard on both pedals. Right, okay, that was a silly mistake but not a big deal. Easy to fix. Just relax, Evie. Relax.

She carefully released the brake pedal as she pressed gently on the gas pedal, and the car lurched forward this time! She braked and sat grinning in her helmet and glanced up to the stands for approval. Both Mr. Dashing and Ms. Velos did not seem particularly impressed. Wheels appeared downright scornful. No. Of course they weren't. Driving an inch forward was probably not exactly a big deal to stunt-car drivers. But Sebastian, he probably was impressed!

Needless to say she was not thrilled to see him wearing an expression of total terror.

*Gee, thanks for the confidence, Sebastian,* she thought.

Okay. It was time to drive.

With fierce determination Evie stared at the track ahead of her and gripped the wheel tightly. She hadn't yet learned how to steer, true, but she was feeling confident now that she understood how to move the car forward. The roaring monster seemed almost like her cheerleader now, and she smiled a little, imagining a big scaly green monster holding pom-poms.

*Let's do this.*

She pressed down very lightly on the gas, and the car began to roll forward. She knew she was going ridiculously slowly, but it still felt like an achievement and also scary, and she gripped the wheel hard. *Don't get hurt,* she thought as she pushed down harder and sped up. After all, Sebastian did have a point. While it would be pretty bad to not convince Mr. Dashing and Ms. Velos, it wasn't as bad as seriously injuring herself, because then what good would she be to her grandfather?

She moved forward along the track and sensed the wind rush around her head and felt a little more confident. She decided to try steering a bit and turned the wheel a little to the right. The car responded immediately, and she quickly rotated the wheel back to the left—but a bit too far, overcorrecting, and the car swung widely to the left. She took in a deep breath and turned the wheel a teeny bit back to the right, and she was driving straight along the track again.

Okay, this wasn't horrible.

It wasn't even bad.

This was actually kind of neat. A little fun, even. She focused on where she was trying to go. She sped up again, remembering they were timing her, and she could see a curve ahead. There was a little lurch, and she was driving faster, and it was a lot scarier, and the wind whooshed more loudly, but she just kept focusing ahead of her at the curve.

*Slow down as you approach it. Drive across it.* Because Sebastian had to be right about this sort of thing. She could feel her already elevated pulse getting faster, and her hands gripped the wheel more tightly. She put less pressure on the gas pedal and slowed down a bit, marveling at how now she actually felt in control and not terrified. Maybe she was getting used to this.

Oh no. The curve. Okay, maybe she wasn't.

She aimed for the far end of the curve but realized that this wasn't quite the same as driving in a straight line. There was a bit of a curve that she had to make, and she did have to carefully turn the wheel. If she had learned anything from earlier, it was to turn the wheel in small increments.

She focused ahead of her, on the almost straight line. She tried to not even plan how much she was going to turn the steering wheel.

She could do this.

She would do this.

She did do this!

She was around the first corner! Quickly she pushed down on the gas pedal and sped up. But even as she celebrated on the inside, she realized she didn't have time. The next corner was coming up quickly.

Right.

With more confidence she drove across the curve, and having succeeded even better this time, pushed down a bit more on the gas. And then a little bit more. She pushed down harder than she had yet, and the feeling was exhilarating. The roaring cheerleader monster was totally on her side now as she came up to the third bend. She was feeling the rush, the thrill, and with a little bit of a flourish, she took the curve.

And was a bit too enthusiastic turning the wheel to the left.

The back of the kart spun out from behind her, and she found herself skidding, spinning too far to the left. Quickly she tried to correct, but this time not going all the way to the right with the wheel like she'd done the last time. Still she found the kart not responding to her, and she drove right toward the wall.

No!

No, she wasn't going to get hurt!

She slammed on the brakes and screeched to a stop, squeezing her eyes shut, bracing for impact.

The car stopped. Her body lurched forward, then back, held in place by her seat belt.

She sat there, quietly panting.

It didn't feel like she'd hit anything. She opened her eyes slowly.

She had managed to stop the kart just inches away from the wall. Evie let out a long sigh of relief and leaned back. She glanced to the side and could see all three of her audience members standing on their feet. And one on its wheels.

Okay. The clock was still ticking. It wasn't over until it was over.

Thinking back to what the mechanic had instructed her to do, she was able to find the reverse. Slowly she pulled herself back from the wall. Far enough that she felt she could turn and aim the car back straight toward the last curve.

*One more, Evie. Then it's the home stretch.*

*One more. And this time, focus.*

Evie once again pushed on the gas pedal and approached the last curve carefully. She did it as slowly as she could, but she knew that she didn't have a lot of time. She squinted in concentration and drove across it, and once she had, she pushed down hard and felt the wind around her helmet, felt the world blur beside her, felt more determined and more alive than she'd felt in days. And she raced along the straight last bit of the track. When she crossed the finish line, she didn't want to stop. She kept going a bit longer than necessary, and then, since it was all over anyway, she decided to turn the wheel hard. The kart spun in a full circle, but this time Evie felt in total control as she brought the monster carefully to a stop.

Then she sat still for a moment. Breathing hard. But it wasn't the same kind of breathing echoing around her helmet. It wasn't fear. It was exhilaration. It was happiness. Even if she'd failed the test, she'd still just done something she'd never done before, and she had really enjoyed it.

There was a shadow crossing in front of the kart, and sure enough it was Sebastian again. She grinned at him, though he couldn't see it, of course. Evie undid her seat belt and pushed herself to standing. Only then did she realize how weak she felt. Her legs were like jelly. Sebastian caught her before she actually collapsed, and helped her find her balance before Mr. Dashing and Ms. Velos came over.

As quickly as she could, Evie pulled off her helmet, her hair a matted mess beneath and not falling nearly as gracefully across her shoulders as Ms. Velos's had. She looked at the drivers with anticipation. She knew she'd made a mistake, a bad mistake, with that one curve. And she didn't know if she'd beaten the clock at all. Did they believe her? Had they fallen for it?

It was too silent. For too long. Why were they just staring at her?

Then Mr. Dashing stuck out his hand, and Evie reached out to take it. They shook.

"Welcome to the SRAC," said Mr. Dashing.

Evie sighed and laughed at the same time. They were in! One step closer to finding the Kid and her grandfather. She hugged Mr. Dashing and then Ms. Velos, and then scratched Wheels behind the ears. And finally gave Sebastian the biggest hug of all.

"You did it!" he said into her ear.

She pulled away and grinned at him. Then she turned to Mr. Dashing. "Thank you so much! Now, we have to talk."

# CHAPTER 10

## In which we experience member privileges.

They had been invited into the main part of the building to fill out their paperwork. Sebastian stood behind Evie, waiting for his turn to sign the register, and stared at the back of her head in amazement. He thought maybe he might have been able to figure out how to drive like she had, but when she'd been heading right for the wall of the track and had then managed to not hit it and make it to the finish line, he was pretty sure he wouldn't have had the nerve to do that. Evie might have had some pretty out-there plans sometimes, but it did seem she was able to make them work.

He remembered her saying something about riding

a llama way back when they'd been escaping the men in black at the zoo. He'd never asked for more about that. He really ought to someday.

"Your turn," said Evie, handing Sebastian the pen. He quickly signed his name and then joined her on the dark red leather couch in a room that was also covered, from floor to ceiling, in red leather.

It seemed like the designer for this place was a big fan of sticking to one idea and one idea only.

Unlike the black-and-white-checkered room, though, there were visible bits of furniture and other colors to be found. Like the coffee table in front of them made out of a huge tire. And the bar in the corner constructed of some kind of shiny metal, with its various beverages held within gas and oil containers, except for one antifreeze can that he thought actually contained the toxic green liquid—until Ms. Velos poured herself a glass and took a sip.

"So," said Mr. Dashing, finding himself another chaise longue and reclining on it with Wheels at his side, "you said you needed to talk."

"Yes," said Evie, all business. "We were told by our director to speak with one of your members. The Kid."

"You are the only kid members," replied Ms. Velos, sitting on one of the barstools.

"Oh no, she doesn't mean *a* kid, she means *the* Kid," said Sebastian.

Ms. Velos looked at him carefully. "I don't know how to make it any clearer. You are the only children members of SRAC," she said slowly, as if he didn't understand the words she was saying.

Once more he was being considered stupid. He really hated that. Especially when he constantly demonstrated time and time again how well he understood so many things.

Then he suddenly understood.

"Oh! Well, that's a nickname," explained Sebastian, finally realizing that of course they wouldn't know him as "the Kid." That had been his Filipendulous Five nickname, and he was going under a totally different name now. Probably a different name than his real name, which, come to think of it, Sebastian didn't actually know.

This could be a problem.

"So what's his name?" asked Mr. Dashing.

Sebastian glanced at Evie. She looked as worried as he did. Had this whole becoming members, putting Evie in danger, been for nothing?

"We only know his nickname," said Evie softly.

"That does present a problem," said Mr. Dashing,

running a hand through his hair and making it look even more windswept.

No, this wasn't it. This wasn't the end. *Come on, Sebastian. Time to step up, solve a problem. Any problem.* It had all been Evie solving everything lately, with her SRAC idea and the database of explorers idea and . . .

Wait.

"Do you have a database?" he asked.

"We do."

"With pictures?"

Mr. Dashing nodded, and he leaned over to the side table next to his chaise longue, a repurposed steering wheel, and honked the horn.

In a flash two men in white mechanic uniforms whipped through a side door, flew over next to Mr. Dashing, listened to him, and then ran back out.

"What was that?" asked Evie quietly. Sebastian shook his head.

The men quickly returned with a large binder carried between them, ran to the car tire coffee table in front of Sebastian and Evie, placed the book down quickly, and opened it to the first page, then disappeared through the door.

"How helpful," said Evie, watching them leave.

"Yes, thank you," added Sebastian. Together they

examined the first page of the book. Three pictures ran down the page, one of Mr. Dashing, one of Ms. Velos, and one of another gentleman named Mr. Uturn.

They flipped the page. Then Evie sat up and looked at Sebastian.

Sebastian felt obligated to do sit up and look back at her.

"What is it?" he asked quietly.

"Do we even know what he looks like, though?" she asked, eyes wide with worry.

"We saw him in the pictures in the puzzle box your grandfather left at the Explorers Society headquarters. Remember? That first afternoon we met?" replied Sebastian.

"That seems forever ago." Evie didn't seem convinced.

"Well, it wasn't, actually. Not really. It was just under two weeks ago, in fact. And anyway, we saw them. Or rather, I saw them."

"But do you remember what he looked like?" asked Evie, looking now quite dejected. Sebastian stared at her, more than a little stunned by her question, but before he could say anything, suddenly Evie, with a laugh and looking a little embarrassed, said, "Oh right, of course. How silly of me. Your photographic memory."

He was relieved. Okay, so Evie might not have had

perfect recall like he had. Very few people did. But he'd gotten worried about her when she'd forgotten his special talent. After all, the men in black had kidnapped him precisely because Sebastian had memorized the key to the map to the waterfall. That's why they wanted him so much: they wanted his brain. That was why Sebastian had been kidnapped and taken across the world and Evie had come after him. Fortunately, she seemed clear about it all now. "Exactly," he said. "And I can't think of any better situation to use a photographic memory than when looking at photographs."

Evie nodded and smiled a bit. "You're right. I forgot. I get all overwhelmed when I'm stressed." She stopped and looked toward the bar. "And hungry. Do you think there are snacks?"

"You investigate that. I'll look at the pictures," he said. Evie paused, then seemed to agree. She stood and crossed over to Mr. Dashing to ask about food. In the background—kind of indistinct as Sebastian flipped the pages and focused hard—he heard the beep of a car horn and a door opening and some quick-paced shuffling. Snacks seemed to be being acquired.

Page after page, Sebastian went through the book. Evie sat down next to him holding a tray of crackers and cheese, but she didn't say anything, and there wasn't much she could do anyway except crunch quietly beside him. Once in a while he stopped to look at a photograph of someone more closely, but then it wasn't the Kid, so he kept going.

More than halfway through Sebastian spotted him. Just like that. So easily and clearly. The Kid. Grinning that same grin from Alistair's pictures, looking very sure of himself, almost too sure. The name beside the photograph: Charles Wu. And then another name: Powell and Son.

"What's that?" asked Sebastian to no one in particular.

Evie looked over his shoulder at the book. "I don't know."

Ms. Velos came over to his other side. Both of them being so close on either side, crowding in on his space, kind of reminded him of being confined in the tunnels of the Vertiginous Volcano. It was fine. He was fine. The walls weren't closing in on him. It was just two curious people who could walk away at any time.

Preferably right now.

"Ah, that's his agency," said Ms. Velos.

"Oh," said Evie and Sebastian at the same time. Ms. Velos stood up and placed her hands on her hips, and Evie sat back in her seat. Sebastian was mercifully free once again.

"Do you know where Charles Wu is?" asked Sebastian.

Ms. Velos shook her head. "I don't. And it's very interesting that you're looking for him," she replied.

"It is?"

"Yes," said Mr. Dashing, joining the conversation but not leaving his lounging situation. "No one's seen him for a while. In fact, no one's seen him at all since his accident. I suppose it makes sense that you're looking for him, since it seems he's disappeared."

"That's not possible. People and things don't just disappear. They have to be somewhere. Matter cannot be destroyed," said Sebastian, shaking his head and looking back at the book.

"True . . ." Ms. Velos trailed off for a moment, then found her thought again. "If you want to find him, maybe start with his agency."

Evie stood up in a flash, moving almost as quickly as the mechanic servant guys. "Yes! Of course, his agency! Yes!"

Sebastian stood as well and then pointed to the book. "Can we get a copy of this page?" Evie looked at him. "To show the others, in case they need proof."

"Oh right. Good idea!"

No sooner had the request been made than the mechanic servant guys appeared, whisking away the book and returning with a photocopied page still hot from the copier.

"Thank you so much," said Evie as Mr. Dashing and Ms. Velos walked with them out of the red leather room and into the black-and-white-checkered foyer.

"Anytime. Members help members. Come back on Friday. This time we're racing homemade go-karts," said Ms. Velos excitedly.

"Maybe," said Sebastian, his hand already pushing open the outer door.

"And if you need any driving lessons to work on your skills, we host workshops all the time," added Mr. Dashing, shaking Evie's hand.

And then they were outside again. In the empty parking lot in front of the large white building and the small-seeming (but not really) black door.

"So that happened," said Evie, staring ahead of her a little blankly, and a little out of breath.

Sebastian stared at their car, waiting for them patiently at the far end of the parking lot. He was relieved it was still there.

"Yeah," he said. "That happened."

# CHAPTER 11

## In which the night reveals all . . . or some things. At least a couple of things.

Evie lay in her bed, wide awake and still full of energy and dinner. The day had started so badly but ended so well. From a morning when the adults had been sneaking out to avoid them to a triumphant afternoon return with right on their side and even Catherine apologizing for not taking Evie's idea seriously, today had definitely been a victory. They had followed up their visit to SRAC with a phone call to the Kid's agency and discovered that the Kid's agent's name was Annalise and that her personal assistant hadn't seen her in the office for a while and had no idea if or when she'd return, which seemed odd. But even better, they'd also discovered that Annalise had plans to meet with some PR firm called C Squared the next day. So that had all been seriously helpful, but what had really put the cherry on top was that neither Catherine nor Benedict had disagreed when Evie had suggested that the four of them crash the meeting.

*Her* plan. No one else's. She'd have been okay if it had been Sebastian's, she supposed, but finally it was starting to feel like things were getting back on track to rescue her grandfather.

Okay, so she still wasn't totally happy with the adults, but she appreciated that they had apologized to her and they'd all made up. It was always impressive to Evie when an adult said "sorry" for something to a kid. People so often held grudges, needed to be right even when they weren't, especially adults when a kid had proven them wrong. And she had to give them credit for apologizing.

More important was the very simple fact that, regardless of the drama surrounding what she and Sebastian did, her plan had worked. It had actually worked. They now had so much more information on the Kid. Heck, they even now knew for sure that he *was* a stunt-car driver, and they were going to go meet his agent tomorrow. They knew the Kid's new fake name, even: Charles Wu. And his real name: Jason—something she'd never even thought to ask Benedict and Catherine. In her head, his name had just been "the Kid."

The point was, she had been right and the adults had been wrong. Which, well, wasn't something she'd normally want. She'd want them all to be right together, but she felt great satisfaction that her plan that had been dismissed had been so successful. Maybe now they'd trust her more.

Or remember that they did trust her. That she was there to help. That she was there to find and save *her* grandfather.

Evie sat up in bed with a grin on her face. Yes! Today she was the queen of solving problems.

Quickly she jumped to the floor and put on her shoes. Then she flew out of her room and went to knock on Sebastian's door.

He answered it, bleary-eyed and blinking. "What's going on?"

"It's time. Let's go to the library and research the men in black!" she replied in an excited whisper.

He took a moment, just standing there. "Evie, I'm exhausted."

"We have no other chance. We'll be on the hunt for the Kid tomorrow, and the library will be filled with people and it'll be harder to sneak in and not be seen," she replied. What was wrong with him? Where was his usual spark, his usual need to solve all problems? It was research! "You love research!"

"Can't you do it and tell me what you find out?" He made eye contact with her finally.

"I . . . I mean . . . yes, I guess." What was happening? Her insides started to squirm. Sebastian's reluctance did not feel good, not at all.

"Great. Okay. Good luck. If you have trouble, I'll help you tomorrow, but you can do it." Evie knew Sebastian wasn't a liar, but the way he had answered did not make the offer sound like the truth. It was probably just that he was so tired. But so was she. Tired had nothing to do with it. They had to find her grandfather in any way possible. They didn't have time to be sleepy.

"Thanks," she said, and she just stood there as Sebastian closed the door. She stared at it for a moment. She felt very alone, more alone than when Catherine and Benedict had gone off without them. More alone than when she'd been living at Wayward School. It was a type of alone you felt when you actually weren't. When there were other people around but you still felt lonely. It was a really bad feeling.

No. She shook out her body, took in a sharp breath, and readied herself. She'd do this with or without him. Besides . . . besides, this had been her idea in the first place. And she was tired of convincing people of things. Time to just do it her way and not worry about sleepy boys.

So she turned around, quietly left the suite, and moved into the hall. The pug was asleep at their door and gave her a look as she tiptoed over it. "Shhh," she said, and it went back to sleep. Not a very effective guard dog, really.

In no time she was whisking her way up to the library level and stepping out into the large open space. It glowed a kind of orange from the lights of the city outside. In many ways it reminded Evie of the library at the East Coast society headquarters. The library was several stories tall, but instead of everything being a dark wood with dark banisters and dusty objects hanging here and there, once more there was a white cleanliness to it all. The balconies were curvy as if they had been formed naturally out of a beige stone. The low walls that prevented someone from falling over the side swooped and bent in a very natural kind of way. Everything looked like it had been carved out of something preexisting. Which of course made no sense, as they were at the top of a skyscraper.

The floor rippled with shadows, and Evie looked up to the skylight high above her. There was no tree growing through the center, just a vast emptiness. The light coming down was constantly moving and shifting. She suddenly realized it was the pool! The skylight was the pool, and the ripples were the water far above moving a little in the wind outside. It was an eerie effect. Like ghosts slipping across the floor.

Evie peered around and saw a sign by the stairs. She approached it. It was a directory. Carefully she read until she came across the words "Society Database," with the number four next to it highlighted by the watery moonlight. With a deep intake of breath, Evie

made her way to the stairs. She climbed to the fourth level, followed signs, and eventually found a bank of computers. They sat along a wall of windows, and the LA skyline glowed behind them. Here Evie could see the orange in full view, lighting up the sky just below the black of night. She sat down as softly as she could at the computer and opened up the database, relieved she didn't have to enter a password or anything. She supposed it made sense; after all, it was hard enough to get into the society building, so members probably assumed that anyone on a computer inside would be allowed to be.

In a few clicks, she was staring at an empty search bar.

Now what?

She didn't know much about these men in black. She didn't even know their full names. But, she supposed, she did have their initials. Evie entered *K* into the last names search bar and felt some satisfaction as the page on the computer refreshed into . . . a list twelve pages long. Okay. Well, she wasn't sure what she was looking for, but it was a start, and she had all night.

She read the first line: "Ka, Jane. 2016. Admitting officer, Algens."

Algens. Myrtle! That was Myrtle's last name. That was kind of neat. What was an admitting officer?

Probably someone who . . . admitted to something . . .
Oh! No! It was someone who approved new members,
who allowed them into the society. It was the person
who let new members in!

That was fun to realize. She continued reading the
*K*s. As she did, she became more and more aware of
how ridiculous this search was. She didn't even know
what she was looking for; she didn't know who any of
these people were. Any number of them could be a Mr.
K. The only times she recognized a name were when
"Algens" appeared as the admitting officer.

Wait.

The Mr.s had a problem with her grandfather specifically . . . obviously. . . . What if . . .

She went back to the search page. Instead of searching for members, she searched for "admitting officer."
The list rearranged itself alphabetically by the officers'
last names, and sure enough Myrtle Algens, the president of the Explorers Society and Evie's new guardian,
was the first entry. She had admitted many members,
and there was something about knowing how important she was that made Evie feel quite proud that she
knew the woman personally.

But that wasn't the name she'd been hoping to find.

She flipped the alphabetical arrangement so that
the first name was of higher importance than the last

name, and immediately the name she was looking for rose to the top.

"Alistair Drake."

She clicked on it, and her grandfather's name repeated over and over and over again. It made her heart sing. And it made the task ahead of her seem less slow and painful. She had the patience to go through the list, if only to see her grandfather's name before her, to know that he'd once been respected enough that he'd been granted the responsibility of welcoming new members. She liked that.

She began the task, staring at name after name. As any members with last names starting with $M$, $I$, or $K$ appeared, she wrote the names down on a pad of paper next to the computer. She went through the list like this for a good half hour, until she noticed something different. Next to the name "Fiona Montgomery" she saw a little $x$ at the end, after the row of information about her. When Evie clicked the $x$, a little window popped up with text that said "Dismissed, Algens" and a date below that. She read the words carefully and then returned to going through the names, this time looking for the $x$. A few minutes later, she found another. This time it said "Dismissed, Butler" with a different date. And then she spotted another: "Dismissed, Algens." And then a fourth: "Dismissed, Drake."

She paused to think. Dismissed.

Quickly she left her page of Alistair Drake–appointed members and went back and typed in a new name: "Catherine Lind."

Catherine's profile came up easily, and the admitting officer was Evie's grandfather. Sure enough there was also a little *x* next to her name.

"Dismissed, Algens." And a date. Twenty years ago.

*Dismissed*. Evie pondered again.

That obviously meant "banned." It meant the person was no longer a member. And the name after "dismissed" was the last name of the person who'd been the one to cut off the person's access to the society.

Evie thought about what she'd just read.

"Dismissed, Drake."

She thought back to her train of thought moments earlier, while she'd been lying in bed. Adults and grudges.

What if . . .

Evie examined all her search options, and sure enough, there was a way to put all the dismissed members into a list, categorized by year dismissed. This list was much shorter, only five pages. She dutifully went through all of them, searching for her grandfather's last name as the person who'd been the dismisser. She searched and searched, and then . . . there it was. And there it was again. And again.

And something else too. There was only a handful of times when Alistair Drake had dismissed someone from the society, but there were indeed three last names that stood out clearly. Mandrill, Indolangur, and Kipunji. M. I. K. One right after another. All around twenty-five years ago.

And all banned by her grandfather.

Evie sat back in her chair and stared at the glowing screen. Adrenaline was pumping fast through her body, and she could feel herself almost buzzing. The feeling reminded her of the thrill she'd felt while driving earlier in the day. She'd found them. She'd finally found the men in black. She was sure of it.

"You seem satisfied," said Alejandro, pulling up the chair next to her at the dark computer to her right.

She jumped at hearing his voice and turned to look at him. "You are very good at sneaking up on people," she said.

"Well, I spent my life exploring sacred sites. One has to be careful and quiet all the time. You don't want to disturb," he replied. "Plus I bought these new shoes, and the soles are very soft."

Evie nodded. She didn't know what else to say.

"You have found something," said Alejandro.

"Yes. I have." She was so excited, she just needed to share, even if it was with someone who wasn't entirely supportive of her and her team. "Three names that match up with the letters of those bad men. Men who were all banned from the society. All around the same time. And all by my grandfather." She thought the way in which she'd phrased that made it sound extra dramatic and exciting.

"Interesting," said Alejandro, nodding. "That is quite the connection."

"Yes! And don't you see? Clearly they wanted revenge on my grandfather because he kicked them out. Clearly also there was something bad about them if they were banned in the first place. They did something they shouldn't have done. It makes sense that these guys want to hurt him."

"Well, yes, in a way. I am not so sure things are as clear as you say they are, though," said Alejandro.

"I think they are," replied Evie. It was pretty obvious, wasn't it?

"Well, let us see here. Your grandfather banned these men. But your grandfather was also banned. Is your grandfather then a bad guy?" asked Alejandro, leaning back in his chair.

"No, of course not. I mean . . . what the Filipendulous Five did wasn't good, of course . . ."

"They created a tsunami that destroyed an island's homes and ruined the lives of many. That, I'd say, is more than just 'not good,'" replied Alejandro.

"No. I know that. I didn't mean to make it sound like it was no big deal. It was. But they didn't do it on purpose. They were trying to save their own lives deep underwater, being attacked by a monster. And they did make up for it and stuff. They felt really bad and gave away everything they had to help," said Evie, feeling immediately defensive of her grandfather and also a little uncomfortable with what the West Coast president was implying.

"So being banned does not necessarily mean one is bad," concluded Alejandro.

"But this is different. We know how bad these men are because they've been doing awful, destructive things." Yes! *Good point, Evie,* she told herself.

"Yes, they have. I just want to make sure you think about bad and good and what that means." Alejandro stood up and placed a warm, steady hand on Evie's shoulder. "You are with two members of a team that many across the world do not think is good. You are trying to rescue a man who many never want to see again." Evie made an attempt to speak, but Alejandro spoke first. "Other people's judgment, my judgment, does not prove fact. But to trust in bad and good and nothing in between is dangerous. Do not be blind to facts. Do not be blind to loyalty. And do not let loyalty blind you."

"I . . . I don't know what you mean," said Evie, turning around and looking at him.

"Today you and the boy went on your own, without Benedict and Catherine. Why did you do so?"

"Because we had a good idea and they weren't listening to us. And it is so frustrating, because, before, Catherine always used to listen to me."

"Who is she more loyal to, then? This is a question you need to ask yourself. Who are you more loyal to? Who is the boy more loyal to? These are all things to think about." Evie stared at him, her heart pounding. She felt scared, though she wasn't sure why. What he was saying was hitting her in a way she couldn't exactly explain. Alejandro smiled a soft smile at her. "Tomorrow. Think about it tomorrow. Tonight it is time for sleep. And the library is closed."

Evie nodded, grabbed her notes as she stood up, and walked with Alejandro as he escorted her out. They parted ways at the elevator, and Evie made the journey back to her suite alone. She quickly kicked off her shoes, climbed under the covers of her bed, curled up onto her side, and stared at the wall of windows and the glowing skyline beyond.

Loyalty.

*Shifting* loyalty.

She hadn't thought about that.

Catherine preferring to do things with Benedict. Sebastian thinking sleep was more important than research . . .

See, that was why families were *so* important, because you always knew who had your back. You always had someone even when other people changed their minds and decided they didn't need you anymore.

Evie closed her eyes and then opened them again. The buildings outside were fuzzy lights in her vision as tears blurred the view.

No. No, she wasn't going to be sad. She had just made a remarkable discovery about the men in black. She should be proud. She was going to rescue her grandfather. And then she'd have someone she could trust who would have her back. Just as she was supposed to have. But not just any someone. She'd have *her* family.

# ➤ CHAPTER 12 ◄

## In which we do lunch.

Sebastian sat silently next to Evie in the backseat of the car as Benedict and his perfect sense of direction drove them toward West Hollywood and the agent meeting. He wasn't entirely sure what was going on. Evie had been so full of life yesterday, full of pride at having been right and at having done a good job, and she'd been almost irritatingly hyper at dinner. This morning she had been sluggish, definitely less talkative than the normal Evie he knew. Maybe she'd worn herself out from the excitement? But still, that didn't quite describe it. She seemed more than quiet, almost sad even. He wished he could read people better.

"Are you okay?" he asked in a whisper. Maybe the key to reading people was just asking them questions.

Evie gave a small smile. "Oh yeah, yeah. I'm good. A bit tired."

Sebastian smiled back and then settled into his seat. Well, there you go. Now he had the answer. He glanced at her again. Despite what she'd said, she didn't seem good. . . . He thought about it. *He* had been lying to *her* about how he'd been feeling. What if—what if Evie was now lying to him? They were lying to each other?

That thought produced a tight knot in his gut. He was so over tight gut knots.

"Did you find out anything?" he asked, trying to loosen the knot. She hadn't said a word about her investigations the night before, and it worried him. Normally she was so excited about sharing things.

Evie nodded.

"Find out anything about what?" asked Catherine from the front.

Evie seemed really reticent. Like she didn't want to share for some reason. Why didn't she want to share with them? What had happened?

"I did some research last night, and I found out that the three men chasing Sebastian were all explorers banned from the society by my grandfather, so this whole thing is probably a revenge plot." She said it all in a quiet, reluctant monotone.

Catherine turned around in her seat. "You did?"

Evie nodded.

Sebastian stared at her.

Why wasn't she excited? Why wasn't she beaming with pride?

"What's wrong?" he asked.

She finally looked right at him. "I'm tired," she replied pointedly, then leaned against the window, closing her eyes.

His stomach got even tighter.

They drove past people lounging on leafy patios, sipping drinks from white coffee cups. It felt a lot more like Sebastian's city on the East Coast, where people walked outside, along the streets, than how everyone seemed to travel by car here in Los Angeles. It was strange. After so many death-defying experiences with scary people, his old self probably would have wanted to avoid humans more now. But for reasons he couldn't quite explain, there was something in him that felt safer having other strangers around. More people to help, maybe? To act as witnesses?

They pulled up in front of a restaurant with a low sloping roof that turned into a slight overhang over the sidewalk. Immediately a valet in a red jacket came up to them to park the car, just like at the Explorers Society. Because people didn't like to park cars themselves here for some reason.

The four travelers stepped out of the vehicle, and it was instantly whisked away while they entered the restaurant.

A harried hostess in a white button-down top and black pants suddenly appeared from out of the darkness, seeming a little run-down and overworked.

"Hi. For how many?" she asked, a little out of breath.

"We're looking for C Squared," said Catherine.

The hostess appraised them for a moment and then, smiling exhaustedly, said, "Please follow me!"

She guided them through the dark low-ceilinged room. They were ushered down a narrow hallway and into bright natural daylight and a wall of sound. All the diners on the patio were, well, to put it plainly, gorgeous. Everyone was dressed to impress, in what appeared to be very expensive outfits. The women all with shiny hair and big sunglasses, the men with shiny hair and big sunglasses. And little dogs were dotted about—lying on the ground, getting underfoot as they made their way through the maze of tables—also with shiny hair. And yes, one even wore sunglasses.

Sebastian and the others were led to a table at the

edge of the patio, where a shiny man and woman were seated. They both looked up at them, and it was really hard to tell what either was thinking, their large sunglasses covering not only their eyes but half their faces.

"Can we help you?" asked the woman, wearing a bright pink suit, with sunglasses to match.

"Are you from C Squared?" asked Benedict. His mild tone must have registered as nonthreatening, because the woman in the pink suit removed her sunglasses. Her eyelashes were astonishingly long. It was almost like she was wearing butterflies on her eyelids.

"I am, yes," she replied. With a perfectly manicured hand she gestured to the very tan man sitting opposite her. "I'm Chase. This is Chester."

The man didn't take off his glasses but extended a tan leathery hand to shake, and Benedict took it, followed by the others. "Where's Annalise?" Benedict asked.

The woman just smiled and said. "This is Orson." She gestured toward an empty chair.

Oh. Oh dear. Sebastian cast a look at Evie, who returned it to him with what he assumed was the same concern. Who exactly were these people they were dealing with, and how delusional were they?

"Well, hello, Orson," said Catherine in her soft voice. Sebastian was confused. The animal expert was hardly someone who played make-believe. "May I?" she asked Chase.

"Of course."

Catherine leaned over, and that was when Sebastian finally understood. There was a little dog in the chair, a dog so small that he had been hidden from view. A scruffy-looking terrier with a sparkly collar and a dopey expression on his face.

"We're here to meet with Annalise," said Evie, trying to get them back on track, as always. It was something Sebastian admired and respected about her.

The two Cs stared at her for a moment. Then they looked at each other. And finally Chester shrugged.

Chase tapped a hot pink nail on the table, then made a gesture to someone behind them. "They're joining us," she announced to a very tired-looking waiter. He nodded, and in an instant had brought over another small table and some chairs. "Sit," Chase instructed with a small smile. Her face didn't move an inch, though, when she did it. Talking to her was a bit like talking to a puppet.

They all sat. Chester leaned over and spoke softly to Catherine, "Do you have representation?" he asked.

"I'm not an actor," she said quickly.

"Just in general. You're fabulous. I'm sure I could get a hair product line to sponsor you," he said.

"I don't like sponsors," she said, glancing at Benedict.

"Yes," Benedict added, "people who control funding can be . . . controlling."

Chester didn't seem to understand, and Sebastian didn't either. He supposed it had something to do with the old famous Filipendulous Five days. They probably once had sponsors themselves, maybe, though it was strange to picture either Catherine or Benedict doing commercials.

"So let's talk about Annalise," said Chase, looking conspiratorial.

"Shouldn't we wait until she gets here?" asked Sebastian.

Chase considered him carefully. It was the first time she seemed to have noticed him. The little dog in Catherine's arms whined then, and Sebastian saw that it was struggling a bit.

"She's not coming. Again," said Chester with an exaggerated sigh.

"Again?" asked Evie.

Chester was about to say something when the waiter returned with two large colorful salads and placed them before Chester and Chase.

Chester immediately reacted with a huff. "Take this back. I can't have orange on my salad."

The waiter practically bowed with his apologies as he took the plate away in haste. Chase shook her head in disappointment.

"I'm allergic to orange," Chester explained to Catherine. Sebastian supposed that Chester had now decided Catherine was his friend.

"Oh, that's too bad," said Evie. "It's a shame you can't have them. Oranges are one of my favorite fruits."

Chester sighed hard. "No," said Chester, looking down his nose at her. "Not oranges. Orange."

Evie glanced at Sebastian, then back at Chester. "I don't get it."

"Or-ange," Chester repeated slowly, enunciating each syllable.

"What, like the color orange?" asked Sebastian, still confused.

"Yes," said Chester with relief. "Anything orange. I have the most violent reaction." He turned to Chase, who nodded seriously.

Okay, this was just plain silly. "That makes no sense," said Sebastian. "So anything that you eat that's the color orange—"

"No. No, you don't understand," replied Chester with a sigh. "Anything orange, if it touches my skin, if I look at it without protection . . . I absolutely dread sunsets."

"I guess also sunrises," said Evie.

"Oh, they're a nightmare," said Chester, reaching over and patting her hand.

"Look," Sebastian said. Maybe people could be allergic to a color. He'd never heard of such a thing, but new discoveries were made all the time. It didn't really matter. What mattered was the Kid. And if Annalise wasn't coming to this lunch, they needed to know where she was. "Do you know where Annalise is?"

Chase looked to Chester, and Chester looked to Chase. Chase eventually looked back at Sebastian. "Maybe."

"It's not actually her we're trying to find . . . ," said Sebastian, but at that, Chase raised her hand and sighed.

"No, we can't tell you where any of her clients are at the moment. It's top secret. We don't even know ourselves, but it's a very exciting project. We were told," said Chase. Each new sentence came out in a fit and not like she totally believed what she was saying.

"Well, I'm not excited," said Chester.

"Chester . . ."

"I'm not, Chase. I'm really not. You don't sign on to a mysterious project and then disappear without a trace. And not without your agent going over the contract first. That's so disrespectful to Annalise. Actors don't know what they're doing when it comes to that kind of thing. They simply don't. And when they pretend like they don't need any help . . . so wrong," he said. He spoke in a flurry, though his voice was oddly flat. Not like Benedict's natural calm pleasant voice, but almost robot-like. With a slight upward lilt at the end of his sentences.

"What are you talking about?" asked Benedict, as calm as ever.

"Annalise has lost all her clients to a mysterious project. She was quite upset about it. That's why we were taking her out to lunch. But now she's a no-show, like she's been a no-show for days now, and I've been dog-sitting for her, and you know how I am around dogs," said Chester, once again to Chase.

"Oh, are you allergic to them too?" asked Evie.

"What? No. How absurd. Allergic to dogs?" Chester stared at her incredulously.

"It's not a weird thing," said Evie quietly, almost to herself.

"I can't stand them. I mean, look how he can't sit still in that fabulous woman's arms," he said. And it was true. Orson the dog had been fidgeting the whole time, which was weird, seeing as how good Catherine normally was with animals. Weirder, and kind of creepier still, the dog kept staring right at Sebastian.

And Sebastian really didn't know why. Did he have something on his face?

There was a loud "Hey, girl!" and Sebastian turned around to see who'd said it. No one was there. He turned back in time to see Chase eyeing her phone. Evidently that had been her message alert sound.

"Oh my," she said with a wry laugh. "You are not going to believe this."

"What?" asked Chester, leaning over with excitement.

"It's Annalise."

"It is?" asked Catherine quickly. "Ask her where Jason . . . that is to say, where Charles Wu is."

Chase waved her off. "She's saying that she's decided to quit the business and move to the South of France."

"That sounds suspicious," said Evie.

"And she abandoned her dog," said Catherine, her voice as cold as ice. Chase finally looked up from her phone, and even her unmovable expression seemed a little frightened at the explorer's tone.

"Let me ask her what's going on," Chase said quietly.

Everyone watched her type away on her phone. Then waited.

And waited.

And waited.

"She's not answering," said Chase.

"It's only been a few minutes," said Benedict.

"Exactly," said Chester, shaking his head. "Well, that's it. I'm done with her. This is unforgivable. Abandoning that beast with me. Not showing up to lunch. I'm never talking to her again. Unless she invites us to the South of France, of course."

"Of course," agreed Chase.

"Right. So she's gone," said Sebastian, trying to figure out their next move, "and many clients of hers have gone missing?"

"Yes."

*Great, just great,* he thought.

Orson started whimpering, and everyone looked at him then. He was staring up at Sebastian with a meaningful expression, but the boy just stared back with his brow furrowed.

"I think he needs to do his business," said Chase.

"Business?" asked Sebastian.

"The dog has to go outside to defecate or urinate or maybe both," explained Catherine.

Chase made a face. "You don't have to be so literal."

"Yes, I think she does," said Evie.

"I'll take him," said Catherine. But the dog bolted from her lap and ran over to Sebastian's side.

"Why is he doing that?" asked Sebastian, watching as the dog gazed intently up at him.

"I think he likes you," said Evie.

"Why?" This was strange. Since when were animals drawn to him? That was not usual. Okay, so maybe the pig in the teeny hat had liked him, but that had been an exception. Or. Maybe not. He didn't know.

"Do you want me to take him outside?" Catherine asked Sebastian.

"No, it's okay. I'll go." He got up awkwardly.

"I'll come too," said Evie, jumping up.

Sebastian looked at her and had the sense that, like him, she was starting to get frustrated with C Squared. They seemed like silly people. Besides, it was a good sign that she wanted to be with him, wasn't as tired anymore. Or whatever it was that had been bugging her.

He nodded and reached down to pick up the tiny dog. It didn't struggle in his arms, and that was good.

"We'll be right back!" said Evie.

And the two of them made their way out of the restaurant.

# ≫ CHAPTER 13 ≪

## In which a walk turns into
## a run.

Sebastian stood at the curb as Orson the dog sniffed about the only fire hydrant in the vicinity. Evie had wandered down the street a little to window-shop, so he was alone with the beast, confused by its decision-making process. It seemed like the animal was trying to decide if he liked this particular hydrant or not, but Sebastian wanted him to hurry up. They were missing important happenings inside! Well, probably not, now that he thought about it. It seemed no one was any the wiser about where the Kid was, but at least the group now had more information. The Kid wasn't the only one missing, and it seemed like he was actually working. Somewhere. It still all felt like too much. How was it that an explorer on an isolated volcano accessible only through a mysterious hidden town had been easier to find than a stunt-car driver in Hollywood?

Orson still hadn't made up his mind. Or at least he had made up his mind that this hydrant was not what he was searching for. He wandered away, and Sebastian followed him along the block to a small caged-in tree popping out of the sidewalk. Orson stopped. Then decided against it and walked again. They stopped again.

What was that?

Sebastian suddenly was aware that every time he started to walk, the distinct sound of footsteps behind him would start as well. And every time he stopped, they stopped. He turned around. No one. Just Evie standing half a block away, giving him a friendly wave and going back to examining the store window before her.

Odd.

Sebastian turned back and saw that Orson was farther down the street at another tree, and Sebastian quickly followed him. He heard it again. And spun quickly.

That was odder.

Sebastian began to breathe a little more heavily. This was a familiar feeling. Not a panic attack. No, it wasn't that. At least not yet. No, it was more the feeling of being chased. Chased slowly, it seemed, by maybe a ghost? No, not a ghost. Those weren't real. He was being followed nonetheless. He had run away so many times from those men in black that it had almost felt like his new hobby. But here in California he hadn't had to worry about it.

Not yet.

Had he been too complacent?

Orson was finally doing his business, one leg up on what seemed to be a rather expensive motorcycle parked along the curb. Sebastian really wanted the dog to hurry, but Orson was going to take the time it took. Sebastian could respect that. But still. They had to get moving.

And then there was a hand on his shoulder.

He whipped around to see an anxious Evie right there beside him. How had she gotten to him so fast? "Run!" she whisper-yelled.

"What?"

"Run!" She pulled his arm, attempting to run while holding on to him, and therefore staying in place, her feet sliding across the sidewalk.

Orson barked then, but not at Evie—at Sebastian. Like he too was saying, "Run!"

So he ran.

"Why are we running?" he asked, already out of breath.

"That man with the eye patch is following you," replied Evie as she dodged around a woman pushing a baby stroller, with Sebastian quickly behind.

"What!" Sebastian turned, but he didn't see Mr. M anywhere. "Are you sure?"

"Oh, he's being sneaky about it. He keeps hiding, but I saw him. He didn't see me because he was stalking you." She looked around frantically. "We can't return to the restaurant. He's in the way. We need to find somewhere else to go. . . . Come on!" Without warning she darted across the street.

Sebastian was hoping that Evie was wrong, but sprinted across the road nonetheless, with Orson at his heels. Even if she had seen someone who happened to have an eye patch, there were plenty of people who need eye surgeries or were off-duty pirates who also looked like that. . . .

"There!" she said, pointing.

It was him. It was Mr. M. Eyeing them from the other side of the street, traffic preventing him from rushing them. But that wouldn't last long.

Sebastian couldn't properly analyze the feelings that were flooding through him in this moment. "Fear" was probably the best description for them. But he also felt stupid. Stupid that he'd let his guard down and forgotten that these men still wanted what he knew.

Stupid that he'd forgotten that he should always be on guard.

Mr. M waved at him and smiled.

Okay, so now fear was winning out over feeling stupid.

"Come on," said Evie. Once again Sebastian hesitated, this time not from confusion but because he was so afraid, he couldn't move.

"What happens if he catches me? I mean, you can't save me every time," he said quietly, now basically engaged in a staring contest with Mr. M, against his will.

"Why not? Anyway, we won't let him catch you," replied Evie.

Orson made a similar argument in bark form, and Sebastian was able to break eye contact with Mr. M and unstick his feet from the pavement. The three of them were running once more.

Suddenly Evie took a sharp right down a side street. "Let's hide," she said.

*Good idea,* thought Sebastian, and he looked around. He saw a shop with a messy storefront window that seemed good. "Inside!" he said.

They pushed through the doorway despite not knowing what kind of shop it was. Sebastian figured all the stuff in the window would block them from being seen on the street.

"Hello," said a soft melodic voice, and a woman in a flowing blue dress and large hoop earrings seemed to float over to him. "Welcome to Delicate Curiosities. Please do enjoy." She extended her hand in a wave of blue fabric, and Sebastian finally took in the contents of the store. There were shelves upon shelves of porcelain figurines. Floor to ceiling, row upon row. All small and intricate-looking. Some were of people dancing, others of children playing with bubbles, and still others of animals. All precariously perched near the edges of their display cases.

Well. Okay, then.

"Oh dear," said Evie. "I don't suppose all these little things here are really sturdy even though they look fragile?" she asked the woman in blue.

The woman smiled a peaceful kind of smile. "No." Then she wafted away to the other side of the store.

"I guess we should hide," said Evie, looking deeply uncomfortable. Sebastian nodded, and they made their way toward the back of the store.

Scared that even the slightest breath would knock one of the figurines over, Sebastian tiptoed along an aisle. He felt a brush against his leg and looked down. Orson seemed very interested in a small cat figure on a bottom shelf.

"No, Orson." Sebastian quickly scooped Orson up

into his arms, almost falling off balance into a row of figures all in different dance poses behind him.

*Steady, Sebastian. Steady.*

There was the tinkling of bells, like a dozen fairies had all blown their noses at the same time, and Sebastian peered through the shelving in front of him. *Please let it be some random collector of extremely breakable little statues and not . . .* He could see to the door of the shop and watched as the woman drifted over to Mr. M.

No. No, no, no, no, no. They were trapped.

"Welcome to Delicate Curiosities. Please do enjoy."

Mr. M did not seem to "enjoy" as he took in the contents of the store and appeared pretty much as uncomfortable as Sebastian felt.

There was a tap on Sebastian's shoulder. Evie was motioning for him to follow her, and, as quietly as he could, Sebastian did, walking beside the row of shelves, turning the corner, and making his way along another one. He stared between two mini-chefs fighting over a tiny cake to see if he could spot the man in black.

And staring right at him with his one eye, from two shelves away, between two pairs of singers standing at little microphones, was Mr. M. Sebastian's instinct was to run, but his strong desire not to destroy everything in the shop prevented him. The staring contest resumed. He just couldn't not stare back at the man.

Sebastian had no plan. He didn't know what to do. He wanted to return to the restaurant, to safety, and to people allergic to the color orange. He didn't want this.

"How did you find me?" he asked instead.

"Hello, Sebastian," said that familiar friendly voice that made Mr. M all the more terrifying.

"You didn't answer his question," said Evie, coming up behind Sebastian's right shoulder.

"I'm good at finding things. You know that," replied Mr. M with a wink. Sebastian couldn't help but wonder if the man ever winked with the eye that the eye patch was covering and so no one ever knew he was doing it.

"We know all about your past with my grandfather, and you're pathetic!" said Evie.

"Uh, maybe don't insult him," said Sebastian, not breaking eye contact with the man.

"I don't care," she replied.

"Well, I do." Sebastian's heart was racing fast. And he was getting quite hot and sweaty where he was holding Orson tight to his chest. He put the dog on the floor carefully. "Stay," he whispered. The dog sat and looked at him with concern.

"Time for you to come with me, Sebastian. You can't win this," said Mr. M, sounding horribly reasonable. It was true. Sebastian really couldn't. They couldn't stay at the back of this store forever. The only thing that could save them was getting out. Getting to the restaurant. But how on earth could they do it? They couldn't run away. They could only run toward. Which was madness.

But sometimes there was a method to madness.

He blinked hard, breaking the eye contact with Mr. M once more, and then looked at Evie. She nodded. It was nice to know she was thinking the same thing, and weird that he knew that. Reading people, even his parents, was hard for him at the best of times, but sometimes just glancing at Evie, Sebastian could guess what she was thinking. He didn't know why, but he appreciated it in moments like these. They slowly walked along the row. Sebastian watched Mr. M carefully.

Mr. M, for his part, was also walking along his row of shelves. Happy little forest creatures played around a pond, and a group of clowns frowned while Sebastian's heartbeat got faster and faster. He and Evie turned the corner and found themselves face to face with Mr. M. They stood there. Staring at each other.

Sebastian knew what to do, and also didn't know what to do. He should run for it, right toward Mr. M, totally throwing him off balance and confusing him for enough time that he and Evie could get away. But if he ran for it, there was the serious likelihood that they were going to knock over some delicate curiosities, and he had a sneaking suspicion that the curiosities were not exactly cheap. Also, he would feel really terrible.

Then again, his life was at stake.

Then again, just because his life was at stake didn't mean he should ruin someone's business.

Then again, some things take priority over others.

Then again, Mr. M was now screaming in pain and kicking out his leg, hopping around on his other one.

What the . . . ?

Orson was latched on tight to the man's calf, growling a small, almost cute, but also very angry, growl.

Sebastian looked at Evie, and they both took the opportunity and bolted. He glanced over his shoulder as they exited and saw Mr. M tumble into one of the shelves. The sound of porcelain falling and smashing on the floor was heartbreaking, but Sebastian was relieved that it hadn't been his fault. Well, not really his fault. Even if they had brought the dog into the store.

"Orson!" he called, and a tiny hairball came shooting through the swinging door to follow them, a look of triumph on the terrier's face.

"That was amazing," said Evie as the two of them raced down the sidewalk and retraced their steps back in the direction of the restaurant.

"And lucky," replied Sebastian.

"Come on. That's not it at all. Orson cares for you and protected you! Good Orson!" she called out to the dog running at their heels. "Also, I mean, thank heavens Mr. M only has one eye."

"Why?"

"He didn't see Orson approach! His peripheral vision is seriously compromised!" Evie grinned at Sebastian.

They stopped at the red light and waited to cross the street.

"I'm sorry I was grumpy this morning," said Evie as they waited impatiently for the light to change.

"It's okay." This really wasn't the time, though he was glad she was feeling better. He glanced back. Mr. M emerged from around the corner, practically pulling himself onto the street by using the corner of the building. Sebastian couldn't stand there anymore, and he couldn't talk things out with Evie first either. His fear had taken firm hold of his gut, and he was in self-protection mode. He darted out into traffic, hoping the cars would notice him and pause.

Which they kind of did.

There was the squeal of tires, and Sebastian froze, much like a deer in headlights. Then Sebastian turned to face the car that had just stopped short of squishing him and Orson. It was black and looked really old-fashioned. Like something people might have driven back when cars had only just been invented. It was peculiar, but he didn't have much time to appreciate how peculiar. His heart was racing, and he stared, wide-eyed, at the driver, who was wearing a dark black cap and what looked like some kind of uniform.

"Sebastian, are you okay?" asked Evie, jogging up to him.

Sebastian nodded and took a moment to breathe

and to sort of communicate his apologies to the driver of the car with his hands, saying "I'm sorry!" loudly.

The driver watched him, looking equally freaked out. And then nodded his acceptance.

Sebastian took a few steps back. He cocked his head to the side and blinked a few times.

"Jason?" he said.

# ⮞ CHAPTER 14 ⮜

## In which we hitch.

Evie was confused. No. That wasn't Jason. It couldn't be.

Was it?

She looked closer.

Wait, it was him!

"Jason!" she said, echoing Sebastian's cry.

The Kid stared at them.

They stared back.

No one moved.

Car horns started blaring around them, and suddenly Evie knew exactly what she had to do. Without pausing to think about it, she ran to the side of the old-fashioned car and opened the door to the backseat.

The door was stiff and tough to pull at, but the Kid didn't drive off, thank goodness. He just sat there as the frustrated traffic refused to wait quietly.

Both Sebastian and he finally seemed to come back to their senses and said "Hey!" at the same time. But by then Evie was sitting on the old torn leather bench next to a large bag of chocolates. She knew Sebastian would join her, and sure enough he was there, jumping in beside her with the dog in tow as the Kid turned around and looked at them.

"What do you think you're doing and how do you know my name?" he asked, managing to look stunned behind his dark sunglasses. "And is that Orson?" he asked, noticing the little dog happily resting on Sebastian's lap.

"Drive!" said Evie, glancing out the rear window for Mr. M. Quickly she turned back and added, "Please. We're being chased!"

"Chased?"

"Yes!"

The cacophony of horns screamed at them with even more urgency. The Kid sighed hard, faced forward, and rolled through the green light. Evie looked out the window and could feel Sebastian staring.

Where is he, where is he . . . Ah! There he was. She could see Mr. M furiously trying to flag down a taxi, but there was none to be found, and she was more than relieved to be in Los Angeles and not in a city where taxis were far more common.

"Thank you!" said Evie as Mr. M disappeared behind them in the distance.

"This isn't good. This isn't good," replied the Kid.

"What?" asked Sebastian.

"I shouldn't stop," he said.

"Where are you going?" asked Evie.

"Where have you been?" asked Sebastian.

"Those are all questions I'm not allowed to answer," said the Kid, taking a corner and then screeching to a halt. "Okay, strange kids who jumped into my car for no reason, time to get out."

Evie looked at Sebastian, who had his hand on the door handle. She didn't want to leave. She didn't think it was right. They had finally found the Kid, and she didn't want to lose him again.

"Can you talk to us first?" she asked.

"I can't, man. I'm late enough as it is. Out of the car, please," he said.

"But we're with Catherine and Benedict!" she added. Come on, that had to mean something to him.

"What?" asked the Kid, staring at her hard now. Staring at her so hard that he needed to remove his sunglasses to do it.

"We need your help."

The Kid looked positively flummoxed and glanced at Sebastian and then back at Evie. "I . . . You need to get out, now," he said.

Sebastian opened the door a crack, but Evie crossed her arms over her chest.

"Make me," she said.

"Make you?" replied the Kid with a little laugh of disbelief.

"Make me."

"Uh, Evie . . . ," said Sebastian.

"Close the door, Sebastian," she said, not breaking eye contact with the Kid. She heard the click as he did so. "Thanks," she said. It was nice to see that he could be on her side, even after he'd let her down the night before.

"Uh-huh," was Sebastian's reply.

"Come on, kids. This is . . . Don't make me make you," said the Kid.

"I'm afraid that's your only choice. You will have to pull us out of here, and I don't think that's a very nice thing to do, especially to kids," replied Evie, staring him down. She didn't much like doing that, as he had very friendly eyes, and he seemed nice too, but she was determined. They were not losing him. Especially since his agent was gone and no one else knew where he was. The luck right now was crazy. She was not going to let it slip through her fingers.

"I . . . have to be somewhere," he said. "I'll get in trouble."

"Then keep driving. We'll go with you," said Sebastian. Evie looked at him and realized how much her eyes were watering. She blinked hard a few times.

"You can't," replied the Kid.

"I think it's your only choice," replied Evie.

"It really is," added Sebastian.

The Kid turned around and stared out the windshield for a long moment. Evie mouthed "Good idea" to Sebastian, and he gave her a weak smile back. She peeked at Orson. He panted noisily next to her. For some reason that gave her more confidence.

"Fine, but when we get there, you have to stay hidden, okay?" said the Kid finally.

"Works for me," replied Sebastian. It didn't fully work for Evie, though. It only made her more curious. Well, she'd cross that bridge when they got there. Just like they'd have to cross the bridge of explaining their disappearance to Catherine and Benedict, who were probably worried about her and Sebastian. But there wasn't anything she could do about it right this minute. The Kid started the car up again, and they were off.

They made their way through West Hollywood and onto the freeway, where the Kid really started to pick up speed. Evie didn't know much about cars, but it seemed like this one was able to go very fast. Much faster than what she imagined an actual old-fashioned car could go. Soon they were moving at a steady pace, and Evie was feeling excited and happy again. She watched the back of the Kid's head and felt a real sense of victory. They had found him! This was amazing!

It was then that it finally occurred to her that the driver's seat was on the right side of the car. That is to say, the wrong side. That is to say, not on the left. Like when she'd been in Australia.

"Why are you sitting on the wrong side of the car?" she asked the Kid, leaning forward.

The Kid didn't answer.

She sank deeper into her seat.

"So, the reason we're here is that we need your help," she said instead. "Basically, we need to put the team back together."

"Can't talk now," said the Kid.

Evie looked at Sebastian, who looked at her with similar frustrated bewilderment.

Orson panted sympathetically.

## ⪼ CHAPTER 15 ⪻

## In which we either travel in time or meet some people very devoted to their hobby.

The journey took them to a different part of the city. It looked deserted, just some old warehouses and storage units. It made Sebastian nervous, and without thinking too hard about it, he squeezed Orson. The dog's warm fuzziness was reassuring for some reason.

"Okay, we're almost there. Time for you to hide yourselves," said the Kid.

"Right," said Evie, sliding onto the floor of the car. Sebastian did likewise, and Orson seemed thrilled that they were properly face to face. He gave Sebastian's nose a little lick. Sebastian stifled a laugh and was quite relieved when the lighting shifted in the car and he had the sense that they'd pulled into some kind of garage. Slowly the car pulled to a stop. They were surrounded by silence.

"Okay, so you two stay here out of sight. I'll come back and drive you home soon," whispered the Kid like he didn't want anyone to hear him.

"Is someone in here?" asked Sebastian quickly.

"No," the Kid replied quickly, and jumped out of the car, but not before leaning over to the backseat and taking the chocolates with him.

"What's going on?" asked Evie once they were alone.

"No idea," replied Sebastian.

"We can't just wait here for him to drive us home," she said.

Sebastian really didn't know what other choice they had. He had to trust that there was a reason why the Kid wanted them to stay put. Probably something to do with their safety, and Sebastian was all about that.

Evie, on the other hand . . .

She popped up from below the seat and peered around the garage.

"Evie, duck down! We promised!" Sebastian whispered as loudly as he could, without speaking too loudly.

"We need to know what's up," she replied. "He refuses to talk to us, and maybe it's because he's scared of something and needs help. Come on." And she scrambled out of the car.

Sebastian didn't know what to do. Okay, he knew exactly what he had to do, but he really didn't want to. He wasn't about to let Evie face all the danger on her own. He knew she could take care of herself, but he felt guilty about the night before, and he'd stayed in the vehicle with her. It was starting to feel like too much. But he didn't have another choice. Anyway, being alone in the car didn't feel all that safe either.

It was his turn to climb out of the car, and as he put a foot out, he saw Orson about to jump onto the ground to join him.

"No, Orson, no," he said. "You can't come with us. Stay."

The little dog stared at him happily. He made to take a step out of the car again.

"No. Stay here."

Now the dog looked at him a little more sadly. He lowered his chin and stared up at Sebastian so that the whites of his eyes could be seen. Man, it was cute. But Sebastian knew this was the safest thing. He crouched down. "Orson. Listen to me. You have to wait here, okay?" He gave the dog a little scratch behind the ear. Orson thought about it for a moment and then curled up on the floor mat.

"Good boy," said Sebastian, surprised. Orson had actually listened to him. Why?

He shook his head. He didn't have time for wondering. He had to catch up with Evie. He closed the car door and turned around. The Kid was nowhere to be seen, and Evie was walking slowly, looking around uncertainly. He didn't blame her. This garage, of all the garages he'd been in, was the most unusual yet.

It was small, and aboveground, if the light coming from the single dusty window above the door was any indication. Evie was heading toward a door, so he walked quietly and carefully past three other old-fashioned cars, which were parked in what almost appeared to be stalls for horses in a stable. In fact, though Sebastian didn't really have a lot of experience with horseback riding or horses in general, he could have sworn they were in a stable.[11]

All of it felt a bit . . . well . . . not of this time. Just like the Kid had looked. Just like the car they had been in. What on earth was going on, and where on earth had they ended up? It seemed like they had traveled

---

[11] I, on the other hand, have had plenty of experience with horses. I had to sit next to one throughout all of third-grade math. He was so distracting, constantly tapping the answers on the ground with his hoof. Which he got wrong most of the time. No offense, Sugarplum, if you're reading this.

through time. And remembering the position of the steering wheel in the Kid's car, maybe . . . to England? Or one of its former colonies?

He caught up with Evie at the door.

"So, have you noticed how . . . odd all this is?" he asked quietly.

"Yes. You don't think we've traveled back in time, do you?"

He looked at her for a moment, but saw that twinkle in her eye. "You're joking."

She grinned. "Still, would be neat if we actually had."

Sebastian wasn't so sure about that.

Suddenly the door was thrust wide open, causing Evie, who was closest to it, to stagger back. She stumbled into a wet spot on the ground, which made her slip and almost do a split. Sebastian winced, watching her.

"Ow!" she cried as she toppled over.

"Cor blimey!" said an enthusiastic blond woman with bouncing curls. She was wearing a dark dress, a white apron, and a cap on her head. "Where the devil did you come from?"

She leaned over to help Evie up, but as the floor was too slick for Evie's soles, every time the woman pulled her up, Evie fell again, pulling the woman halfway down as well, so that eventually, after a few futile attempts, they were a heap on the floor. It could have been funny, but Sebastian was confused, watching it all unfold. Also, had the woman just said "Cor blimey"?

"Oh me goodness! What a mess this is!" said the woman, clambering out of the heap and sitting upright on the floor.

Sebastian watched the woman and winced yet again—not at her ridiculously long fall or her contorted legs beneath her. No, it was the terrible English accent the woman spoke with. It sounded like an American actor trying the East London Cockney accent on and failing miserably.

"Come on, ye wee rapscallion. Let's get ye up off this floor, then!" she said with a laugh and a quick glance toward Sebastian. Then he noticed her glancing up at something beyond his shoulder. He couldn't help turning to see what she was looking at, but there was nothing there. He turned back as the woman finally managed to get herself to her feet and extended a hand to try once more to help Evie.

This time they stepped away from the wet spot, and soon they were both miraculously upright.

The woman placed her hands on her hips and appraised Evie carefully. "Well, yer a small urchin, it seems to me. Maybe yer both some poor children of one of his lordship's tenants?" She gave Evie and then Sebastian a rather meaningful look, the kind of look that said "Now agree with me."

Sebastian really didn't know what to do with that, but as usual, Evie seemed game to play along. "Yes," she said. The woman stared at her hard. "I am," she added.

The woman gave a solid nod at that and said loudly to an audience of none, "Well, let's get some victuals in you, then."

"Some what?" asked Sebastian.

The woman looked at him. "Victuals."

He stared back at her.

"Food," explained the woman with some annoyance.

"Oh, okay," Sebastian replied.

"Blimey, yer neither one much fer speakin'. Must be the hunger in ye talkin'. Come along witcha."

" 'Witcha'?" asked Evie.

"With . . . you . . . ," said the woman, her accent suddenly dropping for a moment and her voice now tinged with a rising frustration.

"Of course. Yeah, of course."

The woman didn't say anything further, just turned in a bit of a huff to the door and led them not into the house, as he'd expected, but outside into a small cobblestone courtyard. A few feet away was another door, beside which stood a pimply teenager in a tuxedo, looking miserable. He watched as they walked past him, and he seemed to mouth something to them as they passed. Sebastian was probably wrong, considering his own mental state, but he could have sworn it was "Help me."

They found themselves in a long, low-ceilinged white hallway, the floor a dark brown wood, and the same wood framing as the interior windows and doors running along the hallway's length. There were other women and men dressed like the woman in the apron and the tuxedoed teenager. They all appeared very busy and also a little depressed. Or anxious. Or . . . even scared, maybe?

The costumed people stared at them as they passed, as if maybe Sebastian and Evie actually were from the future. The house's inhabitants looked Sebastian and Evie up and down as though the clothes they were wearing were strange and unusual. Sebastian was starting to worry that Evie might have actually been correct. Maybe they really had time traveled. And if they had, how on earth would they get back to their own time? And would they affect the future, their present, by being here in the past?

No. That was absurd. He had to think rationally. They hadn't time traveled. That was silly, he told himself as Evie and the woman stopped in front of some windows, through which he saw a very old-fashioned-looking kitchen, with a black iron stove smoking, and a young woman in gray with her arms elbow-deep in a white basin of water that was probably a sink.

Nope. This wasn't the past. Not . . . at . . . all . . .

The woman with the terrible British accent went into the kitchen and spoke with an older woman who was standing at a thick wooden table in the middle of the room. The older woman was chopping up vegetables with a great deal of violence. They spoke briefly, and then the older woman saw Sebastian and Evie peeking through the windows. She stared in that same utterly confused way that everyone else had when noticing the kids. With a guarded, slow, unsure nod, she motioned for them to join her.

They stepped down the few steps into the kitchen. The cook wore a funny expression.

"Hi," said Evie carefully as they approached the two women. "So, um . . . actually, we're searching for the driver."

"The driver?" asked the cook gruffly.

"Yeah, he's a friend of ours."

The cook turned to the other woman. Then looked

back at them. Finally the blond woman leaned in and whispered to both of them. "Stop talking," she said, with no trace of a British accent.

"What?" asked Evie.

"Shhh!" She stood upright, and her eyes flicked up and around the room before she leaned back in. "Stop talking. Find your friend, but do it silently. Your accent gives you away."

She pulled back and then left the kitchen as quickly as she could. Almost as if she was running away from something.

Evie glanced at Sebastian, but he had no idea what had happened either. He just turned and stared at the cook, who stared back.

"So, you've come beggin' fer some food," she said in a harsh tone and a rough accent.

Sebastian knew that the right thing to do was to say "yes" at this moment, but then he remembered their instructions and just nodded. The cook swiveled around for a moment and then turned back and handed them each a cookie. Evie was about to say something, but then stopped herself and nodded too. The cook marched away then, and Evie turned to Sebastian. Another meaningful look, but this time one he understood. She wanted them to go in search of the

Kid. Quite frankly he was more than happy to get out of this kitchen, so he nodded slightly.

They slipped into the main hallway and started walking along it again, looking carefully through the hall windows to see various workrooms. The more Sebastian examined their surroundings, the more confused he felt. At first he'd assumed they were in some kind of historical reenactment place where tourists went to see how things had been in the past, but he'd seen no tourists—and why were all these people still pretending to be in the past if there were no tourists? Then he'd thought maybe, it being Hollywood and all, they were on a film set. But usually those had things like cameras and lights and a crew dressed in jeans and T-shirts and stuff. He assumed.

Time travel still felt like the most reasonable conclusion. And Sebastian knew that there was nothing reasonable about that at all.

Out of the corner of his eye he suddenly saw a blur of black. He and Evie both turned just in time to see the Kid with the large bag of chocolates making his way up a narrow staircase at the other end of the long hall. After a quick glance at each other, they started to move toward him, making their own way down the hallway. Evie started to speed up, so Sebastian did too.

Her fast walking became a slow jog. Then a faster jog. And then she was outright running and dodging maids and butlers, Sebastian panting close at her heels and not nearly as good at not running into people.

"Sorry," he said as he knocked into a butler. And then he said sorry again because he wasn't supposed to say anything at all. He was able to stop himself from saying sorry a third time for talking aloud, and chased Evie up the stairs. They reached the top just as the door the Kid had slipped through shut behind him. Evie threw it open, and she and Sebastian burst into a large, fancy room, where three stunned humans and one mildly confused dog turned to stare at them.

# ➤ CHAPTER 16 ◄

## In which things just get weirder.

"My goodness, and who might this be?" said a man with a plummy British accent. His hair was silver, and he was sitting in an oversized, flowery chair. He wore a suit with a deep blue, almost shiny smoking jacket over it, and a white cravat poofed out under his chin. Next to him sat a corgi wearing a diamond collar.

A woman in a pale peach dress with little lavender flowers on it was leaning against a baby grand piano, her short hair gathered to the side with a dazzling pin. She was playing idly with the long pearl necklace that hung around her neck. "Such strange creatures," she

said, observing Evie and Sebastian. "What on earth are they wearing?"

Evie finally looked to the Kid, who was standing by a small table, on which sat a decorative metal bowl. He was midway through pouring the chocolates into it but was staring at Evie and Sebastian as if frozen.

Evie stared right back.

"Neither of them even answers the question. How rude," said the woman, sounding rather annoyed.

Evie blinked a few times and turned to the woman in the peach dress.

"I'm sorry. What?"

The woman rolled her eyes. Evie thought for a moment and then remembered what the woman had asked.

"Clothes," she said in reply, even though technically the woman hadn't actually been talking to her.

"Maybe they are in costumes for a fancy dress party," said the man, taking a sip of some kind of amber liquid from a crystal glass.

Why weren't they talking to her or to Sebastian? Why wasn't Sebastian saying anything? He was simply standing there, wearing an expression of complete confusion. Yes, all this must seem totally absurd to his very logical brain. It was quite frankly affecting hers as well, and she did think she had a decent

appreciation for whimsy. She would have to keep trying here.

"No. Just our clothes," replied Evie. "Who are you
guys?"

The woman laughed lightly, though it didn't sound
sincere. It sounded more like she was in a community
theater production of some play set in the past and
was trying a bit too hard. "What a strange accent! She
must be from the Americas."

Okay, so these people were either playing make-
believe or they were a little strange.

*More* than a little strange.

"Yes, uh, we are," conceded Evie. "Can you tell us
what's going on here?"

She saw a flicker of annoyance race across the
woman's face. Then watched as the woman glanced
very briefly up at something high above behind Evie.
She turned but saw nothing.

"Well," said the man, shifting slightly to scrutinize
Evie. "We are enjoying a quiet afternoon. Or at least
we were."

"Okay, but why are you dressed like that? And
why are you talking like this?" asked Evie. The
woman was now glancing back over her own shoulder, and Evie strained to see what or who she was
looking at.

"I am dressed in my afternoon attire. And I am talking as I talk," replied the man calmly, but Evie could tell he was getting frustrated with her. His expression reminded her of the one the cook had worn, and the maid before that. The "Stop" expression.

What she was supposed to stop doing, she had no idea. She was asking what she considered extremely reasonable questions.

There was suddenly a firm white-gloved hand on her shoulder. It startled her, and she turned to see a very dignified white-haired man wearing a tuxedo.

"That's enough. Come with me," he said. His British accent sounded less forced. "You too, young fellow," he said to Sebastian.

"But we . . . ," started Evie, turning back to look at the Kid. He was still just staring at her. Why was he just staring at her?

"With me. Now." He then spoke to the man and woman. "I'm so sorry, m'lord, m'lady. Young street urchins to whom Cook was giving a treat. They slipped away."

"Yes, well, make sure to check their pockets before you send them away," said the woman, looking visibly relieved and extra snooty.

"Of course, ma'am," he said with a slight bow of the head. "Come on, children."

"Come on, Evie," said Sebastian with hushed urgency.

She knew he was looking out for her, but this wasn't the time to be easygoing. They needed the Kid!

"Jason! I mean, Charles!" called out Evie, trying to get the Kid to flinch at the very least. To prove he hadn't suddenly morphed into a wax statue. Of course it would have been nice if he'd run over to help her in this moment, but a blink would have worked too.

As it was, he did at the very least furrow his brow as Evie and Sebastian were guided away from the man and woman and toward the door leading to the stairs. Once through the door, Evie made to go back into the room, but the man grabbed her. She saw Sebastian with a bewildered expression, lower down on the stairs in front of them. She looked back at the man. Definitely a butler. Or at least dressed as one. It was strange. There was something about him that made her think that maybe he wasn't being mean to them. That maybe she should ask him for help. "Can you tell me what is going on?"

"No talking. Come with me," he ordered instead.

Those were two things Evie really didn't feel like doing, but the way he kept throwing her quick looks gave her hope that maybe wherever he was taking them would give her some answers. So she nodded and followed.

"He's different, isn't he?" whispered Sebastian as she came beside him. •

"I think so," she replied, happy that he'd noticed it too. The man led the kids along the hall to a door. He opened it. It was a broom closet.

"Wait, what?" said Evie, backing away quickly. She was not about to be locked in a broom closet. That so was not something that she was going to let happen to them.

"Trust me," said the man, still sounding very formal but with a pleading expression in his eyes.

Trust him? That was asking a lot. She didn't know what was going on. Everyone was acting bizarre, and all her life she'd been warned not to trust strangers. Not to go into a stranger's car. Not to go into a stranger's broom closet . . .

Then again, she'd already gotten into several strangers' cars, and some people had been most helpful to her in the past.

Then again, there were scary men after Sebastian and the Filipendulous Five.

Then again . . .

She felt a shove and fell off balance, stumbling forward into the closet.

"Hey!" said Sebastian. And then she saw him stumble forward too beside her. She turned around, but the man had entered the closet as well and was closing the door behind him. He pulled a cord above their heads, filling the space with light. Fine. She'd just have to scream.

"Please don't scream," he said with a look of utter distress on his face. "I need your help. We all need your help."

# CHAPTER 17

# In which things get, you know, even weirder.

"Our help?" said Evie and Sebastian in unison. She was still ready to fight this guy if she had to. No one shoved Evie!

"Yes. We're trapped. We can't leave, see our families. We have no way of getting the message out." The man seemed terrified, his pale face turning even paler and looking extra wan in the shadows of the single dangling lightbulb above them.

"I don't get it," said Sebastian. "What's going on here? Where are we? Who are you people?"

"Why are you all being so strange?" added Evie.

"We're all actors," replied the butler, his voice cracking slightly. "We signed on to this show, *Grand*

*Estate,* to play certain roles in a 1920s household. I thought it was a great honor to be cast as the head butler, and the pay was excellent. Also, as an actor, an immersive experience like this, well, it seemed a once-in-a-lifetime opportunity." He was holding tightly on to the lapel of his shirt, his eyes wide and worried.

"I don't get it. How are they keeping you here? Are we locked in?" asked Evie, suddenly realizing how much danger she and Sebastian could possibly be in.

"No, it's not like that." He was gripping on to his jacket so tightly that his knuckles were white. He must have seen Evie stare, because he looked at his hand, then back at her, and explained, "It's my microphone. I don't want them to hear. There aren't any cameras in here."

"Cameras?" asked Sebastian.

"Yes, there are hidden cameras everywhere."

"Okay. I'm still confused. Can you explain again?" said Evie, trying not to panic. "This is a TV show?"

"Yes. It's a reality TV show where we all take on roles on a British grand estate from many years ago. We received handbooks on how our characters would behave, what the head butler, for example, would and wouldn't do. It's an experiment. We are filmed all day every day and must stay in character the whole time.

We aren't ever allowed to break character, or we get docked pay. And we aren't granted any contact ever with our loved ones. On top of that, we don't even know . . ." He paused for a moment, glancing around the closet wildly, then leaning in toward them. "We don't even know," he whispered, "if we're actually being aired on television."

Evie nodded but couldn't quite believe what she was hearing. It was really hard to know what was true. Though, considering she was currently in a broom closet with a man dressed as an old-fashioned butler in a house with a bunch of people who were dressed similarly and who spoke in British accents and . . .

"Wait, is that a fake accent, then?" she asked.

The man shook his head. "No, I'm actually from England. London. Hammersmith. But the rest of them are American. So, yes, their accents are fake. And . . . generally terrible. Quite painful to listen to a lot of the time. It feels like an added part of the torture."

"Right. Okay," said Sebastian, doing what appeared to be some internal calculations. "So you're stuck in this house, is what you're telling us?" The butler nodded. Sebastian thought some more, and Evie decided it was best to let him think, so she stayed quiet. "Wait," he said suddenly. "That can't possibly be true. We were driven here by the K . . . Jason . . . uh, Charles. Charles drove us here. He was allowed out. He was buying . . . snacks. Very not-appropriate-for-the-time-period snacks."

"Who's Charles?" asked the butler.

"The driver? In the hat?" explained Evie. Did he have a fourth name here? That was one too many names, surely.

"Oh! Parker. Yes, he's new. We didn't have a driver before. Yes, he can leave to pick up odds and ends for the cast. And to drive the actors who are playing the family we are all serving, I suppose. I don't really know where they go. I've been stuck here."

"So the rest of you haven't left since this started?" asked Sebastian.

"Not really."

"Not really?"

"The maids and under-butlers do go for occasional strolls."

Evie stared at the butler, willing him to see the most obvious conclusion to be drawn here. He didn't seem to get it. He just stared back at her, possibly willing *her* to see something *he* was thinking but that she really didn't get.

"If you're not locked in, if the K . . . Jaso . . . Char . . . Parker can drive away, why don't you . . . you know . . ." She stared at him even harder, her eyeballs practically popping out across the closet. "Leave!"

"Oh no, we can't do that," he said, sounding quite affronted by the suggestion.

"Why not?" She looked closely to see if maybe he was wearing the kind of shock collar that dogs wore sometimes when their owners had invisible fences, so that if the dog stepped beyond the line, the collar would give the dog a mild electric zap. Always seemed a mean idea to her. But maybe the cast wore them? It was hard to tell, really. The butler's button-down shirt and tie were very tight and hid his throat.

"Because we're not allowed to."

Really? That was it?

"I don't get it," said Sebastian, perfectly articulating her thoughts.

"We're not allowed to leave."

"But if you're being kept against your will," Evie replied, "surely leaving, even if they don't want you to, is a reasonable thing to do." She glanced at Sebastian. The actors' situation seemed to be a bit like how he used to be when she'd first met him. He'd been afraid of breaking the rules, even if the rules had been unreasonable. But he was different now. He was clearly as confused by all this as she was. Which was kind of awesome. She was proud of him.

"Oh no, we can't break the contract. We signed it!" The butler was staring at her now as if she was crazy, and still Evie didn't get it.

"Why can't you break it?"

"It's a really solid contract. No loopholes. Trust me. I checked."

Evie stared at him blankly.

"What?" he asked.

"It's a piece of paper."

"Yes."

"It's not chains or bars. It can be burned. Or torn apart. It's a piece of . . . paper."

"I know a contract is made of paper, yes," the butler said slowly, still utterly confused.

"You can . . . I mean, what's the worst thing that happens if you break the contract?"

Evie was not prepared for the emotional reaction the question caused. The butler staggered backward (as far as was possible in the small space) and fell against the wall. His left hand still covered the microphone, but he brought his right up to his heart. And he gasped, loudly and full of air and utter horror. Like he'd seen a ghost. Or like she'd told him she didn't actually watch television that much and preferred the outdoors.

Wow. Actors were dramatic.

He seemed incapable of speaking, just standing there as if he was about to faint.

"Well, I mean, maybe I can answer that one?" said Sebastian, looking first at the man and then at Evie. She couldn't help but smile. *Of course he could.*

"The worst thing would probably be that he'd be sued for breaking the contract," said Sebastian. "And from what I understand, most actors, unless they are famous, don't make a lot of money. He could go broke." Evie nodded. She supposed that was true. "Aside from that, there's probably a professional concern too. Reputation matters with work, and I'm assuming that people wouldn't want to hire an actor who breaks contracts." Sebastian looked over at the butler. "Did I get that right?"

The butler nodded, still in a fluster but seeming a bit calmer. "Exactly. It's as you said. I would probably never work in this town again. It would mean the end of a dream, one I've had since I was younger than you are now. I'd go back across the pond—that's a term for the Atlantic Ocean, but in a poetic sort of irony, since it's so huge and you call it something small," he explained.

"Ah, okay, that's kind of cute," agreed Evie.

"Going back across the pond," he continued, "to my family, my friends. Admitting defeat. Failure. Abject horrible failure."

If it hadn't been so over-the-top and kind of sad, Evie would have applauded the performance.

"Look, I just can't do it. You have to help me—help all of us—get out of here."

Evie didn't know what to say. Of course she wanted to help. Mostly for selfish reasons, really. If what this strange butler actor fellow was saying was true, it meant that everyone here was in trouble, and that included the Kid.

"How, though?" asked Sebastian.

"I don't know. If I knew, I'd have done it. I've risked too much going off camera like this. I have to return to my post. Please help us. Thank you!" And he darted out of the closet before either of them even had a chance to protest.

They both stood there for a moment, alone in the quiet.

"Well," said Sebastian finally. "What do we do?"

"I don't know," replied Evie. "I think if we help him, we can free the Kid."

Sebastian nodded. "Yeah, that seems to be the case. But honestly, right now we have to get back to the society. We can problem-solve there."

"Yeah, I agree," replied Evie.

"Let's go back to the garage, and then I honestly don't know what, but figure out what to do next there."

Evie nodded. It wasn't exactly a plan, but they had to do something. They couldn't stay in a closet all day.

With a deep breath she opened the door, and, as casually as they both could, they stepped out of the closet and made their way down the hall. Everyone was still giving them side-eye, but she understood better now. They were scared. They were confused. They'd probably been pretending to be old-fashioned for a bit too long now.

Eventually Evie and Sebastian found their way outside to the small courtyard. She looked around, trying to get some sense of where this house was, if there was a road nearby that would lead them back toward the modern era, with phones and taxis. But the walls were high, and she could only see directly above her, to the sky.

"What did you think you were doing?" asked a now familiar voice.

Evie turned around, feeling a surge of hope. "Jason!" she said.

The Kid came up to them and made a gesture for them to follow him into the garage. They did, and then he opened up the door to the old-fashioned-looking car and made another gesture for them to get in. Which, of course, they both did.

They sat squished in side by side in the front seats. Evie felt something rub against her foot, and jumped. Then she realized. "Orson," she said with a laugh, giving the dog a scratch behind his ears.

"Shhh," said the Kid. He glanced around one last time and then placed his hand on his left jacket lapel, just like the butler had, blocking the microphone.

"Can I talk now?" she whispered.

"Yes."

"We're sorry we followed you into the house, but we needed to know what was going on. We need you, Jason. We weren't kidding earlier. We need your part of the map, before the men in black get to you. And more important, we need your help with the rescue mission," she said.

"My part of the map?" he asked.

"To the waterfall. That man who was chasing us, he's one of three, and they're after the map. We think they want revenge on my grandfather because he banned them from the society," said Evie, her voice getting higher and higher. "And even more than that, they have my grandfather, and he's asked for the team to get back together to help him! We have to save him, and time is going by so fast." Time was going by almost as fast as her words were now falling out of her mouth.

"Who is your grandfather, and what does he have to do with the team?" asked the Kid.

Oh right. This had happened before, with the board at the other Explorers Society. "He's Alistair."

The Kid stared at her. For a long moment. Then he looked carefully at his left hand. She wasn't really sure what he was doing. "I'll be honest with you, Alistair's granddaughter."

"Evie."

"And Evie's friend," the Kid added.

"Sebastian," said Sebastian.

"I'm . . . scared." He laughed a bit and took off his hat, then ran his hand through his hair and closed his eyes briefly.

"You're scared?" she asked. Aha! It was true; he was in danger. "How can we help? Is your life being threatened?"

The Kid stared at her for a moment, and then laughed a sad laugh. "Oh no, not like that. I'm not in danger here or anything. Thank you, though. You are sweet. No." He was quiet and then sighed. "I've faced my own death, a lot, and I got a thrill out of it. But something changed. Hanging off that cliff . . ."

"Cliff?" asked Sebastian, pulling the whining Orson up into his lap.

"It was a stunt that went wrong. After that, something just changed. I was really scared when I was hanging. I was scared that I was going to die. And being scared scared me. Because no matter what I've faced, I always knew I'd get out of it. The rush. The adrenaline. That was fun. But I never asked myself 'What if?'"

"Not even back when you were part of the Filipendulous Five?" asked Evie.

"I was nineteen then. I thought I was going to live forever."

"No one lives forever," said Sebastian.

"Exactly," agreed the Kid.

They sat silently in the car.

"Okay," said Evie once she'd felt enough time had passed for it to not be inappropriate to press her case again. "I understand being scared. I'm scared all the time. I'm scared about the men chasing us. I'm scared about all the dangerous things we have to do, that we've already done. And I'm really scared for my grandfather. If he's okay. If he's . . ." Her throat got tight. "If he's still alive. I'm scared. But that's kind of the thing. I'm sorry. You seem supercool, and really nice, and very talented, but . . . you cheated."

"What?" asked the Kid.

"You cheated. When you did all the crazy dangerous stuff you did, it was like a little kid still thinking that they have training wheels on their bike when they don't really. They think they're doing great, and then they realize they actually don't have the extra wheels, and they fall over. You did all that stuff when you weren't scared. Doing dangerous stuff even when it scares you? That's way more impressive than doing it when it doesn't."

The Kid thought about that. And then nodded. "Well, that's fair."

"This isn't about you and your fear. It's about my grandfather. It's about the old team. It's about doing the right thing even if it scares you. And I know a little something about that."

She was staring at the Kid hard, and noticed she was up on her knees so that she could make direct eye contact with him. She had no idea when she'd moved to that position, but she thought it had been a smart decision. She didn't feel like being looked down on anymore anyway.

The Kid seemed to be seriously considering her words, and she really appreciated that. It was a relief to have someone actually consider what you were saying. He shook his head. "I don't know," he said slowly. "It's tough. It would be cool to see Catherine and Benedict again. . . . I don't want to let them down. Their opinions always mattered to me." He sighed again. "I just don't know. . . . And there's no way Doris is going to . . . I mean, if you're going to do this, you need everyone. The whole team."

He wasn't saying no exactly.

"Did you get a letter?" asked Sebastian.

"A letter?"

"From Alistair."

"Yeah," he said carefully. "Yeah, I did. It was strange. It's somewhere at my place. I mean, I can at least tell you where it is, and my piece of the map. That'll help, right?" he said, thinking about it.

"Sure," said Evie. It would help. But that wasn't the point.

"Not the answer you wanted. I'm sorry. I'm confused. Your energy, man. It's so . . . so . . ."

"Intense?" asked Sebastian. Evie looked over at Sebastian. He shrugged at her. She rolled her eyes. Okay, she knew she could be a bit much at times. She didn't care. But she knew.

"Well, yeah," said the Kid. "That too. I was going to say 'so Alistair.'"

"Really?" asked Evie. She wasn't going to cry; she wasn't going to cry. Okay, maybe a little, but if she did cry, that would be okay. It was a comforting thing, to be compared to her grandfather.

"That man could talk me into anything."

Evie wiped away a tear. *Wait a minute.* "Does that mean . . . ?"

The Kid held up his hand. "No, no, don't get that sparky look in your eyes. No! I . . . well, maybe."

"Maybe! That's great!" Suddenly she was full of energy again. "That's all we need for now. Oh, trust me, Jason. When you actually get to talk to Catherine again, and Benedict . . . and by the way, Benedict wasn't interested in helping until he read the letter, so I bet the letter will help you . . . It'll make you want to come along!"

The Kid laughed. "Yeah, we'll see." Then he looked down at his hand still covering the microphone. "We still have a little problem, regardless."

"Oh right. You're a prisoner," she said.

"We hear it's a really good contract. No way of breaking it," added Sebastian.

"None of us knows what to do. If only we'd had Annalise to negotiate for us, to read it over first, but . . ."

"Annalise has left the country!" exclaimed Evie.

"She has?" asked the Kid.

"Yes! I forgot. She represented some of the other actors here too, didn't she?" Evie said.

The Kid leaned in. "Evie, Annalise represented all of us."

"Whoever did this to you planned it really carefully," said Sebastian thoughtfully. "Made sure you didn't have an agent to look over the contract before you signed it."

"And how bad of Annalise to desert you like that," added Evie, "just for some money and a fabulous lifestyle in the south of France. And to desert Orson, too!"

"She deserted Orson?" asked the Kid, looking at the dog in Sebastian's lap and appearing as upset as Evie was at the news.

"Yes! I'm sorry, but I don't think I like your agent very much."

"It's okay. I never did either. But she got the job done. I was always jealous of performers with nice agents who actually seemed to like them. But getting an agent is hard and . . . Anyway, that's not the point! The point is, how on earth do I get out of this contract?" asked the Kid.

"I have no idea." She felt conflicted. On the one hand this was delaying them from getting to her grandfather. They could, in theory, just get the Kid's map and letter, as the Kid himself had suggested. But on the other hand there had to be a reason why her grandfather wanted the whole team together. And it wasn't only that. *She* wanted the whole team together.

"Maybe the team has an idea," she replied.

"Well," said the Kid. "That is what the team's for."

"So . . . do you want our help?" asked Evie with hope.

"I'll be honest. I don't care much about the contract. I don't care if I get sued, or even if I don't get another acting job. I still have the stunt-car stuff. Plus I can afford it. But I'm worried about the others. I can't abandon them. You know?" he said.

Evie nodded. She did know. She couldn't abandon her grandfather, and who was she to ask someone to abandon others in trouble?

"Okay. It seems to me that first we need to try to figure out this contract problem for your friends. How hard can it be? Let's make this a team effort!" She smiled. "You in?"

The Kid smiled back. "Oh, I'm in."

# PART TWO

## Of Flappers and Valkyries

She knew these curved passageways inside and out, every bolt, every scratch, every heavy piece of metal. But it was the tin echo that was most powerfully familiar to her. Like hearing a song from a moment in your life that you'd almost forgotten about, and then everything comes rushing back in very unexpectedly.

Doris understood this well. No, she wasn't a performer, but she'd worked long enough behind the scenes now that when a new version of an old show went up, the first time she heard the beginning chords of the music, she would instantly recall the production from many years before. She wondered sometimes if the singers got confused, performing the same piece but differently. All the emotions.

But the sensation of hearing this echo always surprised

her. No matter how often she came down here. At least twice a season, she came to make sure everything was still holding together. And she'd been working for this company now for eight years. But the echo only held that one association for her. An association that was so old, such a distant memory. Almost a dream.

A nightmare?

Not entirely. Most of it had been good, if hard work. But some of it had been very difficult. And saying goodbye to some people—almost impossible.

She shook her head. What was with her train of thought today? There was something off. Not a sense of nostalgia but an immediate urgency that she wasn't used to. She laughed to herself and sighed a bit as she tightened the bolt before her with her adjustable wrench—an anniversary gift from Mia, with Doris's name engraved on it.

This feeling. It didn't mean anything. Well, it meant something. It meant she was feeling a little sad, a bit low. But that was because Jack had decided not to come home for spring break, instead choosing to go on a road trip with his friends. No more need for Mom. A new chapter was starting in his life.

A new chapter was starting in her life.

A new chapter.

She finished tightening the bolt and looked up the

passageway. She could see the white throw cloths and the glint of brass and copper around the corner.

Maybe it was the letter. Maybe that's what was getting to her. Why had Alistair had to remind her of a life that didn't feel like hers anymore? Why couldn't he have left her alone?

She didn't want to go back and reread the book. She wanted to turn the page. Keep moving forward.

She pulled out a handkerchief and wiped her hands, looking around, feeling satisfied. Or trying to, at least. She could pretend as well as the performers onstage. Even to herself.

With a nod she turned and made her way back to the ladder and up and out. No time to dwell in the past.

Time for the next chapter.

# ➤ CHAPTER 18 ◄

## In which a plan is made.

The silence that greeted Sebastian and Evie upon their return to the Explorers Society was not entirely what Sebastian had been expecting. And he certainly had no idea what to do with it when they stepped through the door into their suite with the Kid. It was almost like someone had pressed pause on a movie. No one moved, no one said anything. *Come on, Evie,* he thought, *this is one of the things you're good at. Breaking silences.*

But even she didn't seem to know what to say.

In the end it was the Kid who broke it.

"This is awkward," he said with a grin.

"Yes," replied Benedict.

The Kid laughed. "Aw, Ben, as chill as ever. Come on, man, give me a hug." And the Kid walked over to Benedict and put his arms around him. The hug was returned, but not before Benedict said:

"You know I dislike 'Ben.'"

"Oh, I know," replied the Kid, giving Benedict one last pat on the back before breaking their hug.

"Hi, Jason," said Catherine, extending her hand.

The Kid took it, and they shook. "Catherine, it's great to see you."

"Hmm" was her reply.

"I, uh, suppose you'll want to know where we went?" asked Evie, stepping into the room.

"Indeed," replied Benedict.

"You're okay, though," said Catherine, looking at Evie carefully. Evie nodded. A moment seemed to pass between them, but what that was, Sebastian wasn't entirely sure.

"What happened?" asked Benedict.

The magnitude of the question kind of overwhelmed Sebastian. "I . . . need to sit," he said.

He walked through the group and down the stairs to the couch and flopped onto it. His head was swimming. And not just from all the activity. He was just so exhausted by everything. He wasn't sure he could handle any of this anymore.

"So," said Benedict, sitting on the other end of the couch while the others grabbed chairs. "Tell us what happened."

Sebastian looked to Evie, and in that excellent mind-reading way, Evie knew she was the appointed storyteller. She explained about Mr. M's return. About accidentally coming across the Kid. And about the house that was actually a set for a TV show. That all the actors had been locked into contracts that wouldn't let them leave. That the Kid didn't care if he got into trouble, but he couldn't even think of leaving without helping the other actors first. Not that he was sure yet if he was going to come help Evie and Sebastian. But they had to free the actors, basically. Regardless.

She paused for a moment. And then said, "I guess that's 'the end' to the story."

"Very well," said Catherine, leaning back.

"Wow, you kids have been through a lot," said the Kid, looking very impressed.

"That's nothing," said Evie. "That's only a small bit." And she smiled.

Sebastian didn't, though. He thought about everything he'd experienced since the beginning. About seeing Mr. M again this afternoon. It had all brought the very real and very dangerous part of the accidental adventure into sharp focus. It didn't make him feel all warm and fuzzy, or even proud. Yes, sometimes it had been fun, he couldn't deny that. But right now it all just stressed him out. If he'd been through all that already, what else was to come? Would it be worse? Could he handle it?

"So," said Benedict, "how do we save these actors?"

"Good question," said the Kid. "I'd ask Annalise to look over the contract, but . . . she's gone."

"Could another agent at the agency do it for us?" asked Evie.

"Yes, but that would mean waiting until tomorrow because the office is closed now," he replied.

"Good point," said Evie.

"What's the rush?" asked Sebastian. Surely a quiet simple evening in wouldn't be the worst thing after a day like they'd had.

"Every moment that passes, my grandfather could be in more trouble. You know that, Sebastian," said Evie, looking at him in disbelief. "So the sooner we solve the actors' problem, the sooner we get back to my grandfather's."

"Yes, of course, you're right," he said. She was right. But he was very tired and not exactly thinking as straight as he normally did. So. They needed an agent ASAP. Or someone agent-like. Or someone who could just read over a contract. How hard could it be to read over a contract? "I could try," he said. Or rather, his mouth said it. His brain was pretty startled to hear it. Then again, it was half-asleep.

"What?" asked Benedict.

"I can look at a contract. A contract is just a series of instructions about what you can and can't do. I imagine it would be pretty straightforward to see if there are any spots where the logic doesn't add up." He didn't feel that sure of himself, but he didn't not feel sure of himself either.

"I have a copy of it in my email. Let me pull it up," said the Kid, walking over to the computer in the corner and sitting down.

"Perfect!" said Evie, giving Sebastian a smile. He appreciated her confidence in him. But at the same time he really didn't want to let the team down. He'd never actually done something like this before, after all.

"Here you go, man. Good luck!" said the Kid, standing and letting Sebastian take his place.

They all huddled around Sebastian, watching him read the screen. Too close, much too close. *Just focus on the task at hand. Forget about everyone around you,* he told himself. It was easier to say than do.

"Okay, well. I mean, okay. It's all written out here," he said, skimming the paragraphs. "Jason, did you know that you aren't actually allowed to go beyond a three-mile radius of the set?" he asked.

"I did."

"Did you know there were cameras inside the cars monitoring you? And that they keep track of wherever you go?"

"What?" asked the Kid, looking closely where Sebastian was pointing. "We might be in trouble, then. I covered my own microphone, but if they hid one somewhere in the car as well, then . . . whoever is in charge probably knows what's going on. Probably heard our conversation in the garage."

"I was thinking that too," said Sebastian. "But really, they're probably not that worried. It doesn't matter what our plan is. There's very little any of us can do. 'No one from the outside world can disrupt the integrity of the experiment,' it says. You actually signed a contract that said you'd be working until stated otherwise—"

"Well, I state otherwise. There!" Evie exclaimed triumphantly.

"By the production company," continued Sebastian, scrolling to the next page, where the sentence finished. Evie let out a sigh.

"And who is the production company?" asked Catherine.

"Forever Entertainment," said Sebastian, continuing to scan through the contract. There was nothing, nothing anywhere, that allowed any actor or participant to leave the show except with the permission of the company. It was ridiculous. These performers had essentially signed up to be imprisoned.

Sebastian leaned back, and when he did, he was relieved that everyone else took that as a cue to go sit back down. With space around his body, his brain was able to process things a bit more clearly.

"There's really nothing we can do for them?" asked Evie.

"Not that I can see," replied Sebastian, closing his eyes and thinking hard.

"Not even convincing everyone to leave the project?" she asked.

"They'll be sued. For a lot of money. And I imagine anyone who would agree to this job in the first place needs the money," replied Sebastian.

"Not all of us," said the Kid. "I'm okay leaving the show."

"What happens if someone gets sick?" asked Evie.

Sebastian leaned forward and scanned through the pages. "Ah, here we go. Evidently a doctor in costume will come on set and administer 'historically accurate treatments.'"

"Well, that's kind of terrifying," said Evie.

"Indeed. Treatments from the past were not particularly . . . humane," said Benedict.

"Oh! Good news. If you die, you can leave the show. Someone will come and take the body away," said Sebastian, reading on.

"I don't think that's the solution we're looking for," said Evie.

"No. No, it's . . . not . . ." Sebastian stopped and thought about it for a moment. About being made to pretend to be a street urchin earlier. Now he understood. Because of the rules of their contract, the actors hadn't wanted him and Evie to seem to be from the outside world, which would "disrupt the integrity" of the show. They had been "cast" in roles to keep things going and to not get everyone else in trouble. "Huh," he said out loud.

"Sebastian! I don't know what you're thinking, but I think those people would rather be imprisoned on an old-fashioned television show than . . . not living," said Evie.

Sebastian turned to her. "Of course. I'm not that ridiculous. No, I was simply thinking how nothing can disrupt the integrity of the experiment."

"They want to keep the historical accuracy of the show intact," said Catherine.

"Exactly. That's the thing. Whoever is filming this wants it all to be as realistic as possible. The story is everything."

Evie was at his side so quickly, it made him jump. "Sebastian! You're not suggesting—"

"What? What is it?" asked the Kid.

Sebastian shook his head. It was the only way. "We have to save everyone . . . by acting."

# → CHAPTER 19 ←

## In which everyone gets the chance to chant.

"Wow, it's huge," said Evie, staring as they approached the set of *Grand Estate*. Or rather, the house. Mansion. Whatever. It was massive. And like something from a different country. A very large British brick manor house was sitting at the end of a very long driveway lined with trees. To one side there was a small pasture, even a barn. It all looked so surreal, especially in the setting sun. Like she was dreaming.

"Impressive," added Catherine.

There was a narrow dirt path that veered around to the back of the building, which they turned down now, heading toward the garage, Evie supposed.

Evie moved her head to the side. The piece of wood

she was holding was poking into her cheek, scratching her a little. But it was nothing compared to the simple wool dress she was wearing. Everyone was dressed in costume, but no one seemed to be as uncomfortable as she was, nor as itchy. She couldn't wait until they could climb out of this car and she could stretch her legs. Three explorers and two kids crowded the car. (Fortunately, no dog. That would have been one too many things. Orson was being kept safe at the society.) Plus, a bunch of signs attached to long sticks took up a lot of room.

The car eventually pulled to a stop. The skinny pimpled teenager quickly ran around and opened the doors, gaping at them. The Kid shut off the car, and soon everyone was out in the dark dampness.

"Welcome to the past!" the Kid said with a laugh.

"I can't believe we're doing this," said Sebastian.

"Hey, it was your idea," replied Evie with a grin, passing him a pair of signs.

"Yeah. Still. I can't believe we're doing this." He shook his head.

They all followed the Kid through the back door and made their way out into the small courtyard. The pimply boy followed them, just staring.

"Oy, what's goin' on?" he asked.

"Here," said Evie. "Take one!" And she tossed him a sign. He looked at it, then back at her. She smiled. He still stared.

The team gathered together. "Is everyone ready?" asked Catherine, not looking particularly so herself.

"Yes," said Evie and Benedict.

"So, wait. We're chanting, right?" said Sebastian.

"Yes. You've seen this sort of thing on the news, haven't you?" asked Evie.

Sebastian nodded.

"Let's go!" said the Kid.

And they burst into the main servants hall.

"What do we want?" called Evie loudly, her voice echoing in the space.

"Fair wages!" shouted everyone else. Though Sebastian next to her kind of mumbled it.

"When do we want them?"

"Now!"

"Now." Another soft Sebastian mumble.

Evie repeated herself as she walked down the hallway: "What do we want?"

"Fair wages!"

"When do we want them?"

"Now!"

Sebastian was getting a little louder. As they

marched, holding up their protest signs, various maids and butlers and cooks filtered out to see what the commotion was about. They all looked completely stunned.

"What do we want?"

"Fair wages!"

"When do we want them?"

"Now!"

Sebastian was enthusiastically shouting along with them, and it made Evie feel very happy. They marched toward the staircase that led to the large room, chanting in unison. It felt so right. And historically accurate.

The butler emerged at the top of the stairs, appearing utterly baffled.

"What are you lot doing here?"

The Kid stepped forward. "It's time for us to free ourselves," he said. Sebastian coughed meaningfully at that. "Uh, free ourselves from bad wages. We need more money! And these lovely people I met while running an errand for his lordship have shown me a better way. A way where we do not need lords and ladies as masters!" Evie noticed then that he too had a strange accent. *Wow.* His attempt at a British accent was failing miserably.

The butler looked at the Kid and then at Evie. She

gave him a reassuring smile. It seemed to click then, and he grinned back.

"What's goin' on?" asked the blond maid, stepping forward.

"I think these people have come to rescue us," he replied. Then added, "From indentured servitude." He glanced up at what Evie now understood to be a hidden camera.

"We have!" she said loudly.

"Come," said the butler. "Follow me!"

He turned, leading the way, and the protesters climbed after him, continuing their chanting. Everyone, not just the team but all of the actors who had come into the hallway, had joined the chorus. They were all smiling too. Sebastian passed the cook his placard, and Evie turned back around to continue with their march up the stairs.

They burst onto the main floor of the house, flooding into the room where Evie had met the lord and lady of the house. Neither was there. The chanters made their way into a huge vaulted foyer with the biggest staircase Evie had ever seen. Gold-framed portraits of men and women ran along the walls. The group marched up the stairs over the thick flowered carpet and into the dark paneled hallway, until they came to the lord and lady's dressing rooms. The mob rushed inside.

The lord and lady stood hurriedly, the lady scooping up the corgi as she did, and soon all of the servants had surrounded them, chanting. Evie was getting concerned. The lord and lady looked truly scared. And she didn't want anyone scared. She wanted to free all the actors. And that included the ones playing the rich people too.

She jumped up onto a chair and held up her hand. She was surprised how quickly everyone was quiet. She felt rather powerful.

"Join us!" she said. "We know that you also do not think it is right that your servants don't have their freedom. In a way, it must be a bit of a prison for you, too, having to look after them and this large house. Wouldn't a smaller house, maybe . . . in . . . the city . . . Wouldn't that be a wonderful way to live too?" She paused to take a breath and look at the lord and lady. They glanced at each other.

"She is right!" said the butler suddenly. He stood up on a leather footstool. "All of us are in our own prisons. In this house. In our own hearts and minds." His voice was getting richer, a little more musical. He was evidently delivering a monologue now. "Who can really say what each of our own prisons is? But how can we ever break free of ourselves if we are not free . . . ourselves?" He paused, bringing his hand to his heart. Perhaps expecting applause? "Join us! Be free of all restrictions! For, what do we want?" he asked, and Evie felt a little put out. That was her line.

"Freedom?" said the lord of the house uncertainly.

"Okay, that works too," said Benedict.

"When do we want it?" asked the butler.

"Now!" everyone, including the lord and lady, chanted together.

They began their new chant standing in the circle, with the lord and lady getting rather into it themselves. They kept chanting. And chanting. Until they all stopped and stared at each other.

"Now what?" asked the lady.

Evie looked around the room and found Sebastian. Now what, indeed.

"Uh, well," Sebastian said. "I say we do a walkout. A strike. Everybody leaves."

Everyone gaped.

"It's not disruptive. It's a thing that workers do sometimes. In real life. Which this is," he said, explaining haltingly. "And sometimes employers join them, in solidarity." He nodded at the lord and lady.

The butler looked at Sebastian. Then at the crowd. "Let's do it!"

There was a pause.

A rather long, pensive pause.

And then suddenly, entirely in unison, a great cheer went up. It made Evie want to cheer too! Then . . . everyone suddenly bolted. It was impressive how quickly they fled the house, but Evie supposed it made sense. They had been trapped there for a while. This was their chance, and they definitely took it.

"That was fast," said Catherine once her group and the butler were the only ones left in the room.

"Very," replied the Kid.

"What on earth do you think you're doing?"

Everyone turned. Standing in the doorway was a furious woman with a sharp black bob and bangs, wearing a crisp white jacket and short skirt.

"What are *you* doing here?" asked the Kid, sounding stunned.

"Hi, Charles," replied the woman, not even glancing in his direction, glaring instead at the butler. It was almost as if she had steam coming out of her ears, she was so angry.

Evie turned to the Kid. "You know her?"

"Yeah," he said, taken aback. "That's my agent, Annalise."

# ➤ CHAPTER 20 ◄

## In which the butler did it.

"I trusted you, Tom," said Annalise, entering the room, scowling at the butler.

"And I trusted you! I hired everyone for you. I got them all to sign the contract. And then you gave me the role of the butler!" said Tom, storming toward her as she stormed toward him.

"The butler is a great role! How many films and shows are centered around the butler? There's so much you can do with it. You could have been evil if you wanted!"

"Well, I feel pretty evil now!"

They were practically nose to nose.

"You're fired!" she sneered at him. "You're never working in this town again! I'll tell everyone that you broke this contract, and I'll sue you for every last penny you've got!"

"You can't do that. Nothing that was done here disrupted the integrity of the work," he replied with a victorious grin.

"Oh? What about your little chat with the kids?" she asked, pointing at Evie and Sebastian. Evie was suddenly very aware that this was real life and not a soap opera she was watching on TV.

"You saw that?" he asked, not sounding nearly so confident.

"I have cameras everywhere."

"Even the closet?"

"*Especially* the closet!" shouted Annalise. "I let you get away with it because I thought after they left there'd be no more nonsense. I thought things would get back on track. Evidently I was wrong."

"You used me, Annalise!" said the butler. His left eye was twitching slightly.

"I gave you work! Well-paid work!" she replied. "And I'll take it away."

"You'll regret this!" he said in a high-pitched voice.

"Go! Now!" she shouted. The butler stared at her, wide-eyed. "I said now!"

And the butler dashed from the room, tripping a little on his own feet as he went.

Well, that had been a dramatic exit, thought Evie.

"Annalise, what on earth is going on here?" asked the Kid slowly.

"Yeah. We thought you were in the south of France," added Evie. Annalise gave her a strange look.

"Isn't it obvious, Charles?" she said with a sigh, sitting in a tall pink wingback chair.

"Not to me," replied the Kid, leaning against a desk and folding his arms across his chest.

Annalise had an odd smile on her face. Well, if she wasn't going to explain it, Evie was certainly willing to give it a shot. "Did you create a television show for all your own clients, and pretend to quit agenting and leave the country, but instead you've been in charge of this production the whole time?"

"Who are you?" Annalise asked.

"Evie," she said. And then added, "The girl from the closet."

Annalise stared at her for a moment. "That's relatively accurate."

"But I don't understand the rest of it. The contracts, the having to disappear in the first place. All the . . . lying."

"Well," said Annalise crossing one leg over the other, "it basically comes down to a conflict of interest. I have funding for this project, and I take a salary out of that funding. But I also pay my actors."

"And you get a percentage of what they're paid," said Sebastian suddenly. "That's not allowed. That can't be allowed."

"It isn't," said Annalise, turning to him. "Hence the lying."

"But why do any of it?" asked Evie. "Weren't you making enough money already? Do you care that you're breaking the law?"

"None of that matters, my dear. It's about working to realize your dreams."

Evie stared at her. "So . . . your dream was to have a nonstop reality show set in the 1920s?"

"It was, yes."

Well, Evie didn't exactly know what to say to that.

"Why put your own actors in such a bad position with such a terrible contract?" asked Sebastian.

Annalise looked shocked. "Bad? They were acting full-time! They were getting paid! How many actors can say that?"

"But never allowed to leave? That's a bit extreme," replied Sebastian.

Annalise just shrugged.

"Well, anyway, it doesn't matter now. You don't have a cast anymore," said Evie.

"Yes, I know." Annalise turned to the Kid. "You're all in a world of trouble."

The Kid leaned in and smiled. "Maybe I broke the contract, but the rest didn't. Fire me if you like. I really don't care. But what Tom said was true. They did everything by the book. By the contract."

Annalise stared at him. They stared at each other. Evie was getting nervous. Who would break eye contact first? *Oh, let the Kid win,* she hoped.

"Does anyone smell smoke?" asked Catherine.

# ⪼ CHAPTER 21 ⪻

## In which, oh boy, did the butler ever do it.

Sebastian ran to the window, followed quickly by everyone else, even Annalise. They stared down at the garage. It was in flames. Standing in the courtyard, far too close to the garage to be safe, was Tom the butler. He was waving up at them.

"Never, ever trust your secret plans to a temperamental actor!" groaned Annalise.

"He's set the building that *we are in* on fire?" Sebastian gaped. It was quite simply the stupidest thing he'd ever heard of anyone doing.

"Oh yes. What a temper tantrum." Annalise looked like she was ready to explode.

"We need to get out of here," said Benedict.

"How emotional. Actors," said Annalise, leaning against the window and not moving.

"I'm calling the fire department," said Benedict, pulling out his phone and walking to the other side of the room.

"There goes our transport," said the Kid, watching the blaze.

Annalise sighed hard. "My car is on the other side of the house. This isn't a big deal. It's just an expensive one."

Sebastian was frozen in place, eyeing the flames that were swallowing the garage. It might not have been a big deal to Annalise, but it was a terrifying one to him. Even though it was dark outside, he could still see smoke filling the air. What kind of person did something as dangerous as this? How had he ended up in this situation?

"Then let's go. I'm driving," said the Kid, giving Annalise a look. The agent rolled her eyes but finally stood up.

"Fine," she said.

"Wait." It was Catherine. She was standing next to Sebastian, also staring out the window intently. But she didn't seem to be looking outside. She seemed to be thinking hard. "How historically accurate is your production?" she asked Annalise.

Annalise rolled her eyes as if the question was offensive. "I pay *very* close attention to details."

"Do you have animals? Chickens, horses?" Catherine finally turned to look at Annalise.

Annalise slowly nodded. "They're in the barn."

"Okay, everyone to the car. I'm going to set the animals free. We'll meet on the road," said Catherine, and without waiting for anyone to agree or not, she made for the exit.

"I'm coming with you!" said Sebastian. He was? Once again his brain seemed to have a mind of its own. Its own mini-brain. All he knew was that the second he'd heard Catherine talking about the animals, he'd pictured Orson's little face.

"Hurry, then," said Catherine.

Evie stared as Sebastian rushed past her. "See you outside," he said. She nodded numbly, and then he was through the door and chasing Catherine down the stairs.

They were in the main house again, the smell of smoke heavy in the air. But Catherine wasted no time. She raced out the front door. It was calm outside where they were. Aside from the eye-watering smell and the sound of a distant cracking and popping, it was as if nothing was happening at all.

Catherine scanned the darkness. "There!" she said,

pointing. And she started to run. Sebastian once again ran quickly beside her.

"Why did you want to come?" asked Catherine as they crossed the dirt path.

"You needed help. Also, I don't know. I was worried about the animals."

"That woman is horrible. First she abandons her dog. Then she doesn't even think of this."

"Yeah," said Sebastian. "I'm kind of glad we took Orson now."

Catherine nodded. "Me too."

They arrived at the smallish wooden barn. Catherine pulled the door to one side. The animals were making loud noises, all extremely stressed knowing that somewhere, not far off, there was a fire. Sebastian wasn't surprised. If he with his human senses could smell and hear everything, they were very likely overwhelmed.

"What do we do?" he asked.

"Just let everyone out, open the cages, shoo them from the barn toward the road."

Sebastian nodded and set to work.

Evie was following Annalise, and she in turn was being followed by the Kid and Benedict. They were making their way hastily through the house. Evie marveled at how huge and detailed the place was. "You made this all from scratch?" she asked Annalise.

"I did. It was all my design. My crew worked to my very exacting set of specifications. I was very proud of it. Now it'll be gone. And I'm going to be very angry." She led them past a blue drawing room into a large glassed-in conservatory.

Evie didn't say it, but it seemed to her that Annalise already was quite angry. She didn't want to know what "very" looked like.

They ran outside through another door into what appeared to be some very lovely manicured gardens, at least from what Evie could see in the glow of the burning building.

"Where's the car?" asked the Kid.

There was a sudden large crack, and everyone looked up. The fire had started climbing the side of the house, and a large piece of the roof had fallen to the ground.

"I hid it from the cameras. It's behind the hedges," said Annalise, starting to run again. It was kind of good to see her frightened. Though Evie realized that until this moment, she had been a little comforted by Annalise's seeming indifference to the flaming situation.

Another crack, and Evie didn't look back. She kept

her focus on Annalise's white suit in front of her. They were going to do this. They were going to make it out of here.

Sebastian ran to the chickens and opened up all their doors. They quite literally flew the coop, flapping their little wings and running away without him having to shoo them or anything. Which relieved him. He was always nervous about getting too close to birds. They had very sharp talons and beaks.

"Sebastian, I need your help!" called Catherine on the other side of the barn. He rushed over to see her pushing two lazy-looking pigs out of their pen. They seemed in absolutely no hurry to go anywhere. "Take over! I need to free the horses," she said.

Sebastian stared at the pigs and immediately remembered the pig in the teeny hat back at the Explorers Society headquarters. These were so much bigger, with nothing on their heads, but if he hadn't felt a need to help them before, he definitely did now.

"Come on," he urged. And he gave one a firm pat in the right direction. The pig looked at him with indignation, and then it almost seemed like its expression softened. "Hurry!" Sebastian tried again. Then the pig . . . Well, it was as if the pig nodded and it suddenly picked up speed, trotting through the barn and out the open door, followed closely by its friend.

Once again Sebastian was drawn to the memory of his first moment with the pig in the teeny hat, saving it from being hit by a car, its stillness in his arms and how Hubert had insisted that Sebastian had to bring the pig inside since it was never normally that still.

Did he have a special pig appeal? Was that even something that people had?

There was a loud neigh, and Sebastian turned to see Catherine holding on to the reins of one horse as it reared up, forelegs in the air, kicking about wildly.

"Watch out!" he called, but he really hadn't needed to. Catherine had raised her arm and was speaking softly. The horse landed on its feet, and snorted a few times. She placed her hand on its nose and spoke again. The horse shook its head. Then stopped. Then was calm.

"Here. Hold on to her," said Catherine, passing the reins to Sebastian, who nervously took them. She then began to unlatch the next stall, and a giant stallion, without even letting her get close, kicked it open the rest of the way and bolted for the exit. When it reached the door, it seemed to understand what was happening outside and started bucking inside the barn, throwing up its legs. It ran right back at Catherine, and she had to jump to the side just in time as it continued its fury to the rear of the building.

"Sebastian, release the mare outside and meet up with the car," she said slowly, never shifting her gaze from the stallion.

"What? You want me to . . . leave you?" he asked. That couldn't be the right decision. He must be able to help somehow.

"Trust me. Do it," she said.

He couldn't.

She turned to him. "Now!"

Sebastian pulled the mare carefully across the barn as she flinched and whinnied at the stallion's temper tantrum. "That's okay. You're okay," he said, even though he had no idea if that was true. Finally he was able to get her outside. And he stopped and stared. The fire had moved onto the house itself. Almost half of the mansion was covered in flames. He could barely swallow for fear. Where were the others? How was Evie?

"Is everyone in?" asked the Kid, his hands on the wheel.

"I believe so," replied Benedict from the back next to Evie.

Annalise gave another of her frustrated sighs. "Drive already!"

"Okay. Make sure your seat belts are fastened," said the Kid. "I don't want anyone getting hurt." He looked at the fire in front of him. Evie leaned over to do the same. Everything was ablaze. Even their exit. "So," he said. "The driveway, everything, is burning up. That's okay. We're just going to have to off-road this."

"Don't forget about Sebastian and Catherine," Evie reminded him.

"Oh, I won't."

Now that Evie was a little bit more familiar with driving, she observed the Kid's technique more closely than she might have once. He flexed his hands and stared hard over the steering wheel, and she had a feeling she was about to see a true artist at work. At least she really hoped so.

Here. We. Go.

The car roared from behind the hedges until it burst onto the gravel drive. They were parallel to the house, and the Kid was driving like he was racing the mansion. Which maybe he was. Another piece of the roof fell off, this time right in front of them, but he swerved to avoid it. Evie looked over her shoulder to watch the flaming object roll away behind them.

He swerved again, taking them back onto the grass, and they were going down a steep hill. Trees were materializing out of nowhere. He turned the wheel, neatly avoiding each and every one. Like he knew they were coming. If the experience hadn't been terrifying, it would have been beautiful to watch. Then he made a sharp left, trying to get them to the front of the house. All of this at a speed that Evie, after her go-kart experience, could not imagine maintaining.

"Pig!" called out Annalise.

Brakes squealed, and they all flew forward, and, thanks to their seat belts, back again. They all sat there, watching, as two huge pigs sauntered slowly across their path in the beam of their headlights.

"I guess Catherine and Sebastian were successful," said Evie.

The Kid eased his foot off the brake, and they were speeding along the dirt once more, until they finally arrived on a smooth, easy surface. Evie had never truly appreciated just how nice it was to drive on a paved road until now. The Kid pulled to a quick stop, for once without causing them whiplash. They were far enough away from the house that they could see it in full view, entirely engulfed in flames. It was utterly horrifying.

There was a banging at the rear of the car, and

Evie turned to see Sebastian waving at them. He came around to her side, and she slid over so he could get in.

"You made it!" she said.

"Yes," he replied, out of breath.

"Are the animals okay?" she asked.

"Yes," he panted.

She paused for a moment, grateful that he was still alive. Then she realized, "Wait. Where's Catherine?"

Right as she asked that, the explorer came into view, charging toward them riding the biggest horse Evie had ever seen. She galloped up to the car, but the horse couldn't stop or stand still. It stomped and flared its nostrils and looked as antsy as Evie felt.

The Kid rolled down the window.

"Drive!" called out Catherine, as the horse pulled itself up onto its rear legs. The animal expert stayed firmly on its back until it landed on its feet again. "I need to ride him to safety. I'll see you back at the society," she finished, nudging the animal forward.

The Kid didn't question, didn't offer another solution. He gave a sharp nod and peeled out of there.

They were on the road, and Evie turned to watch Catherine riding like the wind following them, the large fire burning in the background. She couldn't ride nearly as fast as their car, but my goodness was she going very fast. It was impressive.

Eventually, though, she fell farther and farther behind, until the red glow of the rear car lights could no
longer illuminate her. And even the glow from the fire
was out of sight.

# CHAPTER 22

## In which things wind down with hot chocolate.

"Well, this is a magnificent story, and I am most relieved to see you all alive and well," said Alejandro, leaning back in his usual dining room chair as the early morning sun filtered into the room.

"Really?" asked Evie.

"I might not approve, I might not like you all, but I still am glad you are breathing." He smiled and took a sip of hot chocolate from a small white cup. "And I am very happy to welcome our new member, Orson, to the society," he added.

The dog snuggled into Sebastian's lap and didn't seem to realize what an honor had been bestowed upon him. Sebastian kind of got it. After all, there was only so much excitement a body could take before you just wanted to go to sleep. He stared down at his hot chocolate. He couldn't drink any of it. Even though the excitement was over, he couldn't unclench his body. His stomach was a complete mess. He was tired. So tired. He felt like he'd been tired for days. No, years. And not just because of everything he'd put his body through, or because he'd barely slept last night, but inside too. Emotionally. It was all getting to be too much. It was one thing after another. After another. And last night he'd almost been set on fire. Was that maybe the final straw?

"So this agent of yours, you reported her actions to the authorities?" asked Alejandro.

"Yes. And the good news is that I got an even better agent as an apology from the agency," said the Kid, drinking his orange juice happily. "And when I told the new agent I was taking a break, you know what she did?"

"What?" asked Benedict.

"She was really nice about it and said that was okay. I really like nice people." He beamed at them all.

"I agree," said Alejandro with a grin. "You, Jason, I actually like."

Sebastian heard Evie scoff, and he looked over at her. Evie. He had to tell her something. Anything. That he was starting to doubt that he could do this adventuring thing. That he'd lied about calling his parents.

She'd be sad.

More than that, she'd be mad.

He had to do it. He had to do it now.

"Evie," he said.

She smiled at him. "Yeah?"

"Can we talk . . . like . . . over there?" he asked, pointing vaguely behind him to what turned out to be a very random spot along the wall of windows next to a support column.

Evie wore a quizzical expression. There was a kind of laughter behind her eyes. She was probably finding him amusing again. Sebastian and his weirdness. This made telling her all the harder.

"Okay," she said, rising. He gave Orson a tiny tap, and the dog looked up at him with sad eyes.

"I'll be back soon," he said, and instantly felt ridiculous attempting to explain something to a dog. But Orson stood and jumped off his lap and Sebastian stood too now, the weight on his shoulders almost holding him down.

The adults didn't really seem to care about what

they were doing, just continued with their conversation.

"The next step, then, is Doris," said Alejandro as Evie crossed over toward Sebastian. She stopped to listen to the adults.

*No, Evie. We really need to talk now!*

"She will prove to be a challenge," continued the West Coast president, before pausing and drinking a bit more hot chocolate. "I also like her."

The Kid laughed and nodded. "Yeah, definitely challenging. But at least we know where she is."

"We do?" asked Evie, eyes wide and hopeful.

He was losing her. She was being drawn back into the conversation.

"Well, I do. Obviously, first we need to go to my place, grab some things, especially the letter and map." He glanced at Evie and gave her a smile.

"Does that mean . . . Does that mean you've decided to join us?" she asked, sounding so hopeful.

"It does."

"Oh, thank you!" she said, launching herself at him and giving him a huge hug. The Kid laughed.

"And you know where Doris is?"

The Kid nodded. "We keep in touch. She's working as the technical director of an opera company a few hours outside of Lisbon."

"That's so neat!" said Evie.

"Portugal?" asked Catherine with a tone that Sebastian didn't quite get.

"Yeah," replied the Kid. He seemed to understand her meaning somehow. "I really haven't heard from her much, just when she got the job."

Catherine nodded but didn't say anything else.

"So I guess we're going to Portugal!" said Evie.

"I suppose you are," said Alejandro with a laugh.

"Sebastian! Isn't that great!" She looked at him with a huge grin on her face. Sebastian really could only give a half-hearted smile back, which seemed good enough for her, because she turned back to the Kid, practically glowing. He couldn't very well tell her now, not when she was so excited and happy. Meanwhile the idea of traveling across the ocean again made him sick to his stomach.

All he had to do was call his parents and go home.

And all this would be over.

He sat back down and took a sip of hot chocolate instead.

## ➤ CHAPTER 23 ◀

# In which there is a
# skirmish and I get to write
# the word "skirmish."

"Three down, one to go," said Evie as she grabbed her suitcase and rolled it along the sidewalk toward the automatic doors opening to the departures level of the Los Angeles airport.

"Yeah," replied Sebastian. Evie was getting used to the distracted Sebastian, but he was making her uneasy.

"Okay. You have to tell me what's going on. You've been weird since we arrived in Los Angeles," she said.

"Well, you've been pretty weird too," replied Sebastian.

Yes, that maybe was true. She had had a lot to think about, about loyalty and family and stuff. But she'd also been herself a lot in other ways. It wasn't the same. And anyway, he hadn't actually answered the question. "You didn't answer the question."

The Kid, Catherine, and Benedict had gone through the doors and were talking among themselves inside. They didn't seem to realize that Evie and Sebastian were still outside.

"I don't know," said Sebastian. He was watching the farewell of two travelers who looked like friends.

"Come on," said Evie. "It's only me."

"It's . . . my parents." He stopped.

Her gut clenched immediately. "Do they want you to come home?" It really oughtn't to have upset her that much. She wasn't alone anymore. She had three of the Filipendulous Five helping her. And yet . . . She glanced at them chatting away.

"No," said Sebastian.

That should have made her feel better, but why did the "no" feel like it wasn't a no? "Are you sure?"

Sebastian nodded.

"Sebastian, if there's something going on, if you want to leave . . ." She didn't want to finish the sentence. She didn't want him to say yes, but the fact was that she couldn't make him do this. And if he didn't want to be here anymore . . . Her stomach got even tighter and she could feel the beginnings of tears.

Sebastian looked down, then toward the airport, then over at a taxi pulling over. Anywhere but at her. "I just . . . ," he started.

"Hey, you two!"

Evie turned to see the guy who worked the car rental desk rushing over, holding his jacket in a bundle in his arms. Even though she recognized him, she really didn't think he was yelling at them. She looked around to see who he might have been yelling at.

"I think he means us," said Sebastian.

Sure enough, the man ran right up to them. He looked pretty angry.

"Uh, yes?" asked Evie.

"You guys can't do that. That's cruel. If you don't take him back, I'm going to give him to a shelter. And let me tell you, I have the full name of that guy who rented the car from me, and I'll tell everyone what he did."

The man was out of breath, and it was hard enough to follow the words he was saying through his wheezing, let alone understand what on earth he was talking about.

"Oh no," said Sebastian. He was staring at the man's jacket, and Evie followed his gaze. The jacket wiggled, and then a very familiar head popped up.

"Orson!" said Evie. "What are you doing here?"

"So, what is it? Are you guys taking responsibility for your pet, or am I going to tell the world how you abandoned him in my car?" asked the rental car guy.

Evie finally understood. Orson had somehow sneaked into the car with them, and they'd unknowingly left him in it.

"What do we do?" she asked Sebastian.

Orson was wriggling hard now, trying to leap out of the guy's arms and into Sebastian's. "Give him to me before he hurts himself," said Sebastian, who was promptly handed Orson. The dog wriggled up and tried to lick Sebastian's face all over. "Okay, okay, calm down."

"That's your one strike. If this ever happens again . . . ," said the guy.

Evie nodded. "Thank you for your help," she said, and turned to Sebastian.

"We can't bring him with us," said Sebastian, sounding totally flustered.

"I mean, we probably could," said Evie, thinking about it.

"How?" asked Sebastian, trying to control the wriggling beast.

"He's pretty tiny. I bet we can take him on the plane."

"We can't bring him along. This is a very dangerous adventure. It isn't safe for a dog," Sebastian replied.

"Well, I could look after him," said a far too familiar voice.

*Oh no. No, not now!*

Mr. M didn't hesitate. He grabbed Sebastian hard by the arm before Evie could even think. Maybe Orson could have helped them again, but Mr. K snatched the dog quickly from Sebastian's arms and held him by the scruff of the neck. There was no hope that Orson could bite any of them this time.

Quickly Evie turned and saw Mr. I approaching from behind her.

"I really, really don't like you guys," she said. As Mr. I went for her, she ducked, but he caught her around the waist and lifted her up so that for a moment she was kicking in the air. "Put me down!"

It was then that Evie saw the black car parked next to them, the back door open and waiting. From somewhere within the car she heard a shout: "Come on already! This place is crawling with cops."

"No!" screamed Evie. If she could make a scene, then maybe the police or security or a pilot or someone, anyone, would see them being kidnapped!

The dog barked loudly. Evie was inspired. She bent at the waist and bit down hard on Mr. I's arm. He released a loud grunt from behind his wired-shut jaw and dropped her. She fell to the ground and looked up in time to see Sebastian being pulled toward the car.

"I don't think so," said Catherine, and suddenly Evie was surrounded by explorers. She was stunned into stillness as Catherine, Benedict, and the Kid rushed to Sebastian's (and Orson's) help. The men in black seemed pretty stunned too, but they were ready to fight back, and fight back they did. It was three on three now, and a small crowd was gathering as the men in black tussled with the Filipendulous Five. In the chaos, Orson had been dropped, and he was now a little brown blur frantically yapping and nipping at everyone's heels. Evie could do nothing but look. She watched as the crowd grew larger, and then, to her dismay, as two uniformed police officers ran toward them.

At this point she really didn't want them anymore. Earlier they could have saved her and Sebastian; now they would just add to the chaos.

That was enough to finally get her on her feet and into the action.

"The police are coming," she announced loudly into the mess. Her shout had the effect of stopping everything, kind of like a pause button. Only Orson kept jumping about. Catherine had Mr. M in a headlock; Mr. I was winding up to punch the Kid, who was ducking out of the way; and Benedict was holding Mr. K calmly at bay with both his hands pressing into the man's shoulders. Sebastian, meanwhile, was on the ground right by the open door to the car. He took that moment to slam it shut. Orson ran to him and snuggled into his lap.

Catherine released Mr. M, who pointed at her, practically touching her nose, and with a grimace said, "This isn't over!"

All three men dove into the black car waiting for them, and they were off.

"I can't believe that just happened," said Evie, out of breath and confused. She made her way to Sebastian to help him to stand.

"We need to follow their example and get out of here too," said Benedict.

"Why?" asked Evie as she and Sebastian joined the adults.

"Do you really want to get in trouble for fighting at an airport when we have your grandfather to save?" asked the Kid, looking over her shoulder toward the approaching officers.

"Oh. Good point."

"Let's go," said Catherine, and they hustled inside as quickly as they could without running, so as to not draw attention.

"What about Orson?" asked Sebastian, speed-walking beside Evie.

"I guess he's coming along," replied Evie. Orson looked so happy in Sebastian's arms that it seemed beyond the right choice. "Also, what were you saying earlier? Before the rental car guy showed up?"

Sebastian stepped to the side to avoid a young woman staring up at the list of departures, totally oblivious to the fact that she was in his path. Evie darted to the other side, and when they came back together, he said, "I don't remember."

Evie's heart sank. They fell in line behind the Kid and waited to have their boarding passes scanned before going through security. If Sebastian had said anything else, if he'd, for example, said, "It was nothing," she wouldn't have felt this way at all. Sometimes we start to say things, and then, when other things happen, we realize it's not worth saying after all. But if there was one thing she knew about Sebastian, it was that he didn't forget anything. He had a photographic memory, for crying out loud. "I don't remember" basically meant "I don't want to tell you." Sebastian was keeping something from her. From *her*, Evie. Of all people.

That didn't feel good. That didn't feel good at all.

# ⋙ CHAPTER 24 ⋘

## In which things
## fly in the air.

Of all the plans Sebastian had experienced on this
journey; of all the plans made in mere moments
and made on his own and made in a group; of all the
plans that had involved playing in a K-pop band, and
ejecting himself out of a plane, and sneaking into societies and freeing animals and climbing through volca-
noes and so on; of all the plans he had experienced of
late, none seemed quite as bizarre as the current one:
going to the opera.

Opera didn't intimidate Sebastian. His parents enjoyed it, and he'd heard many played for him at home.
So it didn't seem strange to him that going to the opera
was a thing that people did. What seemed strange was

how normal it was. There was no sneaking involved, no having to pretend to be an underage stunt-car driver, no climbing mountains. No. Instead the Kid had done a little investigating, and it turned out that the evening they arrived in town, there was going to be a performance of one of the operas Doris was working on.

The group didn't really even need to see the opera at all. They could wait until it was over to speak with Doris. But Benedict had suggested that getting some seats might be nice. After all, they would have to spend the waiting time doing something, since their flight would arrive in the late afternoon, and Evie thought waiting in the audience and seeing the performance sounded cool. And so they all would head to the opera together as if on a lovely family outing. As if Sebastian wasn't a bundle of nerves. As if, had the rental car guy not appeared when he had, he hadn't been about to suggest to Evie that he go home and let her do the rest of the adventuring without him. Even though he was exhausted. Even though he didn't think he could do any more.

Why was he still here? Why did he keep going?

He really hated this. He hated not understanding his brain anymore. He hated always feeling ill at ease. He hated all of it.

So why didn't he just go home?

Because he'd hate that more?

He had no idea.

It was all too much, and he realized that he should go to sleep, let his brain think without him present, and maybe when he woke up, all his problems would be solved.

So with his usual efficiency, Sebastian leaned his head against the cool airplane window, instinctively pulled Orson in close, and fell asleep.

How did he do that? Evie stared at Sebastian in wonder as he fell instantly asleep the second his head touched the window. She was impressed and a little jealous. And she knew how anxious he always was. He had been anxious from the moment she'd met him, but now he was even more so. This was a lot for him. She did understand that, even if he was keeping something from her.

Yet here he was, easily able to fall asleep. He probably was so logical about it, told himself, "It is sleeping time." And that was that. She wished she could do that too. Her brain couldn't stop buzzing. Thoughts flew around like leaves in the wind, and they never really landed or went away, just circled in unpredictable patterns. Joy at being so close to finding her grandfather, fear about what they would find, frustration at the adults not thinking she mattered as much because they had each other, and curiosity too.

"Why does Catherine act like that whenever Doris is mentioned?" asked Evie, leaning over to the Kid, who was sitting beside her. She said it quietly, since Catherine and Benedict were sitting a row in front of them. But she was pretty sure both were napping. Only she and the Kid were awake: he watching an action movie on a tiny screen, and she dealing with an action movie of emotion inside her head.

"What was that?" asked the Kid, pulling out an earbud and looking at her.

A new thought floated through her brain that maybe Sebastian's parents were mad at her for all this, and that was what he was hiding, and she stared at the seat in front of her.

"Evie?" the Kid tried again.

She turned. "Oh! I asked, I asked . . ." She leaned in and spoke in a whisper. "Why does Catherine act weird whenever Doris is brought up?"

The Kid listened for longer than it took her to pose the question. He nodded and was quiet.

"I don't want to talk behind anyone's back," he said at last, "which is what we are literally doing." He laughed a little at that. "All I feel comfortable saying is that they were really good friends and Catherine probably doesn't feel great knowing that Doris is still in touch with me but not with her," he whispered.

Evie nodded. That made sense. She'd probably feel put out about that too if someone she was close to suddenly wasn't in touch with her anymore but was with . . . with . . . well, she didn't have any other friends except for Sebastian, so . . . with Sebastian. Or if Sebastian, say, was no longer speaking to her but was happy to speak with Benedict.

"But why don't they talk?" asked Evie.

The Kid shook his head. "That I don't know. I wish I did. I've asked Doris about it, but she said it was personal."

"What about Catherine?" asked Evie.

"I haven't seen or heard from her in years. Or Benedict. It's a bit like . . ." He stopped, lowered his voice, since it had been getting a bit louder, and then continued. "It was an accident, but it's a bit like the team fractured in two after Alistair left. Benedict and Catherine. Me and Doris. Doris was always like a mother to me. And Benedict and Catherine always had similar personalities? I mean, they are . . . odd in a similar way." He grinned. "But who isn't odd?"

"Kind of detached?" Evie added, totally getting it.

The Kid pointed at her in recognition. "Good word choice. Yeah, exactly. But they're not. Never believe it for a second. They seem distant sometimes, but they're not. When you need them . . . Let's just say they've always been there when I needed them."

Evie nodded. She wasn't so sure they'd be there for her if she needed them. But then again, she really wasn't sure if they were friends with her. She didn't know what she was or where she stood, or really much of anything.

"Now you're doing a weird thing yourself," said the Kid.

"I'm thinking," replied Evie.

"Well, don't think too hard. There's nothing wrong with analyzing stuff, but if you dig too deep, you can end up in a hole you can't get out of."

Evie nodded. Maybe. She wasn't sure. It sounded true, but, well, she wasn't sure. After all, if you kept digging, eventually you'd create a tunnel.

"I think I'm going to try to sleep now," she said.

The Kid nodded. "Cool." He put the earbud back in and resumed watching his movie.

Evie closed her eyes. There was no way she was actually going to be able to sleep. She just didn't want to talk anymore.

Instead she watched as her thoughts danced about, the leaves now spinning faster and faster like they were getting pulled in a storm.

## ≫ CHAPTER 25 ≪

# In which the next chapter begins.

They handed over their tickets and passed through the entrance. Sebastian stopped short and stared. Yes, this was an outdoor performance, and yes, even though that wasn't usual, he'd heard of such a thing before. But never in his life had he ever seen anything quite like this.

The audience seats sloped amphitheater-style down the side of a cliff face until the rows met jet-black water. Yes. Water. They were on the edge of the sea, and the stage itself was floating out on it. There were lights glinting off the water, purple, pink, and orange. But it wasn't just the floating stage that stunned Sebastian. There was also the huge set that had been constructed on top of it. This wasn't a square flat space with a painted backdrop and curtains at the front. No, the entire stage looked like clouds floating on the water. And it wasn't like one platform of clouds that the singers would be standing on, either. The scene was multiple fluffy clouds, creating giant platforms at different heights, almost like the audience was sitting in the sky staring into a forest of cotton candy. But the most impressive element on the stage was the giant sparkly silver-and-gold lightning bolt that stretched from high above the clouds, probably more than a hundred feet up, pierced through the set as it made its way across the main stage platform, and then plunged into the water to the left.

"I've never seen anything like this before," said Evie. "Is this normal?"

Sebastian shook his head.

Evie looked at him. "Have you seen an opera before?"

"Not in person, but my parents listen to them a lot," replied Sebastian. "And we have books about them."

They followed the three explorers down the steep staircase to their row in the middle of the audience, and then slipped along the seats to theirs. Sebastian was careful to hide Orson as much as he could. Even

though they were outdoors, he still wasn't sure if a dog was allowed.

"Is it like in cartoons?" she asked as they sat. "Do they really sing like that?"

"Yes," replied Sebastian, staring at the lightning bolt.

"And there's no talking, no talking at all?"

Sebastian shook his head. To say he was distracted was an understatement. There was something about being at an opera, about all of Evie's questions, that made him think of home. He couldn't help but picture sitting with his parents in the living room as some opera by Mozart played in the background. Their contented faces, how relaxed they were. They probably weren't relaxed right now. They were probably scared silly. Worried about him. They'd probably called the authorities to find him. He hadn't thought of that before. Oh man, now he was defying not only them but law enforcement as well.

"Are operas usually on the water like this?" she asked.

"I don't think so. Most are in theaters, I believe." He looked up to the night sky, to the bright stars overhead. "Fancy theaters."

The floodlights shining on the audience dimmed then, and an excited murmur danced over the crowd.

"And do the singers dress as Vikings with horned helmets?" whispered Evie. Her enthusiasm was getting a little annoying. Especially since the lights were low now and the show was about to start.

"No, that's just a myth. That's not actually . . ." Sebastian stopped talking as a woman dressed as a Viking wearing a horned helmet and holding a sword and shield stepped onto the stage.

"You sure?" asked Evie.

Sebastian looked at the woman closely. He noticed then that the helmet didn't have horns on it but wings. He thought about it. She was also on a set that looked like clouds.

"She's not a Viking. She's a Valkyrie!" he said proudly, and way too loudly. He was shushed by someone nearby and lowered his voice. "The Norse mythological war character, which is mythology from countries like Denmark and Norway. That's also where Vikings come from."

"Ah," said Evie, nodding as a bright white spotlight highlighted the sudden appearance of a bright white bald spot on the top of a head rising from beyond the first row in front of the orchestra seated on the edge of the bank. The audience started applauding, so Sebastian did too.

"I know at least that that's the conductor," said

Evie, clapping as well. "The person who tells the orchestra when to play."

"Yes," he said, and they smiled at each other.

The applause died down.

The conductor raised his baton over his head. There
was a pause. Only the breeze caused the faintest movement, ruffling the soprano's gown and the hair of the
audience.

And then.

The first chord was struck, and the overture began
to play. Orson's head popped up, his ears perked, fas-
cinated. Sebastian gave him a little pat as he watched
the action. Valkyries ran out onto the stage, swirling
around their leader. The soprano nodded and smiled
at them, beginning a pantomime where she occasionally pointed this way and that, and then with one last
flurry they all rushed off the stage. Then a male chorus began singing from somewhere behind the clouds,
emerging as a Viking army stomping across the stage.

And so the opera began. The tenor appeared, then
the baritone, a large man in a ridiculous-looking red
curly wig. Eventually the soprano returned, her voice
rich, her high notes so pure, not a false note. There
was action too, a couple of fights, jealousy, betrayal.
Tragedy. More singing. More tragedy. The tenor was
"murdered"; the soprano sang a sad song about it.

Then it was all over.

The performers bowed to a standing ovation.

The floodlights came back on.

And the audience shuffled around, gathering their things to leave. Sebastian stood too, as did Benedict and Catherine. Evie kind of propelled herself out of her chair.

"That was fantastic!" she said, practically jumping up and down. Sebastian nodded and smiled. The music had been amazing, and the floating set was one of the most incredible things he'd seen. But the logical part of his brain could not shut off thinking how unrealistic it all was. It wasn't even the fact that he had been watching Valkyries and other mythical creatures interact. It was the constant singing. How could he possibly not find that a little silly? No one sings all the time.

"Hi," said the Kid to a passing crew member as the group approached the backstage area. "We're looking for Doris. Can you tell her she has some visitors?"

The stagehand nodded and disappeared behind the wall.

They didn't have too long to wait, but judging by Catherine's expression, Evie had the impression that the animal expert felt a lot more time had passed than actually had. Evie was sorry for her, wanted to go over to her and hug her. But of course Catherine wouldn't like that. So Evie just stayed put until the last member of the team emerged.

Doris stared at them.

They stared back.

She looked just like her picture. Though she was a little shorter than Evie had expected. Doris stood basically eye to eye with her, and there was something comforting in that.

Unlike the performers darting about around them in full makeup and giant wigs, Doris was dressed very plainly in a black T-shirt and black jeans, and her black braided hair, sprinkled with gray, which made it shine almost like silver, was pulled up into a knot on her head. She pulled a blue paisley handkerchief from the back pocket of her jeans and wiped her hands as she appraised each of them.

"This is . . . unexpected."

"Doris!" said the Kid, opening his arms wide and walking over to her a bit like a toddler, bouncy and happy and a little off balance. He took her up in a big hug, and lifted the small woman off the ground. Evie couldn't see her face anymore, but she could hear the laughter.

"You foolish boy, put me down!" she said, and the

Kid did so. She was still laughing, her smile bright and warm. Evie felt at ease seeing it. "Oh, dear boy, what have you done?" she asked, shaking her head and looking around at the rest of them.

"I know you want your privacy, but something's happened, Doris," said the Kid. "And I didn't think seeing old friends would be so terrible."

Doris nodded as she approached Catherine and Benedict. Evie watched closely. She watched most things closely, but in this moment, waiting to see how Catherine reacted, it felt like Evie had taken her eyeballs out and placed them on Doris's shoulder. She grimaced at the thought. *Too far, Evie, too far.*

"Benedict, you seem well," said Doris.

"So do you," he replied. The formality of their exchange didn't seem awkward, more like this was just how they always talked.

Doris turned to Catherine now. The animal expert seemed deeply interested in something on her right boot.

"It's been a long time, Catherine," said Doris.

"Yes."

"Well, it's good to see you."

"Yes."

Catherine took in a deep breath and raised her chin with a determined expression. Then maybe with too much force she stuck out her hand, narrowly missing punching Doris in the stomach. Doris looked at her, then at the hand, and then up again. She grinned and took the hand. They shook.

Evie could feel the awkwardness.

"And who are you?" asked Doris, coming up to her and Sebastian.

"I'm Sebastian," said Sebastian. Because that was who he was. "Uh, this is Orson." Evie smiled. It was cute that he felt a need to introduce him.

"Nice to meet you both. Are you related to anyone here?" she asked Sebastian.

"What? No. Of course not." He didn't sound angry, just completely stunned by the question.

"He's my friend. He's helping me," said Evie, jumping into the conversation. *Don't worry, Sebastian. I've got this.* "I'm Evie. And I am related to Alistair Drake, though he's not here. I'm his granddaughter."

Doris stared at her. And stared at her. And stared at her some more. Then she turned to the Kid.

"This has something to do with the letter, doesn't it?" she asked, her smile fading and being replaced with a thoughtful but concerned expression.

"It does," he replied.

A woman in running shoes, jeans, and wings rushed by, saying, "Great show, Doris!"

"Great show, Emilia!" replied Doris, though her focus remained intent on the explorers. "Well, if we're going to have this conversation, we can't do it here. You guys need a place to stay?" She didn't wait for the answer. "You do. Come on, I'll let Mia know to expect guests."

# ➤ CHAPTER 26 ◄

## In which we get to talk with Doris.

Evie sat with the cup of hot chocolate cradled in her hands. She was starting to realize something. Explorers liked hot chocolate. The other thing she was starting to realize was that putting back together a famous exploring team was a lot harder than she'd thought.

She'd also never considered what would happen if one of the explorers had a family. Which was silly, since the whole purpose behind what she was doing was to rescue her family. Her grandfather had had a kid and then a grandchild, and of course, that's what many adults did. But the fact that Doris had a wife and a grown-up child? Those two things were a surprise. Okay, but it wasn't really Evie's fault that she felt this way. After all, Catherine, Benedict, and the Kid seemed like they were loners, so why wouldn't she have assumed Doris was as well? Yes, it was perfectly reasonable that she'd wrongly expected explorers to be single and not have families, except her grandfather.

"How's the hot chocolate?" asked Doris's wife, watching Evie carefully. It didn't feel like she was judging Evie, only that she was concerned, like maybe the hot chocolate was not up to Evie's very particular standards. Fortunately, it was.

"Oh, it's very good. Thank you, Ms. . . ." It occurred to her then that she didn't remember Doris's last name. Then again, she didn't actually know whether Doris's wife had the same last name. Or if Doris had taken her wife's last name. Evie just kind of stopped talking.

Doris's wife smiled a very toothy smile, almost too toothy—as if her teeth were a bit too big for her mouth. It made her seem even nicer than she already was. "Mia. Just call me Mia."

"Mia," said Evie, smiling back.

Mia nodded with satisfaction and moved over to Sebastian to give him that same scrutinizing look. They were sitting in a small, comfy kitchen at a large wooden table made of the midsection of a giant tree. You could see the grain, and the edge against which her knee now rested was rough bark. It had been polished to a gleam, and running down the center was a bright blue river of resin that Evie really wanted to reach out and touch. But she held back, even though she knew it probably wouldn't be a big deal if she touched it. The feeling in the room was one of calm stillness.

The back doors to the kitchen were open, and a cool breeze blew in from a garden lit with little twinkle lights. It was the first explorer home she'd been to, and she now wondered what the homes of the others looked like. She wondered if Catherine had any pets, if Benedict's walls were covered in photographs, if the Kid decorated his home the same way the SRAC did their offices. She suddenly wanted to know everything about them. Their favorite colors. Their favorite movies. Who were their parents? How had they become explorers?

It was strange when she thought about how little she actually knew. Essentially, she was trusting people who were basically strangers to her.

That thought made her gut clench, so to distract herself she took in the cozy room around her. On the surface it seemed like a regular kitchen, but close up Evie could see all manner of interesting devices. Above the stove hung spatulas suspended from wires like puppets, and as one of them automatically lowered and flipped over a pancake that sizzled in a pan, Evie mentally noted that she wanted something like that in her own home. When she had a home. Everything was automated. Even the hot chocolate she was holding had been poured out of the saucepan and into her mug by the metal burner rising up, thanks to some clever gears, and then tipping the saucepan at the right angle. Then the plate on which the mugs had sat spun to the next empty mug, and the action had repeated itself. Overhead a train raced on tracks through a tunnel in the wall, and reappeared minutes later on the opposite side. Evie wasn't sure what it was for, but thought maybe the empty car at the end was for placing messages in or delivering food to other parts of the house.

In all, it made perfect sense that Doris the engineer would create a home like this and live here, but it was so cool that Evie would have been totally happy to live here too.

"So you want to rescue Alistair," said Doris finally as Mia gave her a cup of hot chocolate and kissed the top of her head. Doris smiled a quick thank-you and then turned back to the team.

"Yes," said Catherine.

"Tell me once more what's happened to him?" said Doris after a pause.

"He's been kidnapped by these evil men who are

seeking revenge because he kicked them out of the society," said Evie quickly, trying to get this part over with. She was getting pretty tired of explaining over and over again. Couldn't they just do things without worrying about the facts? Why did it matter what had happened? All that mattered was that it had.

"Really," said Doris. It wasn't a question.

"Not exactly," said Sebastian then.

Evie turned to him. "What do you mean?" She couldn't help but feel a little offended at the way he'd said that.

"That's not accurate, what you said," he explained.

"Sebastian, it's not about being accurate; it's about being true," she replied. She was getting a little frustrated now. She was trying to convince adults to help her. She really didn't need him making that harder.

"Aren't truth and accuracy the same thing?" asked Sebastian.

Evie sighed hard and watched as Doris stared into her mug. Then Doris looked at Catherine. "Catherine?"

The animal expert had been quiet up until this point, Evie had noticed. Almost like she was shy, which was strange. Yes, Catherine was awkward, and usually appeared slightly confused. But nervous? That wasn't really something Evie was used to.

"There is a lot we don't know. We have some pretty strong speculations. The greatest is that Alistair wants us to work together to help him. That's why he sent us each a letter that, when you place them all on top of each other, gives us a clue as to, we think, where he might be. Where he is, how much danger he's in, even who put him in danger, we aren't sure of. We only know he is not safe, that there are these men chasing us for the map. That this boy, Sebastian, has memorized the key and is now being hunted as well. These are the things we know for sure." She said all of this staring at the blue resin river in the table. Never looking up.

"Well, I did find it strange when I got the letter," said Doris. Mia pulled up a chair next to Doris, scraping it noisily along the floor.

"You don't trust this person?" her wife asked in her plummy German accent.

This person? How could Doris's wife not know who Alistair was?

"He's someone from a long time ago," replied Doris.

"Ah, from your mysterious background. These are your mysterious friends!" Mia seemed thrilled at the thought.

"We're not mysterious," said Benedict in his calm

way that definitely made it seem like actually they really were mysterious.

"You mean you don't know anything about the Filipendulous Five?" asked Evie, astonished.

"Evie," said Catherine, turning to look at her with a warning.

"Oh my. I do not. I do not think I could even say the name," replied Mia with a laugh.

Doris took in a deep breath and sighed with a smile. Then she turned to her wife. "Over two decades ago, I was part of a famous exploring team. We traveled the world. Then we split apart. There were a lot of complicated reasons why," she said softly.

Mia looked thoughtful. "And complicated feelings too?"

Doris nodded. "I never really wanted to go back there in my mind. I tried to pretend it hadn't happened."

"You did it very well," said Mia.

Doris reached out and took her hand. "I'm sorry. I never saw it as keeping a secret from you. It was about protecting myself."

Mia smiled and squeezed her hand. "I know. But you see, the past never really lets us go."

Doris nodded, and Evie felt a twinge in her gut. It

was so true. The past was always there, influencing every decision she made.

"So," said Mia, "now this Alistair from the team needs help?"

"Yes," said Evie.

"Why does everyone need to help?"

Evie sat staring at Mia. She seemed genuinely curious, but Evie didn't get why she didn't get it. She wasn't sure what to say.

"Why not one of you, or two? Why all?" continued Mia.

Evie thought about it. The answer was that she didn't know why. But there had to be a reason. Alistair was probably in so much danger that he needed as much help as possible. That thought upset her more.

"We don't know why he needs the whole team. We just know that he does. That's enough for us," said Catherine.

"Ah," said Mia with that big smile of hers. "Loyalty. I understand this."

The word "loyalty" really made Evie's insides do a number, a really well-choreographed number, with props and everything.

"Doris," said Mia, turning to her wife and squeezing her arm gently. "This is the time. Jack is away now.

He is an adult. Even if he doesn't act like it sometimes. Your friend needs you."

"But you need me," replied Doris.

"I don't," she replied.

"Mia, not everyone here understands your German sense of humor," replied Doris, shaking her head.

"I am not joking. I don't need you. I want you in my life and I love you. I'd be lost without you. But 'need,' no. I will survive without you. I will miss you, but I will survive until your return. Besides, it has been years since I've had the entire house all to myself." Mia smiled that toothy smile of hers. Doris shook her head and laughed a little. "Go. You should go."

Doris didn't say anything. Just kept sitting there.

"I don't get you people," said Evie. This was too much, taking up time they didn't have. All these conversations and convincing people.

"Us people?" asked the Kid with a smile.

"Weren't you a team? Why is it so hard to convince each of you to do this? Don't you care about him?" Her voice cracked; the tears formed in her eyes.

"Don't get emotional," said Catherine.

Of course that made Evie even more so. Besides, what was so wrong with getting emotional? And anyway, it wasn't like she hadn't been emotional before, but the emotion had been anger, and that wasn't what people usually called emotional in a bad way. For some reason people tended to only disapprove when it was sadness. Only tears were considered "emotional" in that negative way, for some reason. She didn't understand why.

"I'll get however I want to get," Evie replied.

"That's a pretty rude thing to say," said Doris.

Evie looked at her. "More rude than being told not to feel my feelings? More rude than you guys having to be convinced to save my grandfather?"

The adults all stared at her. Even the Kid, who was normally supportive of the things she had to say.

"I think it's been a long day," said Benedict, rising carefully. "Let's sleep on this. Doris, Mia, thank you so much for your hospitality."

The other adults stood at that, obviously agreeing. Evie remained seated. Yes, she was being stubborn, but sometimes being stubborn was the thing to be. Or even if it wasn't, it was what she wanted the thing to be in the moment.

No one tried to force the issue as they left the room. Only Mia said, "The light switch is over the bacon maker" as she pushed a button, causing the patio doors to slide quietly into place and lock with a clink.

And soon Evie was alone, sitting under the single light dangling above the table.

"Are you okay?"

Oh. So she wasn't alone. She looked up at Sebastian across from her. He'd stayed behind. For her. That was nice. He could have spoken up to defend her maybe, or not have mentioned the whole accuracy thing, but she appreciated that he wanted to make sure she was okay.

She didn't feel okay.

"What do you think?" she asked.

"I think you're upset, and I think that's why you're being unreasonable," he replied.

"First of all, that was a rhetorical question," she said. "Second of all, I'm not being unreasonable. They are! What's more reasonable than helping someone you care about?"

She kept her voice low as the quiet stillness of the house felt slightly intimidating. But there was still passion in her tone. Still anger seething underneath.

"What if . . ." Sebastian stopped.

Evie stared at him. His face, half in shadow, looked a little spooky.

"What if what?" she asked, unsure if she wanted the answer to the question.

"What if . . . What if they don't care about him?" he asked quietly.

The question lingered in the air.

"I . . . don't understand," said Evie, because she didn't.

"Your argument is that they should rescue him because they care about him. But it seems to me that maybe, I dunno, that maybe they don't."

A rush of rage flooded over Evie now, and she no longer cared about being quiet, or being emotional, or whatever else anyone wanted from her. She was on her feet. Her hands pressing hard into the table in front of her.

"That's not true!"

"But don't you think it kind of is?" asked Sebastian, tipping his chair backward farther into the shadows.

"No. No, I don't think so. Catherine cares about him, and maybe Benedict was unsure, but . . ." She could hear his voice in her head, back on Newish Isle: "It's the right thing to do." She'd thought it was because the right thing to do was helping someone you cared about, but maybe . . . "The Kid! The Kid likes Alistair!"

"He likes adventure," said Sebastian.

"No, he likes him. I mean, yes, he does like adventure, but also . . . He said I reminded him of Alistair!" Even before she'd said it, she could hear Sebastian's argument: That didn't mean that the Kid liked Alistair.

"Well, that doesn't mean—"

"I know it doesn't mean." Evie sat down hard. And Doris was so unsure. So unsure. And that was weird, really, because from the little she'd seen of the woman, Doris seemed so confident and happy.

"It doesn't mean they shouldn't rescue him. It means maybe you're making the wrong argument to convince them." She could hear the worry in his voice. He was so slow and tentative in how he spoke. He didn't want to hurt her feelings, but he kept saying this stuff. That was because he was trying to help her. Even if he did hurt her.

Like when he'd thrown the key into the fire at the Explorers Society headquarters. That had hurt so much—but he had done it to save her. He'd had another plan.

Another plan.

"What do you think we should do?" she asked him.

Sebastian seemed to relax and even smiled. He leaned forward into the light. "Did you notice how much Doris looked at Catherine?"

"Yeah. That was odd," replied Evie.

"It was. But also interesting. I think that when it comes to caring about people, Catherine and Doris were really close back in the day."

Evie nodded. She remembered what the Kid had told her on the plane.

"Doris cares what Catherine thinks," said Evie.

"Yes. So I bet that Catherine . . ."

"Can convince Doris to come along!" Evie was feeling so much better. It was amazing how quickly Sebastian could do that for her. "Come on. We have to talk to her!"

Sebastian laughed as they both stood. Orson, who was sleeping at his feet, yawned and stretched.

"What's so funny?" asked Evie.

"You're always so ready to do the next thing," he said.

"Well, I mean . . . yeah." What was wrong with that?

"Let's talk to her in the morning. Adults really like their sleep. And I think today has been a weird day for more than just us," he added.

Evie nodded. "You know, for someone who claims he has trouble reading people, you're pretty great at it."

Sebastian rolled his eyes but kept his smile. "Well, I've had a pretty great teacher."

And finally Evie smiled too.

# ➤ CHAPTER 27 ◀

## In which an explorer
## is vulnerable.

The hardest part about convincing Catherine to convince Doris was not actually the logic of the situation. Sebastian was relieved about that, as he could never really understand why people would listen to facts and logic and then just say no, as if those things didn't matter. But it was equally confusing that someone who had agreed and said yes to the logic of helping Alistair was still not sure about what they were doing.

"I don't know," said Catherine. The three of them were sitting cross-legged on the twin bed in what looked like a storage room of some kind, which had been Catherine's room for the evening. The morning sun was streaming through the small window above a shelving unit. It was hard not to get distracted by the odds and ends, and ends and odds. At another time Sebastian could have spent hours examining everything. But this wasn't that time.

"But why don't you know?" asked Evie, sounding exasperated. "She's your friend. She'll listen to you!"

"And that's why I don't know," replied Catherine.

"That makes no sense," said Sebastian, more to himself than to the animal expert.

"It does." Catherine turned to him. "I don't want to make her do anything that she doesn't want to do. And because it's me, she would."

"Why is that bad, though?" asked Evie.

"It's bad because . . ." Catherine's face wore an expression that Sebastian hadn't seen before on her. It almost . . . It almost seemed like sadness. But that didn't make sense.

"Are you wondering, what if something happens and then it's all your fault?" asked Evie.

Catherine turned to her so that now Sebastian could just see her profile. She made a little nod.

"Is that what this is about? The earthquake?" asked Evie slowly.

Catherine nodded again.

"The earthquake?" asked Sebastian.

Evie looked at him. "You know, the one they set off, that made the tsunami, that destroyed that island. That made them outcasts in the first place."

That was the one he'd thought she'd been talking about, but he still didn't understand. "I don't get it. What does Doris's decision about helping Alistair have to do with an earthquake?" he asked.

Evie made to answer, but Catherine cut her off. "It's my fault. It's my fault. I didn't want them to harm the creature that was attacking us. It didn't know any better. It was scared, that's all. We didn't know what it was, if it was endangered. I asked them to come up with a better solution than hurting it. Alistair didn't want to. The Kid—well, he was busy driving. Benedict was okay with any choice. It was Doris I convinced. It was Doris I asked for a solution. She came up with the idea of burying it under rocks, with the hope that it would still be alive and eventually dig its way out. But it was me asking her, knowing she wouldn't say no to me. It was all me."

Sebastian stared at the animal expert. She had said it so plainly, but he'd never heard her sound so full of sadness and regret. So full of pain.

"Oh, Catherine, I'm so sorry," said Evie.

"And it's not true," said Sebastian. "It wasn't all you. It was the team. It was the decision to go down there in the first place; it was everything. And Doris is a grown-up. She can make her own choices."

Both Evie and Catherine stared at him.

"Can't she?" asked Sebastian, now feeling unsure. After all, he didn't know Doris well.

"It feels like my fault," said Catherine after a moment.

"I get that," said Evie. "But feeling a thing doesn't necessarily make it true."

"Exactly," said Sebastian.

"Also, I mean, if you think about it, wouldn't convincing her to come along help undo the badness of before?" asked Evie. "You can't take back what happened, but you can do a good deed together, as a team."

Sebastian thought that sounded like a solid idea, even though it wasn't really true. Nothing could undo the bad that had happened. That wasn't how time worked.

Catherine sat very still. Sebastian wondered how many times she'd sat that way, trying not to frighten a skittish animal. She'd probably had a lot of practice at it. Then, finally, she nodded. Even though not much changed in her face, there was a sense that her mood had shifted.

"Okay. I'll talk to Doris." She stood with purpose.

Then stopped. Then turned to look at them. "Thank you," she said. "I didn't realize children could be so resourceful."

"Really?" asked Sebastian.

"Baby animals are," added Evie.

"True." Catherine pondered this. "But, well, you know. Humans."

She said it like they should know, and so Sebastian simply nodded as if he did.

Because, well, he sort of did.

Humans.

# ➤ CHAPTER 28 ◄

## In which secrets are revealed, codes are questioned, and witches are helpful.

Catherine and Doris spoke privately, and when they reemerged into the cozy kitchen, now bathed in the warm glow of the morning sun filtering in from the garden, Evie knew she was on board. Even before Doris nodded her head and said, "Okay. I'm in."

This was it. The moment Evie had been waiting for. And as Doris joined them and presented her piece of the map and her letter, placing them gingerly on the tree table in front of them, Evie tried to take it all in. To remember this feeling.

Only a few weeks before, she had been totally alone, escaping the Andersons' burning house, no family, just confusion and fear. And here she was with four different people she'd traveled around the world to find. And a fifth about to be found—who was family.

She grinned at Sebastian, who nodded at her, and she realized he was probably in problem-solving mode. Time to figure out what the four letters had to say when laid on top of each other, each pointing in a different direction of the compass. And it wasn't like she wasn't ready too. But realizing that it was because of her that the Filipendulous Five had come back together was a big thing.

"So let's figure out where he is!" said the Kid, clapping his hands and making both Evie and Orson jump a bit in their seats.

"Let's look at the letters," Evie said. "Doris, do you have anything we could put them on that would light them up from below?" She was excited. That was an understatement. She was so excited that she wanted to be onstage in an opera right now so that she could sing out her feelings. Thinking that made her feel strange. She hadn't sung in a very long time. She used to sing with her parents a lot but hadn't since they'd passed. Maybe it was knowing that she'd be with her grandfather soon that made her think that way. Maybe it was a good thing.

Doris grinned and left the room. There was some scrambling as the explorers produced their letters and

Doris returned carrying an old overhead projector almost the same size as she was. She placed it in the center of the table.

"Now what?" she asked.

"Put the letters on top of each other and face them in the direction that Alistair has indicated in each," said Evie, leaning in close.

"Not the actual direction," said Sebastian quickly. "More like when you look at a drawing of a compass and north is facing up, east is on the right, and so on."

Evie shook her head. Surely it wasn't necessary to be so specific. But who knew? It certainly didn't hurt.

One by one, starting with Catherine, the explorers placed their letters on the projector. When the letters were aligned with each other, Doris flipped a switch, and the bright light beneath them shone up. Everyone leaned in close so that they could all see.

"Uh, guys?" said Sebastian.

They looked at him. He pointed at the white wall behind them. Everyone turned. Sure enough the projector was doing its job, and a large version of the letters was glowing on the wall. Everyone pulled back and stared.

The darker letters shone through. What the group had assumed to be *W*s turned out to be *E*s. And *Z*s were *N*s. It was impressive to behold, and impressive to think of Alistair putting this much work into sending a message. Sebastian read it aloud.

"'NANNIE DEE WADES AT ZERO.'"

Ah.

Okay, then.

"What does that mean?" asked the Kid.

"I'm not sure," replied Catherine, squinting at the wall as if maybe that would help the message make more sense.

"Nannie Dee . . . ," said Evie.

"Who's that?" asked Sebastian.

"Is it even a who?" asked Evie.

The room fell silent. She noticed Sebastian get up and wander away, lost in thought.

"You mean . . . ," said the Kid.

"Well, is it a name or a job? There are a lot of nannies out there. Maybe this is someone whose last name is Dee?" Evie said.

"Could be," said Doris. "Though I'm not sure that helps us at all."

"Why is the word 'nanny' spelled wrong?" asked Catherine.

"Is it?" asked the Kid.

"Well, either it's spelled wrong or he forgot the *s* to make it plural. Which then would spell 'Nannies Dee,' but that doesn't make sense either."

"No, it doesn't," said Benedict.

"Hey, guys," said Sebastian.

Evie turned. He'd figured it out. He'd used that problem-solving brain of his and photographic memory, and somewhere inside he'd dug out a recollection of a Nannie Dee who . . . She stared. He was sitting in front of a glowing computer screen.

"Evidently, Nannie Dee is the name of a witch from a Robbie Burns poem."

"Oh. You looked it up," said Evie, standing and walking to him. He could do that. Any of them could have simply done that.

Benedict stood and leaned over Sebastian's shoulder to see the screen too. "Ah," he said, a smile crossing his face.

"What is it?" asked Sebastian.

Benedict pointed at the screen. "Her nickname is 'Cutty Sark.'"

Evie wasn't sure what that had to do with anything.

Without anyone having to ask him, Benedict explained: "The *Cutty Sark* is a historic British ship from the 1800s."

"Okay?" said Evie, still confused.

"That explains what 'wades at zero' means," he said, standing upright and turning to the rest of them. He waited, but none of them seemed to understand his meaning. "The ship is now a nautical museum. In London, England. Actually, Greenwich, to be precise."

"Greenwich mean time!" said Doris, snapping her fingers.

" 'Greenwich' means 'time'?" asked Evie. She'd never heard the word "Greenwich" before, nor that it evidently had that meaning.

"Mean time," explained the Kid. "Time zones. You know how the time changes depending on where on the earth you are? Plus an hour here, minus an hour there?"

Evie nodded. She could sense Sebastian nodding in unison with her.

"Greenwich, which is a borough of London, is where the zero time zone is. It's the starting point, where we start adding hours if we go east of it and subtracting time if we go west of it."

"Ah," said Evie.

"What happens when you meet in the middle on the other side?" asked Sebastian.

"Well, that answers that, then!" said Doris. She was smiling broadly. "Alistair wants us to go to the *Cutty Sark*. We can do that."

"I don't get it, though," said Sebastian. "Is he being held in the boat?"

"I'm not sure it matters," said Evie. "He's got to be

somewhere around there. Maybe there's another clue in the boat, even. We can figure things out when we arrive. But we need to leave immediately!" She was up on her feet like she was just going to run there. And right then, with adrenaline pumping through her body, she felt like she pretty much could. That she could run so fast, she could run across water.

"Well, we aren't going there by foot. Please sit down, Evie," said Catherine, ever practical.

Evie sat down hard on the bench, a little too hard. She said "Ow" to herself quietly, a bit embarrassed. "Okay. Let's book flights and get taxis and everything."

For the first time, well, ever, Evie saw Catherine make a sneaky kind of smile. It was so surprising to see the animal expert do that that Evie wasn't actually sure she had seen it. But Catherine's quick glance to Doris, and then the same smile growing on Doris's face, confirmed that indeed Evie had.

"What's going on?" asked Evie.

"Wait a minute," said the Kid, pointing at Doris, his mouth agape. "Wait. A. Minute."

"It's not still . . . That is to say, I thought it was destroyed." Benedict furrowed his eyebrows mildly.

Doris made a slight shrug and winked at him.

"Okay. Come on, you guys," said Evie. "This isn't fair. Tell us what's up."

Catherine's smile grew a bit, and even though Evie was now annoyed with her, she also had to admit that she was getting excited. About what, she had no idea. "Doris still has the submarine," said the animal expert.

Evie's eyes got wide then, so wide that she had to blink them hard because she'd made herself dizzy. "The submarine. You mean *the* submarine? The one from your previous adventures?"

"Yes," said Doris.

"But . . . ," Sebastian interrupted. "But no. No, it doesn't work. Don't the men in black have the EM-7056?" Evie nodded, remembering that horrible day when Mr. K had held her hostage in the society headquarters.

"Good memory," said Catherine.

"It doesn't matter," said the Kid, leaning back.

"It doesn't?" asked Evie.

"Nah, the sub runs fine. We just need the EM-7056 to dive really deep into the trench. But we're not doing that. We're just traveling in it." He looked at Doris. "You are one clever lady."

She laughed.

Well, that was happy news. With the submarine they could find and rescue her grandfather faster. This was amazing.

"Okay, so where is it?" she asked.

"I was always told as a child to hide things in plain sight," replied Doris.

"Smart," said Sebastian.

"Does that mean . . . Have we seen it already?" Evie was in awe. She knew the answer was yes even if she didn't understand how it could be yes.

Doris laughed again. Now that she was on board with the team and she had relaxed so much, her laughter was infectious and very calming. "You have."

"The stage," Sebastian said suddenly.

"Yes!" said the Kid, now pointing at him. "Is he right? Is it the stage?"

Doris looked at them all thoughtfully for a moment, and then with a big grin said, "You know what they say: all the world's a stage. Or sometimes . . . a submarine is."

# CHAPTER 29

## In which Sebastian doesn't lie.

"The good news is that tonight is closing night," said Doris.

"The bad news is that we have to wait for the end of the show to get the submarine, so as not to raise suspicions or alert the thugs to where we are," concluded Catherine.

Sebastian nodded and then glanced at Evie. He wasn't the one who needed things to happen right away. She was the impatient one. He could see her nervous energy manifesting itself right now as her right foot was tapping the ground quickly. It was vibrating the bench they were on.

"Hey, you're shaking the whole seat," he said, leaning over.

"No, I'm not," she replied, confused. Then she looked down. "Oh."

"It'll be okay. It's just a couple more hours."

Evie didn't say anything, just tilted her head forward a little. Sebastian was pretty sure she understood that it would be okay even if it didn't feel like it was okay.

But Sebastian honestly didn't mind taking a bit of a break. It had been a really long time since a day had felt like a day. When they could take a moment, hang out, have conversations. When plans were made and therefore rest was totally cool. And when they could eat three square meals and even snacks!

Sebastian was reading a book he'd found called *How to Make Things Move*. He was in the sunny spot on the faded flowery couch in the living room when Benedict approached him.

"When did you last check in with your parents?" he asked, pulling a book off the nearby shelf and reading the title. *An Anthology of Back-Cover Descriptions*, it said. He flipped it over to read the back cover.

Sebastian instantly went from peaceful reader to nauseated liar.

"Uh, I guess it's been a while," he said, literally lying through his teeth, as he was barely able to open his mouth. "I could go do it now?" He said it like a question, though he wasn't sure why.

"Good idea," replied Benedict, leaning back and opening the book.

Sebastian watched him for a moment, but Benedict seemed really into the book, and so Sebastian slowly slipped off the couch and went into the kitchen, where he knew there was one of those older phones plugged into the wall. Kind of like the phone at the airport, actually. Hanging upright. But this one had no graffiti on it. Didn't look sad. But it did look ominous despite the friendly *It's always teatime even if it isn't teatime* ticking coming from the clock above the stove.

Phones had never really been a thing for Sebastian. While the other kids at school demanded ones of their own, he was happy without one, instead preferring the graphing calculator he'd gotten for his last birthday. He'd never actually disliked phones. He was really more indifferent to them. But now it felt like phones were the enemy. That they were judging him. And he knew how absurd that was, to think that, but it was hard not to. Especially when it came to older hanging-on-the-wall phones. Those ones really did seem to have a superiority complex.[12]

What new lie would he have to come up with now? Would he have to update Evie and Benedict on what his parents were doing? Make stuff up? "Uh, my dad discovered this cool new mind teaser, and my mom has learned how to create matter from nothing."

Or he could . . . he could call them. He could.

He picked up the receiver.

He could.

He dialed.

The ringing on the other end of the line made his stomach do an interpretative dance that would probably get a B review from the *New Yorker*.

"Hello?"

His mom's voice. Immediately the guilt washed over him so hard that he felt the undertow pull him into shame. He couldn't bear the feeling, and he hung up, fast. He was gulping air like he'd just run a race, even though he'd never run a race and could only assume that was how he'd gulp air.

---

[12] Though they weren't nearly as full of themselves as rotary phones: *Oh, don't mind me. I'm just going to take as long as I feel like here, spinning back to the start. Just enjoy my magnificence while you wait. If you didn't want to wait, you shouldn't have dialed a nine.*

He couldn't have a panic attack, not in this moment. Mostly because he didn't want to, but also because then people would ask him what was wrong and he knew he couldn't tell them. Couldn't say the truth.

"What's wrong?"

Of course.

"Nothing," replied Sebastian, turning abruptly to Evie.

"Who was on the phone?" she asked, wandering over to the fridge and grabbing some juice.

"My mom." That much was true.

"Oh! How is she?" asked Evie with a smile.

"Hard to say," replied Sebastian. That was also true.

Evie nodded and returned to pouring her juice. Okay, so this was working, this lying-by-telling-the-truth thing. Why did it feel as bad as the lying-by-lying thing? Logically it shouldn't. He wasn't doing anything wrong. Technically. Yeah, probably having to have the word "technically" in there was the problem.

Okay. It was time. It was time. He needed to decide if he wanted to go home or not. And he really needed to talk to his parents. He just . . . he needed to *decide*.

# ➤ CHAPTER 30 ◄

## In which . . . performing!

From the first row, the clouds looked even more like they were floating in the air. Without anyone sitting in front blocking them, Evie had a perfectly unobstructed view of large fluffy white puffs hovering before her, their reflections in the water creating a depth of clouds below them.

The orchestra was in front of her and off to her right, and she could see them now so much better, each instrument: violins, drums, trumpets, flutes, and an interesting-looking horn that she didn't recognize, which spiraled in on itself.[13]

---

[13] *Oh, come on! A French horn! It's a French . . . Oh, never mind.*

Evie eyed the stage, leaned in, and squinted a bit, trying hard to spot the submarine supporting it all. She thought maybe she saw an outline, but it might have been a trick of the shadows.

The houselights dimmed. The spotlight lit up the stage. There was a moment of breathless anticipation. For Evie the anticipation was about so much more than waiting for an opera singer to appear. It was about how, when the opera started, her search would be on its way to being over, and when it was over . . .

Then it was over.

But nothing happened. Just another breathless moment of anticipation.

And another.

And then another.

Evie glanced at Sebastian, who furrowed his eyebrows and scratched the top of Orson's head in a distracted fashion.

The Valkyrie wasn't coming onstage.

There was another moment, and then hesitantly the conductor poked his head around the makeshift wall to Evie's left. He scanned the crowd and then slowly walked to his spotlit position in front of the orchestra. The audience eagerly applauded, not knowing that something was wrong.

The conductor bowed, then faced the empty, larger

spotlight onstage. There was an excited silence now from the crowd. Evie turned to Doris.

"What's going on?" she asked.

Doris was already rising from her seat, staying hunched low so as not to block the view of the person behind her. The view of the no one onstage. "I don't know. Excuse me." She quickly made her way down the aisle and slipped backstage.

Evie looked at the conductor, who was having a quiet conversation with a violinist. She could feel the energy in the audience shift to one of confusion. Her own energy shifted too. She was getting antsy and a little frustrated. If the lead soprano didn't show up onstage, what did that mean for the show? What did that mean about their leaving?

Oh! Maybe they'd cancel it! Maybe the team would be able to leave right away!

"This could be a good thing," she said, leaning over to Sebastian.

Just as she said it, the conductor turned to face the audience. He spoke, his voice thin and high. First he delivered his message in Portuguese, causing the audience members who understood him to mutter to each other. Then he repeated it in English: "Our most esteemed audience, I have learned that there will be a small delay to the start time of our performance this evening. We apologize profusely, and please enjoy some free refreshments while you wait." He smiled timidly and then slowly made his way toward the backstage area. Then he began picking up speed, until he pretty much ran out of sight.

The house lights came on.

"Delay?" asked Evie. She saw Sebastian looking hard at where the conductor had disappeared, and her gut now clenched with fear.

"It's okay. It can't be long. And if it is, then they'll cancel. Or maybe they'll get an understudy," replied Sebastian. Evie nodded. And then smiled. She couldn't help it. He'd understood that her question wasn't about the meaning of the word "delay" but that she was scared of what a delay would mean for them. That was neat. "What?" he asked.

"Nothing. You're right. I'll wait." She sat upright in her chair, though she still couldn't help but watch the backstage wall for some kind of sign.

They sat for about fifteen minutes before Doris returned.

"What's going on?" asked the Kid.

"It's . . . very complicated. But in brief, we need to get the soprano's substitute."

"Oh. Is she okay?" asked Evie. This was still fine,

everything was fine, it would take a little longer, but that was fine.

"Like I said, it's complicated."

"When will she get here? Maybe half an hour?" Evie thought that sounded like a long time, but bearable.

"The understudy is in Lisbon."

"That's two hours away," said Sebastian.

"Two *hours*?" said Evie, in a total panic now.

"Yes. It'll be a wait. I'm sorry, Evie. Normally we'd cancel the show, but it's the last night and there are people who traveled here from all over the world. It's okay. We'll get going right after," said Doris with a smile before heading backstage again.

Evie turned to Sebastian, who looked just as upset as she felt, which she found comforting. "I . . . I can't . . . ," she said. She couldn't exactly explain. And instead she was on her feet and rushing after Doris before she could clearly realize that this was the doing that had to be done.

Behind the makeshift wall, the serenity and magic of the stage and view vanished. Evie was instantly clambering through a jungle of coiled cables and buzzing generators. It felt a bit like the jungle around the Vertiginous Volcano, only in this case human-made.

The one good thing was that she didn't have to fear dangerous beasts attacking her.

Something furry brushed her leg.

"Ack!" She jumped and looked down. It was only Orson. Thank goodness, but if Orson was here . . . She turned and saw Sebastian, red-faced and out of breath, his usual appearance after chasing after her. She grinned.

"What are we doing?" he asked.

"Finding out what 'it's complicated' means, why they need an understudy. Maybe we can solve the problem without one," she replied.

They made their way toward a series of trailers, which they realized on approach was where the opera company kept costumes and props. Doris wasn't any-where. So Evie dashed up a set of stairs and opened a door to one of the trailers.

The opera chorus of around thirty men and women was crammed into the trailer. A woman with blond hair was standing before them holding a conductor's stick. They were in the middle of singing and stared at Evie. She stared back. They kept singing the same note as the woman held her stick high above her head, star-ing at Evie in confusion.

They held the note.

And held it.

Evie almost wanted to see how long they could sing the one note before losing their breath, but she knew that it was impolite to stare.

"Oh, uh . . . sorry," said Evie, backing out slowly and closing the door.

"Probably shouldn't just barge into rooms like that," said Sebastian as she returned to him.

"Yeah."

He pointed at the next trailer. "Knock first?"

Evie nodded, climbed the little set of stairs, and rapped on the door.

It swung open, and a tall broad man wearing a tattered uniform and a wig of curly red hair stood before them. Evie instantly recognized him as the baritone lead in the opera, the one the Valkyrie saved from death but who then killed her boyfriend in return.

"Is it finally time?" he boomed in English. He looked around, confused.

"Down here," said Evie.

He looked down.

"I don't remember you, tiny stage manager," he said, eyeing her with suspicion.

"I'm not a stage manager. I'm Evie," she replied.

"Ah! Evie." He nodded knowingly.

"We've never met before," she said, confused.

"Ah! Yes, good, good," he replied, and nodded.

"Uh, so anyway, we were wondering, do you know why the Valkyrie needs an understudy?" asked Sebastian, stepping up beside her.

The baritone stared at Sebastian as if this was the first time he'd noticed him. Like Sebastian had just appeared out of thin air.

"Yes," he replied.

They waited silently for more. The faint sound of the chorus holding a different single note could be heard, almost like a punctuation mark on the baritone's pause.

"And what might the reason be?" prompted Evie hesitantly.

"In my many years of performing this great art, I have met extraordinary talents. I have worked with men and women, sopranos, mezzos, basses, tenors, who have been charming, frustrating, demanding, shy, talkative, and boring. But never in all my years have I encountered anyone quite so . . . interesting." He spoke all the words passionately, but none of them actually answered the question.

"And?" asked Evie.

"I will show you, Evie," replied the baritone, sweeping his hand to one side. She stared at him expectantly. "Could you . . . could you move, please?" he asked.

"Oh!" And she hopped off the stairs as the baritone walked with purpose and great drama down the three small steps.

"I am Roland, the baritone," said Roland the baritone.

"I'm Evie," repeated Evie, not really knowing what else to say.

"Yes. You are." He turned to Sebastian and looked down at him now.

"Uh, I'm Sebastian."

"And those are our names. Good. Follow me!" He turned and was striding off before they had a chance to gather themselves. So, quickly, Evie followed him, and Sebastian and Orson joined her. They wandered the row of trailers until it ended, pushed up against the forest that encroached on the backstage area. But Roland the baritone didn't stop. He continued into the dark forest, and at this point Evie paused.

"Should we be doing this?" she asked.

"Generally, I think we shouldn't be doing many things," Sebastian replied.

"I guess we don't have much of a choice."

"We do, though."

Evie shrugged and jogged after Roland, hearing Sebastian's hard sigh behind her. It wasn't as scary as she'd thought. The trees were fairly far apart, and the glow from the theater shone into the sky, illuminating their path somewhat.

And it turned out they didn't have too far to go. Just as the forest was starting to get darker around them, they emerged into a clearing. An ancient-looking wooden house, lit with a single tall spotlight standing beside it, sat in the very middle atop a small mound of earth. It was rather otherworldly, like they had stepped into a dream, and as Evie moved into the light, she could see a fire smoldering in a pit, beside which hung some clothing drying. At her feet lay a large round shield as if it had been dropped there recklessly.

"She's in there." Roland pointed at the house, in case they thought that he meant somewhere else in the otherwise empty clearing.

"Who is?" asked Evie.

"The soprano," said Roland. "The Valkyrie."

Evie looked at Sebastian, who looked at her. He looked back at the hut.

"As I said, interesting, isn't it?" said the baritone.

"Yeah," replied Evie tentatively. "Interesting" was definitely one word for it.

# CHAPTER 31

## In which . . . fighting!

Sebastian stared at the hut.

"I don't understand. What's going on?" he asked.

"Have you ever heard of Method acting?" asked Roland.

"Not really, no," he replied.

"Yes! Method acting. That was the term I was looking for the other day!" said Evie with enthusiasm.

"It is common in film and television for an actor to get so into their role that they become the character. In opera this is less common because we are far less ridiculous," explained Roland.

"Right," said Evie.

"More to the point, we need to maintain the quality of our voice, keep the instrument in shape. Our focus usually is on the music."

Sebastian nodded. That also made sense.

"However, it would seem our soprano is a little different. As you can see. The company humored her because she is a genius artist, built her this hut to live in as a Valkyrie for the length of her contract. But tonight . . . tonight it has gone too far. She has gotten too into character."

"How?" asked Sebastian.

"She refuses to perform. And anyone who attempts to reason with her . . ." Roland stopped talking and shivered in fear. "In fact, I worry that we have been here too long. Come. We must depart!"

Sebastian was more than happy to do just that, but as he turned to go, he felt a hand on his shoulder.

Evie.

"We need her to perform," said Evie urgently.

"We can wait two hours for the understudy," replied Sebastian. He really didn't want to stick around anymore. He wasn't feeling good about all this. He didn't think they were necessarily in danger, but he didn't trust hanging out in a place where some performer had totally lost her grip on reality and thought she was an actual Valkyrie.

"Look, if anyone can logic someone into doing a show, it's you," said Evie.

"Some people are not logical, and nothing you can say to them will change their minds," replied Sebastian. How had she not learned this over the last two weeks and a bit since they'd met? He certainly had.

"Please, Sebastian. Let's try."

Sebastian sighed. What could he do? He'd pretended to be a child stunt-car driver, initiated a fake protest, found himself the protector of an odd little dog—and that was only in the last couple of days. Now he was in Portugal trying to help an opera singer perform, so that the submarine supporting the set could be used to rescue a formerly famous explorer. There was no logic to fall back on. They were officially in the land of the ridiculous. They'd been there for quite some time.

"Okay," he said. "Let's see if we can talk her into doing the show."

"Yes!" said Evie with that satisfied triumphant grin of hers. She never seemed tired of doing it, and it was hard for him to get tired of seeing it. "Roland, we're going to stay here."

Roland the baritone looked at her and adjusted his wig slightly. "Well, I won't stop you, but it is now that I must leave you. My voice needs attention."

"What's the soprano's name?" asked Evie.

"Julia," he replied.

"Does she speak any English?"

"Of course. She's Canadian." He said it like it was the most obvious answer in the world. And then he spun on his heel and disappeared through the forest.

Sebastian, Evie, and Orson were alone now. Alone in front of a hut with some soprano who thought she was an actual Valkyrie.

This was not exactly how he'd expected to spend his evening.

Then again, this was his new normal. Not expecting the unexpected was on him.

"So, I'm going to . . . talk to her?" asked Sebastian.

Evie nodded. "I'll be here with Orson. If you need us, call us."

"And you're not coming because . . ."

"Because we don't want to frighten her. And you're the logical one."

"And you're the one who talked the SRAC into letting us in," countered Sebastian.

"Well, then it's your turn," replied Evie.

He stared at her. "Are you scared? Should I be scared?" he asked, his voice breaking and his breath quickening.

"No! No. I . . . think in this case you should be the one to convince her. And I'll be right here. You are perfectly safe." She smiled. He felt a little better, he supposed. "You should probably take that just in case."

He looked where she was pointing. On the ground nearby was a large, round piece of wood.

"A shield?" asked Sebastian.

"Just . . . in case."

He bent to pick it up. It was heavy, and he felt that maybe this was one too many things for her to be asking of him. Frustration nagged at him.

Fine. Fine, okay, okay. It was only an opera singer. How scary could she really be?

He turned to Evie, who gave him an encouraging gesture with her hands as if to brush him forward, and then he faced the hut. This was silly. They were both acting silly because a dramatic baritone had been dramatic. Time to just get this soprano onstage.

Sebastian stepped out of the darkness and onto the mound.[14] He approached the hut carefully, quietly stepping around the fire and making his way to the door of the little house. He was there. There really wasn't much he could do except knock. So he raised his hand and, leaning as far away from his hand as

---

[14] "Onto the mound" is the beginning of my favorite least inspirational speech.

was possible, considering it was attached to his arm and everything, Sebastian knocked.

There was silence.

He knocked again.

He knocked a third time and also called out a shaky, "Julia?"

Then he stepped a few feet away and held the shield in front of him.

Still nothing.

Sebastian sighed hard, marched up to the door, and raised his hand once more, but the door flew open and Sebastian fell backward, almost right into the fire. Out came the Valkyrie in all her winged-helmet glory. She was carrying a large axe, but the expression on her face was what scared Sebastian even more than the sharp weapon.

Julia looked about wildly and then finally saw Sebastian on the ground. With a spark in her eyes, she lifted the axe over her head and came for him. At the very last minute Sebastian held the shield up to protect himself, and the axe pierced through the wood. Sebastian stared at the metal protruding through the shield inches from his face, and then stared at Julia. She tried to pull the axe out, but it stuck there, fast. Taking advantage of the moment, Sebastian threw the shield aside and ran, while Julia struggled.

"Evie!" he called as he dove to the other side of a low wall surrounding a garden.

Sebastian watched as the soprano got angrier and angrier with her weapon, until she flung aside the axe and shield together. They hit the house and splintered. Then she sang a piercing high note, holding it with perfect vibrato. It would have been impressive if it hadn't been so high that Sebastian was certain his skull would crack.

What. On. Earth.

"Who dares disturb the home of the Valkyrie!" she sang. "Face me, coward!"

What. On. Earth.

She continued to address him in furious song. "I'll find you, you insect. I'll crush you like I've crushed my enemies of yore. You will know pain. And you will suffer for your arrogance!"

This was so very strange. Was he going to die at the hands of an overcommitted soprano?

No, of course not. That would be awful. And embarrassing. He had to use reason and logic. Somewhere in there was the opera singer he'd seen onstage the night before. She was capable of doing her job, of being reasonable.

"Julia, can we talk?" he yelled from his hiding spot.

The soprano let out her high note again.

"I know you not," she sang. "So I refuse to counsel with you, coward! I will eat you for breakfast!" Slowly she stalked her way over to him.

Sebastian plotted his escape route, then stood, hunched over, one foot in front of the other, prepped as he'd seen runners at the beginning of a race. Man, he really wished he'd had proper race experience. Then he said "I'm a friend!" and dashed away from the garden as Julia rushed to where he had been. He wound up on the far side of the little house, noticing how on that side there was less set dressing. But. There were several swords leaning against the building. Not that he could actually fight. He didn't know the first thing about it. But. Maybe . . .

"You are no friend of mine," the soprano sang. "You are a friend of darkness, and I destroy all the enemies of the light!"

Sebastian had no idea what that meant, but it seemed like he needed something to defend himself with. He made his way to the swords, grabbed one, and found that he could barely lift it. Not that one, then. He tried another. This one wasn't nearly so heavy. In fact he was impressed by how light it felt. And how balanced in his hands. Not that he really knew how to hold it.

Now what? If Julia was going to continue pretending to be a Valkyrie, there wasn't going to be much he could do to convince the opera singer otherwise.

He needed a different tactic.

"Face me!" sang Julia from the other side of the house. "Or die like a coward, friend of darkness!"

With a deep intake of breath, Sebastian thought back to standing onstage in front of thousands of fans while playing the drums as part of a K-pop band. The thrill of performing. The power and the excitement. And then. With great purpose. He leapt into the blinding light, holding his sword in front of him. He had no idea where Julia was, but he spoke loudly and, he hoped, with confidence.

"I am Sebastian, friend to both the darkness and the light . . . ness! I am here to ask the great . . ." Oh, what was her character's name again? "The great . . . furious Valkyrie . . . for an audience. I am here to . . . talk . . . and not to fight."

There was a horrible silence then. The kind of silence that was way worse than an awkward silence or an annoyed silence. The kind of silence that spoke of an imminent doom. And then. Julia charged.

The soprano had no weapon, but that didn't seem to matter. Sebastian was pretty sure he was done for. But he stayed where he was, holding the sword out in front of him. Surely the woman wouldn't run into it.

Julia wasn't slowing down.

She—wasn't—slowing—down.

The sword in Sebastian's hands began to shake. Oh, wait. No, it was his hands that were doing the shaking. As Julia the soprano rushed Sebastian, he seriously didn't know what to do.

So he did the only thing his body could think of doing.

He shut his eyes tight and braced himself.

Then his body went flying to the side and he slammed into the earth, hard.

## CHAPTER 32

# In which . . . singing!

Sebastian opened his left eye. Then his right. And then he had to shift his head slightly so that his view was not of the ground but of shoes with little wings attached at the ankle. And another pair of shoes, a smaller pair. Standing between him and the shoes with wings.

"Young daughter of valor," he heard Julia sing. "You saved the boy's life."

Sebastian slowly propped himself up. He took stock of what was going on.

Evie was standing, hands on hips, between the soprano and Sebastian. *She* had pushed him out of the way and saved him! He scrambled to his feet.

And he watched Evie do something she'd never done before. At least not in front of him.

"O valiant one, I did," she sang. Her voice was soft and shaky, but pretty too. "He is a friend of mine. And we are here to speak with you." Her voice got stronger as she went. Sebastian remembered that Evie had once said she liked to sing, but it had been in passing and felt like such a long time ago. And here she was doing it. She was good at it.

"If a daughter of valor wishes to speak with the queen of the Valkyries, then I shall permit it!" sang Julia in return. "And . . ." She held the note as she turned to look at Sebastian. "He may join us."

Julia stayed briefly where she was. Then, with arms wide, she swept past Sebastian toward the door to the house and went inside.

Sebastian turned to Evie. "Thank you," he said.

"Of course," she replied.

"You've got a nice singing voice," he added.

Her face got slightly pink at that, and she quickly said, "Oh, I don't know. Thanks. I mean, it's not that great. I haven't sung since my parents . . . I . . . well, anyway . . ." She glanced at the door. "I've come up with a plan, since clearly logic isn't going to work."

"No, it clearly isn't," replied Sebastian.

"Just follow my lead," said Evie, and he nodded. "Now let's go in there and get this over with."

Sebastian nodded again, though he wasn't sure if he wanted to go to a secondary location with that woman. First he took in a deep breath of relief, and then a second deep breath of "Let's do this." And he followed Evie into the house.

Inside smelled stale and rank. The hut was dark, and it was hard to discern anything in the mess, but Sebastian could make out leftover food lying on the table, and unwashed clothes sitting in piles everywhere.

Julia sat on a wooden chair carved like a throne. She eyed both of them with suspicion. "Speak!" she ordered with a wave of her hand.

Sebastian looked over at Evie. She raised her chin, proud. "I have been sent by our clan to ask for your cooperation." She sang now with much more confidence than before.

"Why should I cooperate?" Julia managed to laugh and sing at the same time.

"Without you my people will be doomed to sit and wait. Without your voice, your heroic actions, we are left in a limbo too frightening to imagine," sang Evie.

Wait. Was her "clan" the audience?

"I care not," sang Julia, turning away. Something in her had changed, just slightly.

If Evie was talking about the audience, then maybe he could talk about . . .

Instinctively Sebastian stepped forward. He did something even more terrifying than playing drums onstage. He lengthened his words and held the vowels. In other words, he sang. "Oh, mighty Valkyrie. There are people depending on you. Without you they fail. They have nothing to bring home to their families."

Evie turned and gaped at him. He wasn't surprised. He didn't sound nearly as good as she did, that was for sure.

"I have cared for my people for centuries, but the one being who cared for me is gone. How can I go on without his love?" sang Julia. There was a shake in her voice, a real emotion attempting to burst through.

"Tell us, oh queen of the Valkyries, whose love has forsaken you?" sang Evie, turning back to Julia.

Julia sat on her throne and looked away. She seemed genuinely hurt and sad. Then the moment passed and she rose, the anger flaming once more in her eyes. She reached down beside her and grabbed a sword leaning against the throne.

"Get out!" she sang.

"But," said Evie.

"Get out!" She held "out" long as she pointed at the door and brandished her sword. Both Evie and Sebastian staggered backward.

"We should go," said Sebastian, grabbing Evie's arm. Evie nodded. They crept toward the door and swung it open.

"Bark?"

Orson was standing at the door. It almost seemed like he was smiling. Then, before Sebastian could do anything, the dog trotted right by them and into the hut.

"Orson, no. Come here," said Sebastian, nervous for the dog's safety. But for the first time since they'd met, the dog ignored him. Instead he scampered over to the feet of the Valkyrie, who still stood tall, her sword held above her head. She watched as Orson sat and stared up at her, panting.

"Orson!" called Sebastian.

Evie placed a hand on his arm. "Wait," she said softly.

Julia looked at the dog. The dog looked at Julia. Her expression slowly changed into that one of vulnerable sadness they'd seen briefly earlier. Her bottom lip twitched, her eyes got watery, and the sword in her hand began to quiver.

She sat on the throne, dropping the weapon to

her side in a clatter. She appeared defeated. The tears flowed freely. Orson cocked his head to the side and then, with the agility of a cat, leapt into Julia's lap. She stared, frozen in place, and then very gently and nervously started to pet him.

"What's going on?" whispered Sebastian.

"Julia?" said Evie, inching closer to the soprano. "Julia?"

The opera singer made a little "hmm" noise, still focusing on Orson, who had now curled up.

"You said something about someone forsaking you. Was it . . . Did you . . . have a pet?" Evie asked slowly. She was now standing right in front of the throne.

There was silence as Sebastian watched Julia cry quietly and scratch behind Orson's ears. Then she said, "My dog, Binky. She was sick. She passed away this morning."

For some reason, hearing Julia speak and not sing now felt more peculiar than the other way around to Sebastian. It was amazing what you could get used to.

"I'm so sorry," said Evie, placing a hand on the opera singer's knee.

"I miss her."

"Of course."

"I didn't think I would get this upset." Julia looked up then at Evie. "But I guess I did."

"Boy, did you ever," replied Sebastian.

"Sebastian!" said Evie, glaring at him. "Grief makes us act in unexpected ways."

Sebastian nodded. He did know that. Only . . . pretending to be a Valkyrie? That wasn't one of the usual stages of grief, at least not one he'd heard of.

"I'm sorry. I really am. I could really have hurt you guys," said Julia.

"Yeah," said Sebastian, nodding.

"Sebastian!" Evie chastised him again.

"No, I could have. He's not wrong to agree." She looked down at Orson. "What's his name again?"

"Orson," said Sebastian.

"Orson." She smiled. "He's very sweet. You're very lucky."

Sebastian watched Orson snuggle more deeply into Julia's lap. Sebastian had never seen Orson more content. Not even when Orson had chosen Sebastian as his new guardian.

Of course.

"Do you want to keep him?" asked Sebastian.

Julia gasped, shocked. "Oh no, I couldn't."

"No, really, it's okay. I think he's been searching for his person. Maybe he thought it was me, but he seems so at home here. More than ever." Sebastian wasn't sure why he felt that way. He just knew it was right.

"Are you sure?" asked Julia with a gasp.

Evie was eyeing him closely now. He hoped she wasn't worried that he was sad to say goodbye to the dog. He was going to miss him a bit, but Sebastian had never thought he'd be keeping Orson forever. Sebastian liked this solution. It felt right. Plus it seemed to make the soprano feel better, and wasn't the whole point to get her back onstage?

"I'm sure." He walked up to Orson and patted him. The dog licked his finger. Then snuggled up again. Sebastian smiled.

"Thank you. Thank you so much. He won't be able to replace Binky, but . . ."

"It'll be a fresh start," said Evie.

Julia smiled. "Yes. A fresh start."

They all smiled.

There was a pause.

"Uh . . . speaking of starts . . . ," said Evie.

Julia's eyes widened. "Oh my goodness! What time is it?"

"Time to get onstage, I think," replied Evie.

"Definitely!"

There was no time to lose. Sebastian and Evie helped Julia get her costume straightened out and Orson settled in to sleep the show away in the now-empty throne. Then all three of them were darting through the forest and past the trailers to the backstage area, where the conductor, the chorus, Roland the baritone, and Doris were all waiting, rather surprised by the trio's sudden arrival.

"Well, what are we waiting for?" asked Julia, smiling at them all. "The show must go on!"

And with that she swept out into the spotlight to mighty applause. Evie looked at Sebastian.

"What?" he asked.

"Thank you," she said.

"No problem," he replied.

"That was weird."

"Yeah. That was really weird."

# ➤ CHAPTER 33 ◄

## In which things end
## and begin.

The show was done. Evie sat alone in the audience on one of the hard seats, her knees bent up into her chest, her chin on them. Sebastian had gone off to say goodbye to Orson, and the rest of the team was working with the opera's tech crew to unbolt the set from the top of the submarine. She was watching them now. They were small out on the giant cloud stage, running around.

She was feeling unhelpful, but sometimes too many people helping was worse than too few. Besides, the team knew how to work together and had quickly fallen into old roles, Doris shouting orders and the rest following them. It was curious to observe, because for the first time Evie kind of realized: the team was a family in its own way.

The Kid was the happy-go-lucky rebellious teenager. Doris was the studious one. Benedict and Catherine seemed kind of like their parents. Who was Alistair, then? Her stomach clenched. He couldn't be the team's grandfather. Not when he was *her* grandfather.

The idea made her feel a little jealous.

She shifted in her seat, folding her legs underneath her. The clouds looked two-dimensional with the stage lights off and the work lights flooding over the water. The lightning bolt was lying on its side on the shore. The magic was gone. It felt a little depressing. But it wasn't. Her thoughts just made it seem that way. She tried to rally herself: this was exciting! This was the last step before they went to save her grandfather! And she'd get to travel in a submarine. How many kids could say that?

But she thought back to that afternoon, to Sebastian getting to speak with his mom, to Doris saying bye to Mia, and now watching the team all together. It was getting harder and harder to push away the lonely feeling. And when this adventure was over, everyone would return to their families. As they always did. Like the kids at the Wayward School did at the end of the year. Or at holidays.

No. No. Things would be different this time. This time when it was over she would have someone to return to as well. Or to journey on with. This time she'd get a family too.

That thought, finally of all the thoughts, helped force the unease out of her body, and her shoulders were able to relax down from around her ears. The stage no longer seemed dull, but neat. Watching the technicians up on ladders and the unfurling of thick black cables onto the stage like hanging vines was really cool.

"Hey, Evie," said Catherine, coming over to her.

"Hi," replied Evie.

Catherine stood beside her and observed the activity as well. Several small boats were darting in and out to deliver technicians to parts of the stage, and one of the larger clouds was being towed to shore. Everything was falling apart for the opera while things were coming together for her.

"Are you okay?" asked Catherine.

"I am," replied Evie, looking at her. She wasn't used to Catherine checking up on her. She felt a familiar feeling, like they were back in Australia. A connection. "Are you?"

Catherine nodded.

"This all must be unusual for you," said Evie.

"It is what it is," replied Catherine, and Evie truly believed that the animal expert was perfectly satisfied with that fact. Maybe both of them actually were okay. For once. "I'm sorry again for how I acted in LA," Catherine said. "I'm trying to figure out how to be around adults and kids at the same time."

Evie nodded. She didn't need another apology, but she felt like Catherine maybe needed to make it. "That's okay. Everything worked out."

"Not yet," said Catherine.

Evie laughed a little to herself. It was true, not everything had worked out yet, and it was important to be specific around Catherine. But Evie wasn't going to let that stop her from feeling a sense of victory. The last of the set was being cleared off, and in front of them the water was empty, still, and silent. It looked so different without the giant clouds. Larger, like it went on forever.

"Hey, they want us on board," said Sebastian, coming over to them.

They walked to meet him halfway. "Did you say bye to Orson from me?" asked Evie.

"I don't know how I'd do that. He doesn't understand English," replied Sebastian, furrowing his brow.

"Oh. Well, maybe you could have told him in Portuguese, then?" asked Evie with a smile.

"He doesn't speak . . . anything. . . . Oh." Sebastian sighed. "Oh, okay. I get it."

Evie laughed out loud this time. The old Catherine and the old Sebastian. It felt like everything was getting back to where it needed to be. It felt like the strangeness in LA had evaporated since they had found Doris. She thought about Alejandro, about his warning. About the question of loyalty. About people being complicated.

Maybe it hadn't been a warning but a kindness. To tell her to be more patient with people. They aren't all good or all bad. They make mistakes. Even Evie made mistakes. Sometimes.

They walked along the sloping grass to a small dock hidden behind where the orchestra had sat. Benedict was waiting for them in a small motorboat, and they climbed into it. They didn't go anywhere, though. Just sat.

"What's going on?" asked Sebastian.

"We need to stand by," replied Benedict.

"For what?" asked Evie.

She watched as Benedict squinted into the dark, and she followed his gaze. There was nothing to see. Even the horizon was invisible in the distance.

And then.

Evie stared as the water began to ripple and then

bubble, and waves were created as the water flowed down and away from the top of the submarine emerging from the deep. It gave Evie a tingle up her spine, not of fear but of excitement. A sense that this was both an ending to something and a beginning.

Once the hatch door was fully out in the open, the water calmed, and there was stillness again.

"Can we go now?" asked Evie, turning to Catherine.

"In a second," she replied, watching for something. So Evie watched too, waiting for something mystical maybe, something thrilling, something . . . special.

The hatch of the submarine opened then, and the Kid could be seen grinning in the faint light from within.

"All aboard, mateys!" he called.

# ≻ CHAPTER 34 ≺

## In which we get to
## experience the submarine.

"You made it," said the Kid as Evie hopped onto the floor of the submarine. It echoed her landing with a dull tin bonk sound.

"It was just a ladder," she replied with a smile. Certainly it was nothing compared to climbing down the inside of the Vertiginous Volcano.

"True."

The other explorers had gone ahead, but she and the Kid waited for Sebastian to join them. Once he was in, the Kid hit a large yellow button on the wall and the hatch closed above with a loud shocking clang.

"Follow me!" he said, and they did.

Their steps were tinny as they walked. You definitely couldn't stalk someone in here; you'd hear them a mile away. Probably a good thing, considering that the men in black were still after them. The corridor was narrow, and the ceiling low and made from a dark metal held together with huge bolts like someone had really taken the job of "this thing has to go underwater" very seriously.

Then Evie realized that that someone was Doris, that she had built this whole ship. Evie was suddenly super-impressed. As they continued to make their way to the front, Evie was astonished by the size of thing. It hadn't seemed quite so big on the outside.

Soon they were in the main cabin. The "bridge." Evie looked around. It reminded her of something— the thick wooden table, leather chairs and couches, dark green painted walls—and then she saw the photos of the team, including her grandfather. That was it! It felt like home, or at least like the Explorers Society building that she now called home.

The Kid marched ahead of them and hopped onto the raised platform by the large curved windows that gave the slight impression that the group was inside a giant fishbowl. He pulled at the drop cloth hiding something lumpy in the middle and uncovered a console of brass, with glass dials and a large leather swivel chair that turned a little with the enthusiasm of the reveal.

"Cool," said Evie.

"Yes," agreed Sebastian.

The Kid sat down in the chair and swiveled to face them, grinning so widely that he looked pretty ridiculous. But it was nice to see him so happy.

"The leather still fits the shape of my butt!" he said with enthusiasm.

"Oh, Jason," sighed Catherine as she walked around the console and handed him a notebook.

"It does! It's like coming home again!" he said, opening the book. He turned to the console, and with his back to them said, "Hello, old friend."

Evie smiled.

He glanced over his shoulder. "You wanna come see?"

Evie nodded, and she and Sebastian made their way up to the Kid, passing Benedict, who was unfurling a map on the long table, and Catherine, who was going over to help him. Evie and Sebastian climbed the two steps. Evie stared at the blackness before them. It was a little creepy, not knowing what was out there.

Then she came up behind the Kid, taking his right side, and Sebastian took his left. Up close she could see

a series of dials behind glass and a large compass in the middle jiggling a bit when the Kid placed the notebook next to it. In front there were two large levers, one, it seemed, for each hand. There were also buttons that ran the length of the console. They glowed different colors.

The Kid looked up. "Want to see something neat?"

Evie nodded, and Sebastian said, "Sure."

The Kid pushed the large glowing blue button directly ahead of where Evie was standing. Suddenly it was no longer dark outside the glass. A bright turquoise blue shone before them, and a passing yellow fish stared at the windows in shock and swam off in haste.[15] In the distance, Evie could see some shapes, almost like she was looking at mountains along the skyline.

"Whoa," she said.

"Headlights," replied the Kid.

"So what is that, exactly?" asked Sebastian, pointing to the book.

"Some old notes I made back in the day. Funny to look at paper, isn't it? Kind of nice, though. It's been ages since I've driven this thing, so it's some reminders, a little advice to myself. And of course a few num-

---

[15] And also in the water.

bers. Can't go below sixty-three right here, see?" He pointed to the page in the notebook and then pointed to a dial on the left.

"Okay, yeah. What's that?" asked Sebastian.

"Pressure. Outside the submarine. As you said, we don't have the EM-7056 anymore, so we can only go so deep. It's not a big worry. We're at the level for a normal submarine at present. We can handle the pressure. But I'm used to being able to go way lower, so, you know, have to remind myself. Don't want to kill everyone on board!" He laughed heartily at that.

Neither Sebastian nor Evie did.

He noticed that.

"You kids have been through a lot, haven't you?" he said, becoming serious.

Evie nodded. "I mean, it's been fun at times, and fun maybe after the fact. But sometimes . . ."

"It's been scary," finished Sebastian.

"Well, you guys are very brave, and very smart. And you're lucky to have each other. You're a good team."

Evie smiled and looked at Sebastian, who looked back with an expression that was kind of sad. She didn't get it.

"You guys should come up with a team name!" said the Kid, now smiling again.

Evie's gut twisted. "Oh," she said.

"Oh?" asked the Kid.

"I thought we were part of your team."

The Kid paused for a moment. A moment that felt a bit too long, and then his eyes widened and brightened. "Yeah! Of course. You totally are, of course!"

"I mean, that doesn't really work," said Sebastian a little quietly.

"Why?" asked Evie. They were totally part of the team. They belonged. They . . . did.

"I mean, the name of the team is how many people are in it. And it's alliterative. The same letter starts each word. So 'Filipendulous Five' makes sense. Filipendulous Seven . . ." He stopped talking when he made eye contact with her.

"Ah, what's in a name?" said the Kid, waving off the argument. "Anyway, I actually have to get to work here, so . . ." His voice faded and he stared at them.

"I guess we'll go, then," replied Evie. She turned and looked toward the rear of the cabin. Catherine and Benedict were hunched over the map, and Doris was off somewhere tinkering. Evie felt a little useless, so she wandered over to the glass windows and sat down in front of them. The way the glass curved and how close she was to the ocean made it kind of feel like she was floating in the water too. A pair of jelly-fish bobbed past her in a very chill manner.

Sebastian sat beside her.

"I'm sorry," he said.

"For what?" she asked. She squinted at the blue before her and saw an outline of a school of fish all swimming together in perfect unison.

"For . . ." He paused. "You got upset."

Evie shook her head. "I'm not upset." She was, though. She knew she was, but she didn't like that she was, so maybe if she pretended that she wasn't, she wouldn't be.

"Do you . . . Do you want to come up with a team name?" he asked. "Like, our team name, just you and me?"

Evie had to look at him now. She was rather sur-prised. That was not a Sebastian thing to ask. It was too . . . creative.

"No, that's okay."

Sebastian glanced toward the explorers doing their various jobs and then back at her. "The Fearless Duo?" he asked.

Evie guffawed then.

"What?" asked Sebastian.

"No, it's cute that you want to do this. Okay. Well,

we should probably make it like the Filipendulous Five, with the same letter at the start." She was humoring him humoring her. It was strange. But also a bit fun.

"So something that starts with *D*?" he asked.

"Yeah." Evie thought for a moment. "The Daring Duo?" she said.

"Hmm . . ." Sebastian seemed unsure.

"Come on. We're pretty daring," she said.

"I don't feel it. I feel like everything we've done so far was simply what had to be done."

"Sebastian! You've hung out of a helicopter on a rope! You played drums onstage in front of thousands!" How could he not see it?

"But it was necessary."

"Not everyone would do that, you know." Sebastian seemed super unsure. "They really wouldn't."

"I guess." He seemed more scared than anything.

"Well, I think that's our team name. I have decided."

"The Daring Duo?" asked Sebastian.

"Yes." She grinned at him. "The Daring Duo."

# CHAPTER 35

## In which we're off!

"Okay. We're ready to go! Everyone, seat belts!" announced Doris, appearing from a hatch in the middle of the wooden floor in front of the large table.

Sebastian jumped at her sudden appearance and was up on his feet instantly. If there was one thing he believed in, it was being strapped down inside a moving vehicle. No one had to order him twice!

The only problem was . . . "Where do we sit?" he asked.

"Ah!" said Doris with that mischievous grin. "Jason, if you please!"

The Kid mirrored the grin with one of his own and then hit a yellow button on his console. There was a rumble from somewhere below, and then four chairs emerged from within the platform and rose next to the console, two on each side. They settled to a stop. And the rumbling ceased.

"Cool," said Evie, going over to one to check it out. Sebastian did too and noticed on closer inspection that one brown leather chair had an imprint of a fox on the back of it.

He looked at the one Evie was staring at, and there was a camera tooled into the leather. They both made their way to the other side and saw a wrench on one and a compass on the last. Evie touched the imprinted material softly with her hand.

"Would you like to sit in Alistair's chair?" asked Doris, placing a hand on Evie's shoulder. Evie didn't say anything, just nodded. She carefully climbed into it and sat, her arms on the rests. A bit like a little queen. She smiled at Sebastian. "Sebastian, take my seat," said Doris, pointing to the chair with the wrench imprint.

"Oh no, that's okay," he said. Though, as he said it, he glanced around for where exactly he could sit that would be safe and had a seat belt.

"No, please do. I have to stay with the engines and keep a close eye on them. I haven't driven this gal such a distance in a very long time." Doris wiped her forehead with a handkerchief and looked around the room with pride.

"As long as you're sure," he said.

"I'm sure, I'm sure. Sit, sit," she said, and without actually waiting for his answer, she turned and made her way back to the trapdoor in the floor.

Sebastian watched Evie, who seemed to be really enjoying sitting in her grandfather's chair, and then he turned and climbed into his. It was a very comfortable chair, he had to admit, and it was hard not to put his arms on the rests as if he was on a throne. He peered down to one side and was thrilled to see a seat belt. He grabbed it and attached it into its other side.

To his left, beyond Evie, Catherine and Benedict were sitting down too. Benedict seemed engrossed in his map, hardly caring where he was, but Catherine had an odd look on her face as she got comfortable. Almost like she was scared the chair was going to eat her. Which was strange, since for one thing, chairs don't do that,[16] and for another, even if the chair were alive, there was no one better to tame the beast and not get eaten than Catherine.

There was a whirr then as the engines came to

---

[16] Though, quite frankly, how would anyone know unless there were witnesses, I suppose. . . .

life. Through the window Sebastian could see a rush of bubbles stream past and then subside. There was a sudden loud metal clunk that reverberated through the vessel. He instinctively looked up, but all he could see was the shiny copper ceiling above, reflecting his worried face.

"And we're free!" said the Kid. "Doris has unlatched us, and we're ready to sail."

It certainly seemed like they were no longer attached to whatever had been keeping them in place. The view out the window was bobbing slightly now.

Sebastian watched the Kid closely. From his angle he could see the Kid pushing various buttons and staring at the glass window. He really hoped the Kid remembered how to pilot this thing.

"And we're off!" The submarine moved downward and then jerked to a stop. The view in front of them floated a bit to the left. "Wait. One second. . . . Now we're off!" said the Kid, and this time they pulled downward smoothly and slowly through the water. Sebastian thought it was very helpful that the Kid liked to narrate as he went, but maybe at this point all his attention should be on his driving.

Fortunately, there weren't any more false starts. They carefully glided down and forward through the water, and as they did, fish scurried away from the window this way and that, and sometimes even the other way.

"We're doing it," said Evie softly beside him.

He turned to her. She was staring out the window, and he wasn't entirely sure if she was speaking to him or to herself.

"We are," he said.

Nodding, she gave him a look closely followed by a smile. She leaned in. "I can't believe this is happening," she whispered.

"Honestly, me neither." There was so much about this that he couldn't believe. That he of all people was on a submarine, that he was with an exploring team on a rescue mission, that he still hadn't called his parents, that he was lying to Evie about that, that he was no longer sure about pretty much anything he had ever been sure of . . .

It was a lot.

He was grateful the journey wasn't going to be long and that it wouldn't be deep. He didn't need to imagine the weight of all the water on top of them added to the weight of everything he was feeling.

When had he gotten this dramatic?

"We're going pretty steadily," said the Kid. At that,

both Benedict and Catherine rose from their seats and returned to the table.

"I guess that means we can get up," said Sebastian, unbuckling himself from his seat and glancing at Evie. She was sitting still in place. Staring ahead. "I mean, not that we have to."

"I think I just want to sit here a while longer. You can explore, though," she said, not really paying that much attention to him.

"Okay." For some reason it felt strange standing and walking away from her. Especially when she was acting so "off" at the moment. He made his way over to Benedict and Catherine.

"Is there much of a plan?" he asked, examining the map they were staring at. It was of London and the river that ran through it. The Thames, it was called, and Sebastian knew it pretty well. He'd looked at a lot of maps of London over time. He'd liked watching the evolution of the city from ancient Roman and medieval eras to now, how the waterways were used for transportation and how that changed with technology. It was neat.

"Well, that depends," said Benedict, bending over a portion of the map.

"On what?"

"On what you are referring to. If you meant a plan for traveling to the *Cutty Sark,* we do. It's straightforward enough. If you mean anything to do with Alistair . . ." Both he and Catherine looked over Sebastian's shoulder, and he turned around. They were staring at the back of Evie's head.

"You can tell me," said Sebastian, turning back quickly. If there was something he should know, that Evie should know, he needed them to share it.

"There is a lot of uncertainty," said Catherine. "We don't know exactly where he is. And we don't even know if . . ." She stopped.

"What?" asked Sebastian.

"We don't even know if he's alive," replied Benedict coolly.

Sebastian's heart dropped. It was true. It was very true. They had no real knowledge of anything. At all. He thought back to this entire experience. Everything he had gone through. It had all been to help Evie. But now here he was, in a giant machine underwater, traveling somewhere to help someone he wasn't even sure needed his help. Someone who the rest of the team weren't even sure needed help. And, worse, who could be beyond their help.

How on earth had he put himself in this situation?

Because of a love of adventure? He wasn't even sure yet if he did love adventures. Right now he was feeling pretty darn tired of them. They took longer than you expected. There were lots of boring moments, lots of tedious traveling from one place to another. And then, when things weren't tedious, they were downright dangerous. Life-threatening. Okay, maybe you got to go to a K-pop concert and an opera. And, okay, maybe getting to know new places and people was kind of exciting.

But . . .

What was his point again?

"Sebastian, are you okay?" asked Doris, joining them at the table.

"What?"

"You look . . . odd," she said.

"Oh yeah, I'm okay. Uh, is there some place I could lie down? I'm very tired."

Doris was on her feet immediately. "Oh, you're right! It's very late, for all of us. Follow me!" She turned and called out to Evie still sitting in her grand-father's chair. "Evie, do you want to join us? I'm show-ing Sebastian his quarters."

"I'm okay, thanks," replied Evie.

"Okay, great!" Doris turned back to Sebastian.

She led him off the bridge and into one of the passageways. After a little walking they arrived in front of a low curved door. "Here's your quarters. It's one of our guest quarters. Pretty nice, really. We always treated our guests well."

She turned the metal handle, and it squeaked loudly, as did the hinges as she pushed the door open. "I should probably get some WD-40 for this, huh?"

Automatic lights flickered on in two wall sconces, revealing a cozy room. Though it was small, there was enough space inside for a bunk bed over a simple mahogany desk. And on the far wall was a porthole.

"If you need us, you know where to find us," she said.

"Thanks," he replied, stepping into the room.

"You have a nice sleep." The door closed in a slightly too loud squeak and slam.

He climbed up the short ladder to the bunk bed and lay down on his back, feeling utterly mentally exhausted. Maybe it was time to create a pros-and-cons list. To work toward making an actual decision. He'd been coasting for too long. Did he want adventures, or didn't he? Was he the same Sebastian as he had been before he'd met Evie and started working for the Explorers Society? Or had he changed? If he had changed, had he changed since he'd changed? That was a new one. Had he maybe once thought adventuring was fun but now was over it?

What about the simple fact that the team was back together and no one really needed his help anymore?

His eyes closed heavily, but he forced them open again, wide.

No! This time he wasn't falling asleep. This time he'd find out the answer first!

# CHAPTER 36

## In which decisions
## are made.

Evie awoke with a start. She blinked a few times at the blue in front of her, but when a lazy octopus swam by as if on its nightly stroll, everything came flooding back.

"Hey, you're awake," said the Kid, looking up from his book. He was sitting sideways across his chair like a teenager, knees over the right armrest, back against the left.

"Yeah. How long was I asleep?" asked Evie, trying to get her eyes to focus. She and the Kid were the only two on the bridge. The lights had been dimmed, and everything was painted in a blue glow from the ship's headlights illuminating the water ahead of them.

"A few hours," replied the Kid. "It's probably around four in the morning Portugal time."

"How are you still so awake?" asked Evie.

He shrugged. "It's my job. I'm also a bit of a night owl. You want to go to bed? I can take a break and show you to your quarters."

Evie shook her head. She knew deep down that she was being silly, but she didn't want to leave her grandfather's chair. It almost felt like if she did, it would vanish or something. Which was ridiculous, of course. She curled herself sideways into a ball so that her head was on the armrest and she could see the Kid and out the front window.

"Jason?" she asked quietly.

"Yeah?"

"What happens when this is all over?" She watched as bubbles from the engines blew past the fringes of the window. The bubbles were kind of hypnotic.

"What do you mean?" he asked.

"What happens? After we rescue my grandfather? To you guys?"

"Oh." There was silence, and she heard him softly close his book. "Hmm. Well, I have a new agent, so I'm excited to work with her. And I guess Doris will return to her family and the opera, or maybe they'll move somewhere else. They do love traveling. And Benedict, well, he'll go back to the university, and Catherine has all her animal rights causes. . . ."

"So everyone will simply do what they were doing? Nothing will change?"

"Change?" replied the Kid.

"Yeah. Now that you've seen each other again, spent time together. You're all just going to split apart again like this never happened?" The thought made her feel sad.

There was silence. Evie shifted her position so that she could see the Kid better. He wasn't looking in her direction. Instead he was staring off into the distance, seeming, well, kind of sad himself.

"I think there are too many bad memories. I think . . . they want to forget," he said, lost in thought.

"What about you?"

"Me?"

"You said 'they.' What about you?"

The Kid dropped his head, and she couldn't see his face. "I've missed them. I have. But I can't change them."

"You're making new memories. Maybe that will change things. Maybe I can change things!" She was starting to feel energetic again. The bubbles were less hypnotizing now and more like they were propelling her. She sat up.

"Evie, you can't fix everything," said the Kid with a small laugh.

"Wanna bet?" she asked with a grin.

The Kid's laugh got bigger. "I like your attitude, Evie, I really do."

She grinned back at him as he returned to his book. She ran her fingers over the etched-in compass symbol in the chair. Things *were* going to be different. The Filipendulous Five would be back together. She would make sure of it.

Sebastian woke up and, after climbing out of his bunk, made his way back toward the bridge. He was mad at himself for having fallen asleep. He hadn't meant to. He thought back, trying to recall when sleep had taken him. Oddly, it's almost impossible to recall the exact moment when you fall asleep.[17] That split second between being awake and not was always erased. Like if you were to remember it, it would reveal the secrets of the universe. Or at least some really good gossip about it.

---

[17] Which is why I try to stay asleep as much as possible.

But finally his memory knocked itself back into place and Sebastian did think of one thing. A decision he'd made. An important one at that.

When he arrived at the bridge, Evie gave him a big wave, and he was happy to see her standing at the table with the others and not still sitting in Alistair's chair.

The Kid was pacing while the others were looking at a map.

"I don't think this is fair. I definitely do not think this is fair," the Kid was saying.

"What's going on?" asked Sebastian, quietly slipping in beside Evie.

"Evidently the person meeting us and getting us into London is the Kid's archnemesis," replied Evie just as quietly. She was smiling, though. It seemed extremely unusual. Weren't archnemeses a bad thing?

"Sounds serious," he said.

"Not really. Apparently there was a short period when the Kid went missing back in the team's heyday, sneaked off to his own adventure mountain climbing. The team replaced him with this other explorer briefly. And . . . Jason did *not* like that." She raised her eyebrows at Sebastian.

Oh. "Well, I mean, that was his own fault," replied Sebastian.

"Yeah," said Evie.

"Look. Let me go ahead. I'll get us a boat, return with it, and pick everyone up." The Kid stopped and turned, his eyes bright and excited with the idea.

"Or we could not waste precious time waiting for you and simply use the help we can get," replied Doris, crossing her arms.

The Kid's face fell. His expression turned to mopey. He pouted. "So unfair."

"You're acting like a child," said Doris.

"Hey!" said Evie at that. "We're not the ones pouting over here."

*Exactly,* thought Sebastian.

The Kid glanced at her, shook his head, and laughed a little. "Ugh. Whatever. Fine. But don't expect me to be nice."

"Okay, Jason," said Doris. "Enough's enough. Bring us up."

The Kid slouched his way to the driver's seat and pushed a few buttons. The submarine shook more violently than Sebastian had known it to, and everyone looked over at the Kid. "Sorry," he said, not seeming particularly so.

Water rushed outside the windows, bubbles burst

past, and the rumbling got louder and louder. And then stopped. Suddenly. With a little bounce.

There was the sound of chain against metal as the anchor was dropped.

"Okay, everyone," said Doris, clapping her hands together. "Time to go!"

# CHAPTER 37

## In which we go from boat to boat.

Evie could barely contain everything she was feeling. If she'd been thrilled before, which she had been, what on earth was this feeling now? It was too much, way too much, and she bounced a little on her feet beside Sebastian and (she couldn't help it) gave him a big sideways hug.

"Whoa!" he said in surprise.

"I'm sorry," she said with a laugh. "I'm just so excited!"

"Yeah," he said.

It was hard to know exactly what was going on there with him. After all, he'd been weird for days now. But she also knew that Sebastian experienced excitement completely differently than she did, so she was okay with his withdrawn response.

"Did you sleep okay?" she asked as they followed the explorers toward the exit hatch.

"Yeah." But he stopped speaking. Like he didn't mean it. Like there was more to say.

"What?" asked Evie.

"I made a decision," he said. He eyed her closely.

Maybe this was it. Maybe this was what he'd been keeping from her. "About what?"

"Come on, you two," said Catherine, motioning for them to hurry.

They started walking again. "Please tell me. We don't need to be standing still to talk. And we're always going to be interrupted somehow." There was never a perfect time to say anything. He really needed to *say* it already. They approached the ladder, and Catherine stood to the side to let Evie up first. "Tell me on the boat," she said as she started to climb.

She hoisted herself into the open air. It was so good to feel it against her skin, feel the spray from the sea, smell the salt in the air. She looked toward what she assumed was England, the sea crashing against the shoreline. Approaching the submarine quickly was a really fancy-looking speedboat, zipping its way over and creating a white tail in its wake.

The hatch closed behind her, and she turned to see Sebastian next to her. The Kid was standing, still pouting, staring at the black-and-red speedboat.

They all watched as it slowed to a stop. The driver stepped forward and tossed them a line.

Benedict caught the rope easily and pulled the boat alongside the submarine. "Okay. Everybody in," he said.

Doris climbed down the submarine's external ladder first and with the driver's help hopped easily onto the deck of the speedboat. Well, if Doris could do it and she was the same height as Evie, that meant that Evie could do it. She felt so confident that she said, "I'm next!"

Catherine nodded and helped her slowly over the side of the submarine. Evie took each rung of the ladder step by step, now more aware of the cold wind that nipped at her cheeks. When she arrived at the bottom, she turned to see the driver's outstretched hand. She grabbed it and jumped on board. Evie looked up and waved.

"Thank you!" Evie said to the driver.

The woman smiled back at her, pushing a strand of brown hair behind her ear. "You're welcome." Evie moved to the side as the driver prepared to help Catherine, who really didn't need any help. "So," said Evie to the driver as they waited, "you're the Kid's arch-nemesis."

"Is he still going on about that?" replied the driver with a laugh.

Evie laughed too. "Oh yeah."

Soon Catherine was there, and then the Kid was quick to follow, landing on the deck with a flourish.

"Hey, Jason," said the driver. She didn't look particularly nemesis-y. She seemed nice, her brown hair back in a ponytail, her smile friendly.

The Kid said nothing but moved over with a har-rumph.

Sebastian was next, peering down as he went. He was so focused, Evie could see, on each step, and then on the hand of the driver, as if he wanted to memorize everything. He didn't even make eye contact with the driver, didn't even look up, which Evie thought was a bit rude, but could be forgiven, she supposed. He'd been through a lot.

Last was Benedict, who after clambering aboard gave a big shove against the submarine to push them off.

"Take your seats!" The driver indicated the back of the boat, where a soft couch-like sitting area curved along the shape of the boat. Everyone started making their way to the cushion, except for the Kid, who stayed near the front on his own.

And except for Sebastian.

Evie looked at him, standing there holding on to a side rail. He seemed extra confused. She felt bad for him. "Okay. Tell me the thing you wanted to tell me earlier."

"What?" he asked.

"Clearly it's on your mind, this decision of yours," she said.

The engines started up, and Evie was thrown a bit to the side. She reached out and grabbed the rail just in time. They were blasting away from the submarine, bumping over the choppy gray waves. It was amazing how fast they were traveling. It took her breath away. It also made the wind ten times colder, and she zipped her sweatshirt all the way to her chin.

"No, it's not that," said Sebastian loudly over the roar of the engine and wind.

Evie was so confused now. And she really wanted to not be on her feet. "Let's sit!"

Sebastian nodded, and they stumbled toward the back as the boat passed out of the North Sea and into the Thames. And suddenly the wide-open water narrowed, and banks could be seen in the distance on either side.

They sat for a while in the noise. It was hard to speak, and really, when she thought about it, what could anyone say? It was all anticipation at this point. Waiting. It felt like everyone was relieved to have this moment of time to themselves, even though they were sitting side by side.

She didn't know how long they'd been going, maybe an hour, when the boat got slower and the sound got softer. The banks were so much closer to each other, and Evie could see buildings along their edges. Now and then they passed under bridges. They were getting closer to London. That was certain. Closer to the *Cutty Sark*. To her grandfather.

Evie finally turned to Sebastian.

"Tell me," she ordered once it was quiet enough to talk again.

"I'm having a weird sense of déjà vu," he replied.

"I don't get it," said Evie. Was that the decision he'd made?

"It's when you feel like you've experienced something before," he explained.

"I know what déjà vu is. It's French. Like 'already seen,'" said Evie, a little exasperated. "But what does that have to do with anything?"

"The driver. There's something familiar about her . . ." Sebastian trailed off.

"The driver?" asked Evie. "You know her?"

"I don't know. It's weird. I'm so good at remembering faces . . ."

"Yes, you are."

He looked concerned, but it appeared as if it wasn't with Evie or the driver or anyone else, but with himself. Like he was scared about why he couldn't remember.

"It's okay, Sebastian," she said.

He nodded. But it really didn't seem like he believed her.

# CHAPTER 38

## In which Sebastian remembers.

The buildings had become larger and more densely packed as the boat had gone along. There wasn't a specific moment when they entered the city and went through some official gates or saw a sign that said YOU'RE IN LONDON. But there was a very specific moment when Sebastian realized that they were in fact in the city itself.

First the boat slowed down and the traffic on the river increased. Secondly, there were tall buildings here, and in the distance he could see a city skyline. It hadn't felt like it had taken them long to get into the city, but he was surprised to discover it had been almost two hours. He supposed his brain had been trying to solve the puzzle of why he wasn't remembering properly, or why he was remembering something that he wasn't supposed to. Or . . .

It was definitely a time-consuming, and exhausting, activity.

They turned a bend, and a dock appeared on the left. Sebastian could feel Evie get bouncy beside him. He saw a modern building and then, as they crept into the dock, the tall masts of an old-fashioned ship behind it, nearby, but not anywhere on the water's edge.

"I don't get it," said Evie.

"Get what?" asked the Kid.

"Why is the *Cutty Sark* so far back?"

"It's a historical site, a museum," replied Benedict, standing and stretching. "If it had been kept in the water, it would not have lasted the centuries. As it was, it was burned to ashes in 2007."

"Wow," said Evie, sounding as astonished as Sebastian felt.

"Yes, this one is completely rebuilt. But it's an accurate replica," Benedict said, tossing a line to a waiting man, who caught it deftly.

Sebastian stood and watched as their driver made her way over to help.

Maybe he didn't know her. Maybe he did. Maybe he was going crazy.

Maybe he was just putting off telling Evie that he had decided a big thing. That he had finally decided.

That he wanted to go home.

That it was time for him to go home.

They all disembarked onto the modern sleek dock, with the Kid muttering something under his breath.

"Thank you so much," said Doris to the driver. She smiled and gave them a small salute as they made their way toward the boardwalk. Doris linked her arm with the Kid's. "That wasn't so difficult, was it?"

The Kid shook his head. "I never trusted her," he said.

"We like you so much better," replied Doris, giving him a squeeze. He smiled at her and seemed calmer.

Didn't trust her. Sebastian looked over his shoulder and stopped. The driver was bent over, working on something in the boat. He turned and watched as the gang made their way onto the boardwalk without him, not seeming to notice that he'd been left behind.

He turned once more to look at the driver. Or at least at the back of her head.

That jogged a memory. Much more than the front of her head had. Of another back of a head. In the driver's seat of a taxi. In Seoul.

"Guys!" he called out, still staring.

He spun to search for them, but they'd disappeared. They were on land somewhere, making their way to the *Cutty Sark*.

He felt a familiar panic, and he rushed off the dock and onto the boardwalk. He began to carefully examine everyone in the crowd. It was afternoon, and there were a couple of large school groups with kids a few years younger than Sebastian. All of the kids were dressed in matching uniforms, and they were blocking his path.

"Guys!" he called out again as he saw the explorers buying tickets and heading toward the ship.

The ship! It was amazing. It was a large beautiful old thing with tall wooden masts, and sails furled on high. Like Benedict had explained, it wasn't sitting on the water. Instead it looked as if it was sailing on glass. There was a glass building at the bottom holding it. The ship was sitting inside it, like a tissue standing tall inside a Kleenex box. It kind of gave the impression that it was sailing on a glass sea, even though it wasn't. It was pretty impressive, really.

Sebastian ran to the others by the entrance.

"Should we split up?" the Kid was asking.

"No!" said Sebastian, huffing and puffing as he arrived. When was all this running to catch people going to start getting him into better shape already?

"Are you okay?" asked Evie.

"I remember," wheezed Sebastian. He couldn't get words out fast enough. What were the best words to use that would take as little air as possible? "It's a trap."

"A trap?" Catherine peered at him closely.

"Arch . . . nemesis . . . She's one of them. . . ."

"What do you mean?" asked Evie. He could hear the panic now in her voice.

"It means she's one of us. It's not that complicated."

Sebastian felt his heart drop. They were so good at sneaking up from behind. He turned. They all turned.

"Mr. M." Sebastian said it. He didn't know why he said it. It wasn't to identify the one-eyed man. Everyone knew who he was. It was more . . . It was more like he was saying, "Of course." Which he supposed he could have just said instead.

"Of course!" said the Kid. He almost looked happy. "I knew there was a reason not to trust her!"

# ➤ CHAPTER 39 ◄

## In which we witness a reunion.

Evie stared. There he was, Mr. M. And flanking him, as they often did, were Mr. I and Mr. K. Of course. Of course they would be waiting for them. But she wasn't scared. She had four tough explorers and one fellow member of the Daring Duo behind her.

"Where is he?" she demanded. "Where's my grandfather?" She was so ready for a fight that she balled her hands into fists and held them in front as if she'd totally know how to punch someone if she had to. Which she didn't.

Mr. M stepped forward, and she took in a breath. She wouldn't be intimidated.

"We know he kicked you out of the society and

that's why you want revenge. He had better be okay! Where is he?" She was getting a little desperate, a little scared, thinking that maybe he wasn't okay. What if he wasn't okay?

"Evie," said Catherine. Here was the typical warning Evie was getting pretty used to, that she was behaving badly, but how could you behave badly in the face of evil thugs? The only way would be to not behave badly. Yes! Behaving not badly was behaving badly.

"We'll take you to him," said Mr. M in his customarily pleasant way. "Follow me, please." He extended his arm.

"It's a trap," said Evie.

"What do you want with him? Ransom? The map? Is that why you're holding him hostage?" asked the Kid. Evie could hear the emotion in his voice.

"If you come with us, we'll explain everything. Away from the tourists," replied Mr. M, giving them a meaningful look with his one eye.

"We don't trust you," said Catherine.

"You don't have to. But you don't get to see him if you refuse."

Evie stared at him. Then at Catherine. At Benedict. The Kid. Doris. And lastly, Sebastian. They'd taken these men on at the airport. They could fight them again if they needed to.

"Okay," said Evie.

"I agree," said Benedict.

"But tell me first," said Evie quickly. "Tell me . . ." She swallowed and then raised her chin. "Is he still alive?"

Mr. M stood, frozen for a moment. Then finally he said, "Yes."

Evie felt every muscle in her body relax, so much so that she almost collapsed, and had to steady herself.

"Okay," she said. "Let's go."

They were led away from the ship by Mr. M, with Mr. K glowering at them in the middle of their group, and Mr. I following in the rear. They must have appeared quite interesting to the tourists, walking along as they did. Seven solemn adults, two scared kids. Everyone in interesting outfits that didn't seem practical for visiting tourist attractions. But Evie didn't mind standing out. It made them memorable, and being remembered was important because, well, because . . . in case.

They went back toward the boardwalk and turned and followed along it until they reached a very modern apartment building, low, with only three floors, made of glass and ironwork. They passed through the front doors and managed somehow to squeeze themselves together into the elevator.

It was kind of funny. Especially watching Mr. K trying to keep his scowl while shifting about to get more room. Mr. M just seemed to be enjoying the whole thing.

The door opened. All of them tumbled from the elevator into what turned out to be an apartment. Not even the hallway. Evie would have been impressed if she hadn't been shaking with anticipation.

"Where is he?" she demanded again, and then realized, right at this moment, that she was the only one demanding, and also that the others didn't seem to be stopping her from demanding.

She searched around, making her eyes wide so that she could see every nook and cranny. She took in the space. It was all white and gray, with windows that overlooked the Thames. A large gray world map was framed on the wall, and a big, silver globe sat in the corner. All the furniture was also white with gray, and had black accent pillows. And a spiral staircase in the middle of the room led to more space above. It was all very fancy and also kind of cold and impersonal.

"Lots of maps," said Sebastian under his breath,

and Evie turned to him. He looked at her. She remembered sitting in his room, examining all the items from the puzzle box. The look of Sebastian's maps on the walls. It felt like so long ago.

Map on the wall . . .

Why did it seem familiar?

"What's going on?" asked Catherine. Her voice had a hard edge.

Evie saw that she and Sebastian were standing ahead of the group. The adults were standing in a row, slowly looking around in different directions, taking in the apartment, and then it clicked in her mind—where she'd seen the map before.

In a picture.

Behind the team.

There was just one person missing.

"My old friends," said a voice from above.

And suddenly time stopped. And Evie looked up.

"Alistair," said Catherine, stepping farther into the room. "What have you done?"

# CHAPTER 40

## In which we meet
## Alistair Drake.

Her grandfather was dressed impeccably and very much in the same style he had had in the photos she'd seen, with a tweed vest and tweed trousers, a crisp white shirt with a paisley burgundy cravat, and polished tan leather shoes that clicked as he walked down the spiral staircase. His face was a little more lined than in the photographs, but not much, and his slicked-back hair was whiter, though he still sported that well-groomed goatee.

Evie felt light-headed and rooted to the spot. It was as if every single emotion she had ever felt in her short lifetime had come flooding up inside her and created

the equivalent of the color brown. Just a sticky mud of feeling.

"Catherine, it is so good to see you," said Alistair. His voice was warm and calming, and it was then that Evie realized she'd never heard it before. This was the first time, and she didn't know what to do with the hugeness of that thought.

"Alistair, I . . ." But Catherine stopped. Evie was surprised. The animal expert was a woman of few words, but she was rarely speechless.

What was going on?

Why were the men in black simply standing off to the side like that?

Alistair reached the floor and turned to take them all in. He smiled, and it was exactly like his voice, so very warm. There was a twinkle in his eye. He smiled at his former team and nodded as he appraised each of them, as if he approved. And then he finally looked at her. At Evie. He stopped.

The smile faltered.

His eyes got wide.

Evie's heart was in her throat.

"Evie?"

It was her name. It was who she was. But for a moment the muddy-feeling soup inside her made her feel like maybe it wasn't and maybe she wasn't. She had to think about it. Yes. The answer was yes.

"Yes."

"My goodness. You look just like your parents. Both of them." Alistair stared at her as if he was seeing a ghost. He approached her carefully until he was right there. Close enough that she could smell him. He smelled like pine trees.

Then he reached out as if he was going to touch her face, and Evie instinctively flinched. He withdrew his hand. "I'm sorry," he said.

"No, I'm sorry," she said quickly. He was her family. Why was she feeling so strange right now? Why was she feeling a little afraid? She shouldn't have recoiled like that. "Are you okay?" she asked, moving toward him. There didn't seem to be any signs of a struggle, of bruises or anything, though maybe his sleeves were covering them.

"I was going to ask you the same thing."

"I'm okay." She smiled. He cared about her. Because of course he did. He was her grandfather. He smiled back, though his eyes still looked sad. His whole face that had seemed so full of life was now sunken and drawn. Like he'd been through too much. She didn't want to think of what those evil men had done to him. She started to feel angry again.

"Why . . . I'm sorry. . . . I'm so stunned. Why are you here?" he asked.

This question confused her. It was pretty obvious, wasn't it? After all, he'd asked for her help, and here she was. Maybe he couldn't believe that she'd actually followed through. Especially since her parents had done so much to keep them apart. "I'm here to rescue you."

Again he stared at her. This was not the joyous reunion she'd anticipated. There was way more staring and looking and furrowing of brows than she had anticipated.

"But . . . why?"

"Because you asked me to," she said, her voice accidentally cracking and revealing the emotions she was so desperately trying to hide. Didn't he want her to rescue him?

"That's not true," he said, shaking his head firmly.

"You did!" said Evie. It was impossible to stay calm now. The mud feelings were separating back into their distinct parts, and her anxiety was rising to the surface. "You sent me a letter."

"No." Alistair said it more to himself than to her.

"You did. Mrs. Anderson gave me the letter." She was not going to back down. This was important. She had done what he'd asked.

"I sent the Andersons a letter, yes," he said slowly. "I sent them a letter asking them to protect the key. And I sent the team letters. . . ."

"But in the letter to the Andersons you said . . ." Evie stopped. Her hand went over her mouth in shock. It was her turn to stare at her grandfather, wide-eyed.

"What's going on?" asked the Kid, removing his sunglasses and pinching the bridge of his nose.

"I know," said Benedict, slowly and calmly, as always.

Everyone stared at him. Except Sebastian. That was when Evie realized that he was watching her. It made her feel even more vulnerable. For the first time in their short friendship she kind of wished he wasn't there.

"Oh yes, Benedict. You do know everything, don't you?" said Alistair with a heavy sigh, something akin to a roll of the eyes. This attitude really startled Evie and seemed so out of character for such a dignified man.

"Tell me I'm wrong, then," Benedict said.

"About what?"

"About how you were never in danger to begin with. That this was all a trick to get the team back together, that you need us for something. You knew that the only way we'd join up again was in response to our misplaced sense of loyalty to you. To each other. Tell me I'm wrong about how these men work for you. About how you have threatened the lives of children, of your own granddaughter—"

"I had no idea about Evie or that one over there. None," said Alistair, walking over to Benedict. "What kind of monster do you think I am?"

They were standing almost nose to nose now. Her grandfather was clearly upset, but of course Benedict was as calm as ever. "Don't ask me questions you won't like the answers to," Benedict replied.

Evie couldn't stand it anymore. "I don't understand,"

she said, and only then realized that tears were welling up. She choked them down as best she could. "I don't . . . Are you in danger? You said you were in danger."

"He's not in danger, Evie," replied the Kid, sliding his sunglasses back on and sighing.

"But the letter to the Andersons. The secret message in the letters to everyone else about the *Cutty Sark*. He said he was in danger." It didn't make sense; none of it made sense.

"It was a lie," said Doris.

"No," whispered Evie.

"Yes," said Alistair to her. "Oh, my dear girl, I'm so sorry. I had no intention for you to find yourself in this mess."

"I . . . thought you were dying. I thought . . . You lied?" Evie was shaking now. Her whole body was shaking.

Alistair came over to her and crouched, placing a hand on each of her shoulders.

"Don't touch her," said Sebastian.

Evie didn't turn to look at him. She was so mesmerized by her grandfather actually holding her. "It's okay," she said to Sebastian softly.

"This is a very complicated situation. And yes, I lied. But not all lies are bad," he said. His face was still sad, but his voice was warming up again. It was hard to know what to feel. A moment ago it had been really scary, watching him attempt to stare down Benedict, but now he seemed so kind and caring.

"I don't know," she said. She didn't really like most lies.

"Will you let me explain?" he asked.

She nodded. She definitely needed an explanation, that was for sure.

Alistair stood. "Will you all let me explain?"

Nobody said anything. No one made a sound. And then something that Evie never would have imagined happened.

Benedict did the most astonishing thing she'd ever seen him do.

He started to laugh.

# ➤ CHAPTER 41 ◀

## In which the past is revisited, but not in that fun time-travel way, or even that *Grand Estate* reality-show way.

At first Sebastian worried that Benedict was choking on something. He raced through his memories, trying to recapture the facts of that one health and safety class he'd taken at school that one time. But just as he found the memory, he realized that Benedict wasn't having trouble breathing. He was laughing. Actually laughing.

It was really strange. Even unsettling. And Sebastian was clearly not the only person who thought so. No one said anything. Even the men in black, who had now made their way to the long white sofa along the wall and sat on it next to each other a bit like birds on a wire, looked concerned. Even Mr. I, who was still wearing his reflective sunglasses.

Everyone allowed Benedict to finish, watching as the man finally sighed and wiped the tears from his eyes. "I knew it. I knew it. I thought maybe he had changed. I thought he truly needed my help. It's laughable, isn't it?" He looked at Alistair, who was frowning at him now. "No, please. Please, Alistair. Explain. I'm sure whatever you have to say will make your actions perfectly acceptable. I'm so sure there's a very clever explanation. As there always is."

There was another long pause.

"Well, I don't know about the rest of you, but I need to sit down," said Doris, marching over to a tall white wingback chair and flopping down onto it. Her legs didn't quite touch the ground.

"Good idea. And I'll make tea for everyone," added the Kid. He walked over to the open-concept kitchen, all gleaming steel and black marble, and began to hunt around as if it was his own apartment.

"So come on," said Benedict, sitting on a hard wooden chair at the dining room table. "Tell us."

Sebastian watched closely as Alistair rose from his crouch in front of Evie and took a deep breath. It looked like he was trying to calm himself down, though why he needed to, Sebastian didn't understand. Sebastian thought everyone was being pretty reasonable. Especially considering that Alistair had tricked them all.

"Let's sit," Alistair said calmly. And he gestured for them to follow him into the living area, where Doris and the men in black were already waiting. Catherine took a seat on a small gray chaise longue, and Evie sat on the low ottoman next to Doris. Alistair took the second wingback chair. There was nowhere else really to sit, aside from the couch with the men in black on it, so Sebastian sat down on the shaggy white carpet and crossed his legs.

No one said anything, just waited for Alistair to start. After a moment, he did.

"It's been a very long time since the team disbanded. And yet in that time there hasn't been a single day when I haven't thought of you, haven't longed to see you. Some of you were more willing to communicate than others." He looked at Catherine, who was staring at him hard. "And all I could think about was how fate had ended such a profound friendship. All I could think about were the explorations left unexplored, the plans left unfulfilled. It was hard."

He seemed genuinely upset as he spoke, but there was something Sebastian didn't trust.

"Get to the point, please," said Benedict. He was calm again now, back to his old self.

"This is the point, Benedict," replied Alistair.

"I understand your philosophy, and your longing. I want to know why you brought us together. Why we're here. Why you lied to us." Benedict leaned back against the wooden chair so far that the front feet rose off the floor.

"I had to, don't you see?" said Alistair, mirroring him by leaning far forward and gesturing with his hands. "None of you would be here if I'd just asked. Because of your own shame. I have tried so hard to convince you, to tell you that we are the good guys. We didn't do anything wrong. We weren't monsters."

Benedict shook his head but stayed perfectly neutral. "This was always your problem, Alistair. You always thought that things were so easy to divide between bad and good. But good people can do bad things. We did a bad thing."

"No, we didn't!" Alistair was up on his feet, his face turning red. It was a little scary. "It was an accident. Accidents happen."

Sebastian looked over and stared at Evie hard. Hoping maybe the intensity with which he was staring would get her to look at him. He knew that made no sense. But short of calling out her name . . .

"It *was* an accident," said Catherine, finally speaking up. She looked calm and composed. "But it wouldn't have happened if we hadn't been there. If we hadn't pushed so hard. If I . . ."

"It wasn't your fault," said Doris gently, standing up and putting a hand on Catherine's shoulder. Doris whispered something into Catherine's ear that Sebastian couldn't hear.

The Kid started laughing. "Oh man, I remember this," he said from the kitchen, filling a teapot with steaming water from the kettle. "I remember this. Yeah, this was why, this was why."

*Why what?* Sebastian asked himself. Oh, forget letting the adults talk. They weren't actually saying anything. "Why what?" he asked out loud. "Say things. You guys don't say things!"

Finally Evie looked at him. He was only just learning how to read expressions, and the look she gave him was too advanced for him to understand.

"They don't, do they?" she said to him. Then she turned and asked the Kid, "Why what?"

The Kid walked into the room with the tea tray and placed it on the glass coffee table in the middle of the room. Then he took his cup and wandered to the windows overlooking the river. "Why I left. I'd forgotten. I'm not sure you're old enough to have memories that look better than they really were. But when time passes, you forget about the petty stuff. The fighting. The egos. You only want a real adventure again."

"Yes, exactly!" said Alistair, jumping in. "That's what I thought. You need adventure in your life. We all do."

The Kid raised an eyebrow at him. "You could just have asked, man. Because this is not the way to do it. I'm probably the only one who would have said yes, and now it's a no."

"Yes to what?" asked Sebastian.

"Who *are* you?" asked Alistair, finally turning to look at Sebastian.

Sebastian was startled by being suddenly so noticed. It was also strange to be asked a direct question. "I'm Sebastian. I'm Evie's friend." He glanced at the men in black. Mr. M smiled at him. "They didn't tell you about me?"

Alistair stared at him for a moment. Then something seemed to occur to him. His eyes got wide, and he turned to the men. "This is the key," he said. He even pointed to Sebastian to make it very clear.

"We told you," said Mr. M, sounding a little hurt.

"You didn't tell me it was a little boy," replied Alistair, exasperated.

"I'm not a little boy," said Sebastian. There was no need to exaggerate.

"Please. You can't be older than twelve." Alistair dismissed him with a wave.

"That's not little," replied Sebastian, but Alistair was completely ignoring him.

"You told us by any means necessary," said Mr. K gruffly.

"Within reason. Obviously within reason," replied Alistair.

Mr. I grunted. Mr. M glanced at him and then nodded in agreement. "Exactly. You never *said* within reason."

"That's not something I thought needed to be said out loud." Alistair's voice cracked in frustration.

"Maybe that's the problem," said Evie. Once again she startled everyone into noticing her. "I mean, that is to say . . ." She sort of shrank under the gaze of her grandfather. "All I meant was, you still haven't explained why you did what you did."

Alistair nodded slowly. "My granddaughter is right." He smiled. "I needed the team back together because I wanted to redo our final voyage. It's time. Our names have been tarnished too long. And the waterfall could have been helping the world all these years, not remaining undiscovered and unused. Think of the lives that could have been *saved*. It's time. Will you join me in one last adventure? Will you help me set things right?"

He looked at each of the explorers. At the Kid leaning against the window sipping tea. At Doris standing protectively behind Catherine. At Benedict still on his chair.

No one answered.

Until someone did.

"No," said Catherine.

# CHAPTER 42

## In which there's a fight.
## A really bad fight.

"No?" asked Alistair, staring at Catherine. Evie stared at her too. Of all of them, she had always been the one most keen to help, most ready to "save" him. Back when they'd thought he needed saving, that is. But to be the one to say no? That didn't make sense.

"We are not going back down there. It was a mistake from the beginning. We never should have gone. And we should never go back."

"It was your mistake, not mine," said her grandfather. He was calm, but Evie could sense that he was angry.

"That's not fair, Alistair," said Doris.

"Can we please stop pretending? Catherine's love

of animals is very admirable, to be sure, but it's still no excuse. It was and is the reason all of this happened," said Alistair. He sat down hard in his seat.

"It's not," said Benedict. There was a slight thud as the front feet of his chair touched the ground again. "From the beginning, we knew the journey would be very dangerous. We knew we couldn't predict what was in the trench. We all took the risk. Catherine prompted all of us to act in a way that could save an animal that might otherwise have become extinct. Saving that animal was our only choice."

"The beast's life was not worth more than ours, and not worth the damage inflicted upon the island," insisted Alistair.

"Ha!" laughed Doris, but it didn't sound like a real laugh. It was strange. It came from the same place as laughs do, but maybe from a slightly different, less happy neighborhood. "*Now* you care about the island?"

"I never didn't."

"You seemed at one time to care more about losing our fortune," she replied.

"They didn't need us to fix everything. That wasn't the first tidal wave to hit their community, and it wasn't the last." Alistair was extremely frustrated. Evie hated seeing him like this. Everyone was ganging up on him.

And he wasn't wrong. On the other hand, they weren't wrong either. Sometimes the most violent arguments happened when both sides weren't wrong.

"Stop! Please!" she called out. She turned to Sebastian, to reasonable, logical Sebastian. "You aren't being fair to him," she said to the others. "There are two sides to every story. Right, Sebastian?"

She stared at him hard, willing him to help her out. He seemed a little lost and kind of scared for some reason. But finally he spoke: "Yes . . . ," he said slowly. "There are."

Somewhere in the silence that followed was a lingering "but" floating in the air.

"What? What is it?" she asked, her stomach in knots.

"Logically there are always two sides to every story—at least two sides. But it doesn't follow that they are both right, or that one isn't the better version. And also . . ." He paused.

"Also what?" She could feel anger mixed with disappointment rise up out of the muck and in behind her eyes.

"Of all the people in this room, who was the one who lied? Who pretended to be in danger? Who lured everyone here for his own personal need? It seems that trusting the liar over the people who have been there for you, for us, over this entire journey . . . doesn't make the most sense." He stopped. He stared at her. She could see he knew that what he had said was going to hurt her.

Impressive that he had learned that.

And that he was right.

"So you're basically saying you don't trust my grandfather," she said carefully.

"I . . . I'm saying that when trying to decide whether to trust someone, we need to consider their history," he replied.

There was a long, uncomfortable pause. For the first time the adults didn't have an opinion. How convenient. "Well," she said, pushing her tears back as far as she could. "I don't know his history. I don't know anything about him. I didn't know he existed until basically half a month ago."

Alistair rose out of his chair and looked at Evie. She couldn't tell what he was thinking, and she was frustrated about that. How was it she could understand everyone else in the room better than she could understand her own grandfather? Better than her own family?

"I'm sorry, Evie. I wanted to know my granddaughter. I did," he said. He reached out his arms to her. She stared at them.

"Why didn't you come find me? After they . . . after they died?" she asked, so quietly that she wasn't sure he'd heard her.

"It wasn't what they wanted," he replied. He was also quiet. She could see now the sadness in his eyes. He was better at hiding it than she was, but still. She could see it.

Evie was trying very hard not to cry. Her whole body had started to shake now. "I miss them." She could barely get the words out.

"Me too."

She couldn't hold back now. She ran into his arms, and he drew her in tightly as she sobbed into his chest. He held her close. She'd never felt this completely wrapped in a hug before. No, that wasn't true. She had. With her parents. But that seemed a lifetime ago. Like a different Evie. Everything she'd been feeling, not only since she'd discovered the letter but from before that, from her time at the Wayward School too, from before even that, from the moment of leaving her home with the few things she owned. From hearing the news about her parents' deaths. Everything, all of it, it burst out of her, and the release made her knees weak. She crumpled, but her grandfather caught her. He caught her.

"I'll come with you," she said into his vest. "I want to come with you."

"I'd love that. Family together at last," she heard him say into her hair.

Finally she pulled away. He reached up and wiped her tears with his hand, smiling as he did.

"We don't need anyone else," she said.

Alistair laughed. "You're right. We don't. It will be much harder, and this isn't how I wanted it, but my people can get us there. We have the pieces of the map."

"I won't let you do this," said Catherine. Evie looked over and saw the woman stand. She was intimidating, not just because of her height but because of her expression. Even Doris seemed a little afraid.

Alistair looked at Evie and brushed away one last tear on her face before rising and looking at the animal expert. "This isn't about me. It's about her. It's what she wants. And it happens to also be what I want. And you can't forbid this."

They stared each other down. Evie was getting frustrated. Here was Catherine, again, trying to decide what was best for her when she had no right to. Hadn't Evie proved more than capable? What more did Catherine want from her?

"I want to do this. Stop getting in my way," Evie said angrily. Yes, maybe it was a bit mean, but it was the truth. And what did Catherine really care anyway? She just wanted to prove a point to Alistair. To get back at him. Even though Catherine was the one who'd done the bad thing, even if it hadn't been on purpose.

Catherine looked at Evie, then at Alistair.

"Fine. Then I'll come too," she said, her jaw tight and her chin held high.

"You will?" said Evie, stunned.

Catherine nodded, not breaking eye contact with Alistair.

"She's not some helpless creature you have to protect," said Alistair.

"Do you want me on the mission or not?" asked Catherine.

Alistair nodded, and as he did, Doris spoke up. "Well, then obviously I'm coming too."

"Me too," said the Kid.

Evie looked around the room at all of them. She was confused. Were they doing this for her grandfather? Or for her? If they were doing it for her . . . why?

Everyone looked to Benedict now. It was his turn to speak. He sat for a long time, his calm expression telling them nothing. Then finally: "Okay."

It was all he said, but Evie knew it meant he was coming too. She turned excitedly toward Sebastian to celebrate. But he had a peculiar expression.

"What is it?" she asked. It was strange. She should have been the one angry at him, not the other way around. If that was what was going on.

"I can't go," he said in a monotone. His shoulders sagged, his expression both sad and almost scared, it seemed to her.

"You can't?" she asked.

"No." He didn't look at her.

"Or . . . or do you mean you don't want to?" She was starting to freak out a little bit.

"I don't think I can do any more adventures. It's getting too hard and scary. And all of this, it's . . . too much. And anyway, I have to go home, to my parents. They've got to be terrified about me by now." He still didn't look up.

"Why? They know you're here. They knew the risks," she said.

Finally, finally he looked up at her. He looked really sad and also really, really tired.

"No. They didn't. I never called them."

Evie stared. What? That made no sense.

"But you did, many times," she said.

Sebastian shook his head. "I didn't. I pretended to.

I didn't know what I wanted, and I knew they'd convince me to . . . *make* me go home. And I didn't know if I wanted that. But now I know what I want. I want to go home."

It was like the words didn't really reach Evie until a moment after they'd been said. She had been right about her earlier suspicion that he'd been keeping something from her. But she had been oh so wrong in another way. She had never ever thought that he would actually lie to her. Like, tell her one thing but mean another. Maybe he wouldn't tell her everything—everyone has secrets. But to lie! To lie to *her*!

It was too much. It was one too many feelings for a very confusing afternoon, and she just couldn't take it. Not Sebastian. Not him. Out of everyone. It had hurt enough when Catherine had seemed to favor adults over Evie in LA. But Sebastian? All this time.

The pain swirled around inside her.

"You lied to me," she said. It was the only thing she could say.

"Yes," he said quietly.

"You *lied* to me. How horrible! What kind of person are you? You pretend like you're all logical and what you see is what you get, but no. You lie to people. That's not what a real friend does. You're not my friend!" She'd never felt this angry before in her life.

Her whole body was hot and buzzing. Her brain was hot and buzzing.

Sebastian stared at her, wide-eyed. "That's not true! I was confused."

"Then you tell me about it! You talk to me. You don't do this. You're supposed to be my friend! You are a liar!"

"You don't mean that," he said, his voice shaking now like her whole body.

"I do! I really think I do. I never want to see you again!"

"This makes no sense!" His voice was cracking and getting louder. Maybe for once he would actually get emotional. For once. "*He* lied to you way worse." Sebastian pointed to Alistair. "Way worse! He's still lying to you! But I'm the one you can't stand? Me? I helped you when I didn't need to. I've been there for you the whole time. I did things I would never normally do. I have almost died so many times, or at least been seriously injured, and you hate *me*? Me?"

"It's different," said Evie. She didn't know how or why, but it just was. Her gut told her so. She felt out of breath, like she was running a race or something.

"It's not."

"It is. He's my family! You're not my family. You're not my friend; you're no one!" The last bit seemed to hang in the air, and she could feel that everyone in the room was practically staring at the words as if they were printed on the wall or something. It wasn't true, of course. She regretted them instantly, wishing she could pull the words back inside her. But she was still wildly upset, and saying "I'm sorry" didn't feel right either.

"Oh," said Sebastian.

He was hurt. She knew he was hurt. She hated that he was hurt. But she was hurt too.

"Now, Evie, that's not true," said Alistair, placing a hand on her shoulder. It felt nice, though she was in no mood to be calmed down. "He's not no one."

He was right, of course. Sebastian was so much more than no one. He was her best friend. She should apologize. She should fix it. Even if he'd lied and was deserting her now. He didn't deserve what she'd said. She'd gone too far. Her grandfather was right.

But before she could say she was sorry, Alistair spoke again. "He's the key."

# ➤ CHAPTER 43 ◄

## In which no one
## likes the plan.

It was the first time that Sebastian truly understood the meaning of the word "ominous." Considering he'd been in some pretty scary situations with scary people a lot lately, he'd never really realized up until this point that he hadn't. But the way in which Alistair had said that Sebastian was the key, and the way in which Alistair was looking at him right now, made Sebastian's insides feel more concerned for his outsides than they had been in a very long time.

"What do you mean?" Sebastian asked, because he didn't understand. That is to say, he did understand, but he couldn't really process what was happening.

Yes. He was the key, or at least knew what the key looked like in his memory. And also yes, he was not no one. Obviously. He was a person. With bones and skin and stuff. But still . . . everything was happening so fast and things were being said to him and about him that he didn't really like and his gut was all clenched and stuff, so the question was the only thing he could really think to say.

"I mean, unfortunately, despite what you wish to do, I'm afraid I cannot allow you to do it," said Alistair.

"You mean . . . go home?" Sebastian was starting to get it now.

"Exactly. We need you, Sebastian. We need you most of all."

Sebastian glanced around at everyone else in the room and saw expressions he didn't fully understand. There were too many different people looking at him, too many owners of individual brains and opinions and emotions being communicated to him with eyebrow raises and frowns and muscle twitches.

"But you don't. I'll just write it down for you," he said. Easy enough to do. That had been his plan since he'd decided last night that it was time to return to his parents.

Alistair shook his head and smiled sadly. "I'm afraid

I don't trust you, Sebastian. Not after everything you said. Not after you betrayed my Evie this way."

That made Sebastian mad. She wasn't his Evie. She was herself. She didn't belong to anyone.

"This is ridiculous," he said.

"You said it yourself, Sebastian. You have to judge someone by their history. From everything I've heard, you've made the lives of my assistants very difficult," said Alistair. Sebastian turned to the men in black. Mr. K nodded enthusiastically.

"But they kidnapped me!" said Sebastian.

"And then you lied to my granddaughter, the person you were supposed to help. No. I think I need you to come along with us. It's the only way." Alistair thought for a moment, then nodded. Like he was agreeing with himself.

"We can trust Sebastian," said Catherine.

Alistair shook his head. "At this point I trust no one. Except my own blood." He looked down at Evie and smiled. She looked up. Sebastian could tell she was feeling confused. He knew it. He knew it and Alistair did not. *Take that, Alistair!* he thought.

"You can't kidnap a child like this," said Doris.

"That's not what I'm doing."

"Sure looks like it," said the Kid, peering over his sunglasses.

Alistair snapped his fingers in the air suddenly. And in a flash Sebastian was experiencing the very familiar feeling of being grabbed hard by Mr. I. "For everyone's sake, especially the boy's, I hope we all can agree . . . that is not what I'm doing."

It *was* what he was doing. And what he was doing now was making a threat. At Sebastian's expense. And Sebastian didn't like it one bit. Neither did the other explorers.

"Evie," said Sebastian. But she quickly stared at her feet.

"None of us agrees with you, Alistair," said Catherine through a clenched jaw. "But we understand your meaning." She turned to Sebastian. "Don't worry, Sebastian. We'll protect you."

"Well, what a noble and completely unnecessary thing to promise," Alistair said. "Now, I don't think we should waste any more time. Time to head to the submarine. Time to restore our good names." He smiled widely at the group.

No one smiled back.

# PART THREE

An Inappropriate
Adventure

# $\succ$ CHAPTER 44 $\prec$

## In which things are uncomfortable.

They were retracing their underwater cruise from Portugal. London was far behind them, and all that surrounded them was the darkness. The mood on the submarine was just as dark.

Sebastian stood beside Benedict, studying the pieced-together map. He didn't dare say anything about the situation. Mr. I was sitting on the couch opposite, glaring at him in that usual glaring way of his. Instead Sebastian thought he'd simply talk maps. Or something. Anything to take his mind off the fact that Evie didn't think he was her friend anymore and that he'd been kidnapped again.

"So, we're going to the Mariana Trench," he said, knowing that the answer was yes.

Benedict nodded.

Well, he was now out of conversation topics.

"The EM-7056 has been installed, Jason. Would you mind testing it out?" asked Doris, reappearing at her hatch in the floor and climbing up onto the platform next to the Kid. The Kid nodded and pushed a button. Nothing happened. Or nothing seemed to happen. Clearly something did, though, because Doris said, "Good. We're set to go once we get there." She looked at Alistair, placing her hands on her hips. "You ready?"

Alistair nodded. Doris gave a sharp nod and disappeared through the hatch once more, closing the trapdoor loudly. More loudly than she had before, Sebastian noted.

"What was that all about?" asked Sebastian, returning his attention to Benedict.

The cartographer and photographer gave him a sideways glance and then faced him. "You like maps, correct?"

"Yes," replied Sebastian.

"Do you know where the Mariana Trench is located?"

Sebastian thought for a moment, mentally recalling

the maps at home on his bedroom walls. Then: "South of Japan. East of the Philippines."

"Very good."

The reality of the situation dawned on him. "But . . . we're in a submarine."

"Exactly."

"It's going to take us a long time to get there!" He could feel panic rising within him. Not only had he been kidnapped again, but now it would be weeks before he could even possibly think of going home. "We have to go around continents." The thought was overwhelming.

"In a submarine, yes," replied Benedict.

Suddenly, as if on cue, the entire ship started to shake. At first Sebastian worried that they were in the middle of a tsunami or earthquake, but then he noticed that none of the explorers seemed the least bit worried. He did see Evie briefly look over at him. She clearly didn't know what was going on either. But she quickly looked away. She'd been avoiding making eye contact with him and the others since they'd boarded the ship. To be fair, he hadn't been that keen on trying to communicate with her either. Still, seeing that she was concerned too about the shaking reminded him of their being a team, the Daring Duo or whatever they had called it. And how they weren't a team anymore.

She didn't like him anymore. She thought he was no one.

"Come, boy," said Alistair, motioning to Sebastian from his chair on the platform, the one with the compass imprinted on it. Sebastian really didn't like that man, for many obvious reasons—how he treated Evie, how he had been responsible for kidnapping him three times. But he was also very curious about what was going on. And it wasn't like there was anything else to do or anywhere else he could go. He reluctantly went over to Alistair.

"What's happening?" asked Sebastian as the shaking got more intense.

"Watch," replied Alistair, examining their world closely out the front curved window. If Sebastian hadn't already decided that he didn't like the man very much, this would absolutely have been the tipping point for Sebastian. When people are scared about the unknown, not telling them what's going on in order to be dramatic is really the last thing anyone should do. It was selfish.

Sebastian glanced across to the couch on the other side of the room where Evie sat buckled in. This would have been the time to exchange a look, and he was getting very pleased with himself that he understood that to be the case. But she was staring intently toward the front of the ship. Almost too intently. As if her not looking at him was a message.

His heart sank.

It was a message.

Sebastian turned so that he could more comfortably join everyone else in staring out front. He wondered what Doris was doing belowdecks. He wondered what all the rumbling was. He wondered if everyone else except Alistair and maybe Evie was feeling as low as he was. But all he could see were the backs of their heads.

Sebastian had no idea. No idea about anything. He used to think he knew pretty much everything there was to know, and that the things he didn't know he would learn easily enough. But now he knew: he didn't understand anything about people, about the way the world worked. And knowing facts and figures evidently wasn't enough. You needed to know those people-and-world things.

It was a scary feeling, not knowing.

The rumbling got more intense; the shaking as well. Bubbles were raging outside the window, hiding the rest of the sea from view. Everything was frothy and quaking, and it didn't feel safe.

Then it felt like the submarine was moving forward, but he couldn't see out the window and had no clue how the Kid could either. Sebastian supposed that the

Kid had to be using radar to see where he was going. That would have to be it.

The water outside the window seemed to be getting brighter, the white frothy bubbles getting more white, the blue less black.

What?

They were going forward . . . and up?

"We're going up," he said out loud. He said it so Evie would hear him. He said it so that she'd look at him.

She didn't.

The ship kept ascending.

Why? How would that get them to the Mariana Trench faster? They'd still have to go through the waterways and around the continents and . . .

Oh.

Oh my goodness.

*We* are *going up*.

As in . . .

Up.

Sebastian held his breath as the water rushed away from the window. He could see the line between water and air as they rose. He could see the North Sea and England in the distance. There was a louder rumble, and the shaking was getting more intense. They continued rising. The water got lower and lower against the window. The submarine was now on top of the water like a regular ship. So they were going to go along the surface now?

No.

Because they didn't stop. They kept going . . . climbing out of the water.

"Are we . . . going into the sky?" asked Evie.

"You betcha," said the Kid, not turning around but sounding pretty thrilled at the prospect.

"If we can fly, why didn't we do it from Portugal?" asked Sebastian in awe, utterly flummoxed.

"Because it's extremely risky," replied Benedict. "Because it can harm the integrity of the ship and is only ever meant to be used as a last resort. And because flying over Europe is a lot more noticeable than flying over wide bodies of water."

Alistair swiveled in his chair, seeming not to hear any of that. "Amazing, isn't it?" he asked his granddaughter with a smile.

Evie nodded shyly in return. Sebastian was still not used to seeing her act like that. It was unusual. Another thing to add to his list of why he disliked Alistair.

Alistair faced forward again, and all of them watched as the submarine flew forward. Sebastian stared through the glass as they got higher and as the Kid maneuvered the ship slowly so that England went on a bit of an angle and then disappeared from view when the ship turned eastward.

All that lay stretched out beneath them was the deep blue of the North Sea.

"This is wild," said Evie. Sebastian looked over at her, not expecting anything, but he was pleasantly surprised to see she was looking at him. She quickly looked away, almost embarrassed that she'd been caught.

They mounted higher and higher until they were enveloped once more, but instead of deep blue and black it was white. And then it was very bright, so bright that Sebastian had to shield his eyes with his hand. The Kid leaned over and pushed a button, and the glass in front of them turned a shade darker and the outside world became more bearable. They were flying above the clouds now in the sunlight. The shaking was much less and everything felt rather calm.

Though Sebastian didn't want to seem interested, he nonetheless was, and he walked up onto the platform and past the explorers right to the windows. The sight was rather astonishing, to say the least. Up against the windows, with nothing but the vast view before him, the impression he got was as if he himself, and not the submarine, was flying. Clouds spread out before him, and he experienced a really mysterious mind thing. It seemed almost as if they were the clouds from the opera set, that maybe all of this was fake, that they were in a show.

But that wasn't true.

"We're flying," he said.

"We are."

Sebastian started. Alistair was standing right next to him, looking down at him with a smile. The explorer was probably trying to be warm and friendly, but from this angle, the skin drooped off his gaunt face and only made him seem more like a villain from a nightmare.

"This is amazing!" said Evie. She had jumped onto the platform and was standing on the other side of her grandfather. "I had no idea the submarine could do this!" Sebastian watched as Alistair reached and took her hand in his. Evie startled and stared at their hands intertwined, then gazed up at him with watery eyes.

Sebastian's insides writhed with anger. This wasn't right. He was manipulating her. Taking advantage of her feelings. *Don't fall for it, Evie!*

"We're flying steadily," said Doris, appearing on the bridge. Sebastian turned to see that the other explorers aside from the Kid were on their feet, standing together in a small group looking toward him. Or, more likely, toward Alistair.

"Excellent," said Alistair, turning to face them and still holding Evie's hand. "What an excellent team I have."

"It's not your team," said Sebastian.

Alistair just smiled more widely and walked past him with Evie. Neither even glanced in his direction.

"We have twelve hours or so of flight. I suggest we all rest. The journey ahead is going to require us to be alert and ready for all possible eventualities." Alistair stopped next to Catherine and put a hand on her shoulder. "Wouldn't you agree, Catherine?"

Catherine nodded, but her expression seemed pained. Sometimes Sebastian really wished people would say what they were thinking and be done with it.

"So we're really going to do this?" asked Sebastian, following behind Alistair as he walked over to the table with all the pieces of maps laid out on it. "We're just going to do it?"

Alistair sighed but said nothing.

"Sebastian, we agreed. That's all there is to it," said Benedict. "You should get some rest. We're going to need your help soon enough."

"That isn't all there is to it, though. That makes no sense. You can reevaluate the situation, change your mind—"

"Enough!" Alistair's voice rang out and reverberated in the metal room. Sebastian took a step back in shock. The man looked severe. He let go of Evie's hand. "Go to your room."

Sebastian couldn't help it. He started to laugh. How absurd. His room? He wasn't some kid at an adults-only party. Plus, Alistair wasn't his grandfather. He had no authority over him. And if the men in black couldn't convince Sebastian to follow their orders, this tired-looking old man certainly couldn't.

Speaking of the men in black . . . Mr. I suddenly materialized behind Alistair's right shoulder. Evie looked up at him in fear. So did Sebastian, for that matter.

"Take him to his room," ordered Alistair coldly.

"I really hate you guys," said Sebastian as Mr. I gruffly grabbed him by the arm and started to drag him toward the exit. "I don't think I've ever said I hated anyone before, but I really do hate you guys."

Mr. I grunted. Sebastian was pretty sure the man was saying "Likewise." For the briefest of moments Sebastian wondered what it was like to be these thugs, being ordered around to do whatever some mean former explorer told you to do. He wondered if they had goals of their own, things they wanted to achieve in life.

Mr. I yanked him hard.

"Ow!" said Sebastian.

"Hey!" called out Catherine, taking a step toward them.

"Stay back, snake lady," said Mr. K, pointing his ancient gun at her.

"It's okay, it's okay," Sebastian told Catherine. No one was getting hurt here because of him. That was one thing for sure. She looked furious but didn't move. Her hand twitched and then rested on the whip at her side. To avoid any more explorers coming to his defense, he stopped struggling, walked with Mr. I to his room, and went inside without fighting back. The door slammed behind him, and the lock clicked.

Sebastian stomped over to the porthole and stared out in frustration. The view was still astonishing to him even though he'd been in so many planes and helicopters in a few short weeks. There was something about knowing that the view had once been of undersea life and was now of the sky that was awe-inspiring.

He couldn't fight it, could he? He had to go along with everything. Just like everyone else was doing. Even though it was wrong. Even though they were all being put in a lot of danger. There was nothing that would change a madman's mind. Sebastian had to stay and protect himself and Evie. Even if she hated him right now. Because there wasn't anything else he could do. A man like Alistair could not be intimidated. And he certainly could not be reasoned with.

There was nothing he could do.

It was out of his hands now.

Until he could think of something else, that is. Even though it felt impossible in this moment.

But he would.

He had to.

## ≻ CHAPTER 45 ≺

## In which we experience the opposite of feelings.

Evie was used to feeling a lot of feelings. This was kind of her thing. Even when the feelings were so many that they turned muck-like, she still had a sense of what to do with them. She was less able, however, to understand not feeling feelings.

Watching Sebastian being taken off by Mr. I had made her numb, hollow inside. Now staring at the back of her grandfather's head as he sat in his chair and watched as the clouds glided past, she felt like even more of a shell. Where had her feelings all gone? Had she left them behind when the submarine had taken off into the air?

It felt like she was floating as she walked over to

Alistair. He didn't see her at first, just stared out ahead. And she didn't say anything at first either. She examined his profile. The jutting jaw, the strong nose, the white beard and hair. Then he started, and noticed her staring. He furrowed those thick eyebrows of his and looked angry for a tiny moment. Then—realizing it was her, she supposed—his face relaxed.

"How are you doing?" he asked.

She couldn't answer truthfully since saying she was numb was probably a strange thing to admit to. At least to him. She probably could have told Sebastian, though. Not that she was speaking to him anymore. Even though she kind of wished she was.

"Okay," she said. She leaned against his armrest.

"It must feel strange to see me, after all these years," he said, smiling tentatively.

"It is. I didn't even know you were alive," she replied.

Alistair's face fell a bit, and she realized that maybe that had been a bit difficult for him to hear.

"Uh, not that I'm not happy that you are. I'm so happy to have family again!" she was quick to add.

"I know that. I understand," he said with a sad smile.

"They didn't tell me about you," she explained once more. Now she was starting to feel something again, something small. It was the same grief that always overcame her when she talked about her parents. But it was tiny, almost like it was still trying to hide itself behind the numbness.

Alistair nodded. He placed a hand on hers. "I understand," he said again.

The problem was that Evie didn't. Why would her parents have kept the truth about his existence from her? They were kind, smart people. They weren't closed-minded like the people at the Explorers Society. They wouldn't have banned him too, would they? And yet for some reason she hadn't known about him

until the Andersons had given her the letter Alistair had written to them.

The problem was, of course, that she couldn't ask Alistair any of this. How would he have the answer?

Also, maybe she didn't want the answer.

Maybe it was better to believe that it was all just a mistake on her parents' part rather than something else. Maybe it was better to live in hope.

"I'm glad I found you," she said.

"I'm glad you found me too."

She took in the moment, watching the clouds before her, the setting sun making them look pink and blue like cotton candy. The numbness was going away a bit. She was able to feel some happiness now. The only problem was that the grief had fewer places to hide. And behind it her anger at Sebastian was quietly diminishing, was becoming more a confused and messy kind of frustration. She still couldn't believe that he would desert her, but at the same time she could totally understand his desire to go home, to be with his family, just as she'd needed so badly to be with hers. But he'd also lied to her, and that was almost the bigger thing. How could he not have trusted her? After all this time? That was so unkind of him. That's not what a teammate does.

But she also couldn't believe that he'd been

kidnapped, again. And this time kind of by her. Or if not by her . . . by her grandfather . . .

The feeling she had was anger, yes, but it was mixed with . . . shame. That was the last feeling. Shame.

Evie sighed hard. She leaned her head against her grandfather's shoulder.

"Evie," said her grandfather.

"Yes?"

"Would you mind moving? I have some planning to do," he said.

"Oh!" She stood upright and took a step away. Of course, there wasn't time for the big reunion she'd hoped for. Not yet. They'd have to wait until they were home. Until all this was over.

Even though they had more than ten hours still to pass.

Evie wandered to the large table and sat on one of the couches. She felt awkward. And kind of useless. Her whole purpose up until this point had been to convince people to rescue her grandfather. Now, well, they hadn't really had to. He hadn't needed her at all, really. It had all been a bit pointless, even. But now he was with them. And now she didn't actually know what to do.

And no one really wanted to talk to her. And she

was kind of upset with them still too. And it was all kind of a mess.

And . . . and . . . and . . .

She lay on her side and watched Benedict and Catherine sit quietly talking with each other. How she wished she had someone to talk to. Could she really miss Sebastian even though he was still adventuring with her and it had only been a few hours since they'd fought?

The anger within her stood up.

She could. But she wasn't ready to forgive him.

Not yet.

# ➤ CHAPTER 46 ◄

## In which we experience
## a variety of states.

The hours passed.
It's what hours do.

Sebastian slept through them in that kind of sleep where it doesn't seem like you've slept at all but you must have because if you hadn't, you'd have been really bored for all that time.

Still.

It didn't much feel like he'd slept.

But at some point he must have fallen asleep, because otherwise how could he be woken up? And woken up in such a fun way as having Mr. I yanking on his arm again?

"Is this really necessary?" asked Sebastian, sitting

up as he slid across to the end of his bed and managed to hop off and land on his feet. "Can't you tap me? Write me a message?"

Mr. I just pulled at him.

"I guess it is," muttered Sebastian to himself.

It felt annoying, being dragged back down to the bridge of the ship as if he had no idea where he was going, as if he was being taken somewhere new, when in actuality he knew the route better than the thug pulling at him. It really ought to have been the other way around. But he'd never make anyone do anything they didn't want to do. That was the difference.

Okay, there were many differences between him and Mr. I.

Sebastian was thrown unceremoniously toward the large table, where he stumbled and, fortunately, was caught by Catherine and helped to stand upright again. "That was quite unnecessary," she said.

"That's what I said!" Sebastian was pleased to hear her defend him. He knew the other explorers were on his side. Still it had felt a little like he was on his own.

Alistair was standing at the head of the table, with Evie beside him. Once again she wouldn't make eye contact with Sebastian. His heart sank. Not that it had risen before this at all. It just sank lower. Into its own little trench.

"Well, Sebastian, I hope you had a good sleep and are a bit calmer now that you are well rested," said Alistair. Sebastian had not and was not. But he was pretty sure that Alistair didn't want to hear the truth. "It's time for you to help. The first step." He leaned over the map pieces. They were placed together carefully to create one large map. In the bottom right-hand corner was a missing square. That was him. That was Sebastian.

The missing square.

Benedict was on the opposite side of the table, and he pointed to the top of the map. It was then that it finally clicked for Sebastian. This was not a map like a world map or a city map from the top down. This was instead a cross section. This was like opening up a doll's house and seeing all the rooms and the levels. But this was a cross section of the trench and what lay beyond and around it. There were dotted lines running along the paper, and solid lines. And strange markings here and there. And numbers too.

Sebastian looked where Benedict was pointing. There was a triangle and a diamond, small, drawn right at the top, at the waterline. He did the math in his head.

For a moment Sebastian thought he should lie about what he knew as the key to the map, to send

Alistair off in the totally wrong direction. He was getting really good at lying. And quite frankly, he didn't think that anyone could have a worse reaction than Evie had. Sebastian would probably be willing to have a finger cut off, or maybe even an ear. It was way better than the feeling he felt now, like his heart had been torn from his chest.

"Two hundred and twenty-three degrees," he said in a monotone.

He could sense that Alistair was staring at him hard. Then the old man looked down at the map. He thought long and carefully.

"Good," he said.

There was a flurry of movement as the explorers made their way to their seats on the bridge. Evie went to the couch against the wall, and Sebastian suddenly felt himself being yanked across the room to the other sofa by Mr. I.

"Please just ask me to go to places," said Sebastian as he was pushed into the seat between Mr. I and Mr. M.

"We'll try to remember that," replied Mr. M, seeming to actually mean it. "How are you doing, Sebastian?"

Sebastian turned to him. "Oh, you know, great," he replied. Sarcasm, he was learning, could be deeply satisfying to use even if it was rather confusing to understand.

"Awesome," said Mr. M, smiling. Sebastian had no idea if the man got it or didn't. He didn't really care.

"Jason, are you ready?" asked Alistair.

The Kid didn't answer, but Sebastian did see him give a little nod. Sebastian glanced over at Evie, who was staring intently toward the windows. Almost too much so, like she was trying to prove how intently she could stare at something.

"Then let's take her down," said Alistair.

It was Sebastian's turn to stare intently out the front windows. He leaned forward a bit so that he could see around Mr. M's bulk. Sure enough, they were beginning their descent. The nose of the ship dipped slightly so that the view was no longer of clouds on the horizon but of a vast lake of clouds they were about to plunge into. Sebastian held on to the side of the couch instinctively.

As they passed through the clouds, they were surrounded by whiteness. It felt almost like the world around them had been erased and they were zooming across a blank page. It was off-putting.

Then the dark blue of the ocean materialized before them, and Sebastian found that slightly more off-putting.

As in pretty much terrifying, really.

His knuckles turned white, clinging on to the couch as he was, and he noticed so were Mr. M's. It really seemed like they were approaching at too steep an angle. Like they were falling to their doom. And who knew? Maybe they were. Maybe the Kid had decided to sacrifice them rather than go along with Alistair's absurd plan. Or maybe the Kid wasn't very good at flying this ship. That was also a possibility.

Either way, Sebastian wasn't ready to die.

The water was coming up to them fast now. Or rather they were coming down fast on it. He could see individual waves. He could wave back.

They got closer and closer.

He couldn't help himself. He closed his eyes.

Contact with the water was sudden and sharp. There was a loud whoosh-splash rushing sound as the water shook the ship. It didn't jar him nearly as much as he thought it would. It was practically gentle compared to flying in a helicopter that had been attacked by a soccer ball. Hmm. His bases of comparison were very different than they used to be.

He was still alive too, so that was cool.

He opened his eyes.

It was a bit strange that the dark before him felt familiar. He'd never thought he would be used to being underwater in a submarine. Never imagined being in one ever, let alone having any kind of "Oh yeah, that's what this feels like" memory of it.

The Kid turned on the headlights, and the outside world glowed before them. Everything stayed pretty dark, as Sebastian realized they were traveling down, not along. Down deep, it seemed. Very deep.

There were some parts of the ocean that had never been explored before. Some parts that no human had ever been to. Creatures that had never been discovered. And of the ones that had been, Sebastian knew, some didn't have eyes, because it was so dark that they didn't need to see. Seeing wasn't important.

That thought really messed with his mind.

The Kid leaned over and pushed a button. "Doris," he said into a speaker, "we'll need to activate the EM-7056 in T minus eighteen minutes."

A staticky "Roger that!" replied.

The quiet that filled the submarine made Sebastian almost as uncomfortable as the dark depths they were diving into. He looked around, and it appeared that his fellow travelers were statues, frozen in time. He glanced at Evie. He could see her fingers twitch a little. It made him feel a bit better.

He knew how deep they were going. He knew it because he'd seen the finished map. He knew that the trench itself went to a depth of 36,070 feet. The thought of going as far below the surface as mountains are tall filled him with a very strange feeling. A feeling of being very small and unimportant, and at the same time really not wanting his unimportance to end.

Strange creatures started making appearances, passing by the windows. An anglerfish with long pointy teeth and a little lamp-like hanging lure followed along with them for a while until it got bored. Soon a small orange blob thing with tentacles danced its way across their view.[18] And he wasn't sure if he'd seen what he thought he had, but a school of almost see-through small fish raced them for a moment and then vanished as if they'd never been.

---

[18] "Small orange blob thing with tentacles" is the name of my pet octopus.

No one said anything the whole while. No one commented on the creatures or the slow descent or even the weather, of which, Sebastian supposed, there wasn't any. No, instead they sat there in silence for a very, very long time. His back started to spasm from sitting in the same position without moving. It was only then that he realized how dry his mouth was, that he was also getting hungry. How long *had* it been? Maybe time had no meaning in here. Or out there. Maybe the deeper you went, the more zero time became. Like Greenwich mean time.

No, that made no sense.

At all.

He was starting to get a little loopy, clearly.

*Blip.*

Oh great. Now his brain was making blip noises.

"Did anyone else hear that?" asked Evie from the front of the ship.

Okay, so maybe it wasn't his brain.

"Hear what?" asked Alistair.

"I heard a beep sound, high-pitched. Just for a moment. Maybe I'm hearing things." She stopped, and he knew she was doubting herself. Even though he knew she wanted nothing to do with him, he didn't want her to think she was wrong.

"I heard it too," he called out.

"A beep?" said Catherine.

"Just listen," said Evie.

They all sat in silence once more, but this time listening for a blip.

*This might be a useless attempt,* he thought.

*Blip.*

"There!" said Sebastian and Evie at the same time. This time she glanced over her shoulder but then turned away quickly.

"I didn't hear anything," said Catherine. She sounded frustrated. Not because she didn't believe them, but because she couldn't seem to hear what they were hearing. Maybe the small sound was one that only kids could hear.

"Wait," said the Kid. "You said it was a high note?"

Evie nodded.

"Okay. Let's listen again," he said, pushing the autopilot button. He got up and walked to the far end of the console and looked down at it, shoulders hunched. Sebastian had no idea what he was doing.

They listened.

And waited.

And waited.

*Blip.*

"Did you hear that?" said Sebastian.

"No," said Catherine.

"I did," said the Kid. "And I saw it." He stood upright and looked at them all. "There's something on our radar."

## ➤ CHAPTER 47 ◄

## In which . . . *blip.*

Evie leaned over the Kid's shoulder and looked at the screen. Doris was on his other side, and next to Doris was Sebastian. It took all of Evie's willpower to keep her focus on the dot and not on him. To not exchange a worried glance.

"Keep going," said her grandfather from his seat. He sounded tired and frustrated.

"But what if it meant something?" said Evie, turning to him.

"The radar only picks up things of a certain size," said Doris. "You know that, Alistair."

Evie's grandfather rose with a sigh and walked

to them. "I do know that. I also know that a single blip that no one else heard is not something to end an entire exploration over. I'm rather surprised at you, Jason. Never took you for a coward."

The Kid looked up at him. "I'm not. I'm doing my job."

"Your job is to drive. So drive." Alistair huffed back to his seat. Evie glanced at the other explorers and could see they were annoyed with her grandfather. She really didn't need them to add another thing to the list of why they disliked him. He wasn't a bad person, just determined. Focused. Like she was. Sometimes you had to push through your fears.

Even if it meant being mean to people?

That didn't sit right with her.

She made her way to her grandfather. "It's okay. We're not turning around," she said with a smile, trying to make him feel better.

He didn't smile back. "What happened to my team, Evie? What happened to them? They used to be fearless, and now . . ." He shook his head. "It hurts when someone lets you down, doesn't it?" Alistair gave her a knowing look.

He was talking about Sebastian.

Yes, it did hurt. A lot.

But . . . after so much time and sleeping on it and

everything . . . she was starting to wonder how badly Sebastian had really let her down. She didn't say any of that to her grandfather, of course. He wanted her to agree with him, and he needed someone on his side. She was family. And your job as family was to have each other's back.

"It does," she replied.

"I saw it!" said Doris from the console.

Evie rushed to her side. "Where?"

Doris pointed to the upper left portion of the screen. "Watch closely," she replied. Everyone leaned in, including Benedict, who had joined them. Evie tried hard not to blink, in case she missed it. Her eyes were watering and she held them wider. She was also holding her breath, though that probably wasn't necessary.

"You all look foolish," said Alistair from behind them.

A tiny green dot blipped on the edge of the screen, almost falling off it. Evie saw it, though. She saw it. "No, Grandfather. No, look!"

She heard him stand and felt his presence as he too leaned over. She pointed where the dot had been, a little farther up from where Doris had pointed.

They waited.

And waited.

*Blip.*

It was a bit more to the right but still on the fringes of the screen.

She turned to Alistair. "Did you see it?"

He nodded but didn't say anything. Instead he turned around and sat back down in his chair.

"What do we do?" asked the Kid.

"Tough question," replied Doris. "We don't know what it is, and we do have to remember that we all have a bias."

"A bias?" asked Evie.

"Yes. After our experience with the monster last time, we are obviously jumping to the conclusion that it's the monster again this time. There is no indication that it is."

"Just something big that is moving deep underwater," said Benedict.

"It can't be happening again," said Catherine quietly. "It just can't."

"Why not?" asked Sebastian. "If you repeat the same thing, you get the same result."

Evie couldn't help but look at him.

"Well," said Alistair, leaning back in his chair, "if it is, at least you can reassure yourself, Catherine, that everything you put us through did save the creature's life."

"Stop blaming her," said Doris sharply.

Alistair shrugged but said nothing.

"We should turn around," said Catherine decisively. Evie kind of felt like she was right. It wasn't worth risking everything, was it?

"Absolutely not," said Alistair, rising and marching up to her.

Catherine faced him and, standing up on the platform as she was, towered over him. "Alistair, this isn't a dictatorship. This is a team. We'll vote."

"No."

"All in favor of turning around, raise your hand!"

Evie saw one, two . . . four . . . and then five hands in the air, with Sebastian's added last to the group.

"All in favor of staying the course," said her grandfather. He raised his hand high. Behind him so did his three thugs.

"They don't count!" said Sebastian.

"Of course they do," snapped Alistair. "They're explorers too. They are on this mission too. They deserve a say."

"He's right," said Benedict.

"But . . . but . . . they're evil," said Sebastian, glaring at them.

"So," said Alistair. "It's four to four."

"Four to five," said Sebastian, raising his chin slightly higher than usual.

Alistair turned to him with a smile. "I believe you're the one who said you weren't part of the team. And you're not. You're a piece of a map. That's all." Sebastian sputtered at that, but said nothing. Evie for her part really thought that that was unfair. Sebastian had more than proven that he was a part of things. Plus he was on her team. The Daring Duo.

Alistair looked at Evie. She realized only then what had happened. She was the deciding vote. She hadn't meant to be. She'd been so busy watching the action unfold that she had forgotten she was a part of it.

She looked at Catherine, whom she'd always trusted so much. Who had been by her side in Australia, who had risked herself for Evie so many times. But the animal expert also had disregarded her. Ignored her advice.

She had apologized.

But she'd still done the thing.

Evie thought harder. Catherine always did seem to want to do the less risky option, and hadn't Evie been right and Catherine wrong so many times? Or at least a few times? When it had counted?

Then there was the simple fact that her grandfather was her grandfather.

"Evie," said Alistair, almost like he was reading her

mind, "I'd never put you in harm's way. You're family. Trust me."

It was tricky, seeing as she really disagreed about what her grandfather had said about Sebastian, and even more than that, she really hated his thugs, and they were the only ones taking his side. What did it say about someone when their only friends were the bad guys?

But he wouldn't let anything happen to her. She knew it.

"I vote we stay the course," she said. Her voice was less sure-sounding than she would have liked. She made eye contact with Catherine. It was good that the animal expert was so hard to read, because Evie could now pretend Catherine wasn't disappointed in her.

*Blip.*

"It's back," said Doris.

Everyone rushed to the radar. Everyone, that is, except for Evie. And Alistair. Who smiled at her in this way that made her feel warm inside. He was proud of her. She turned to the screen and saw that one other person hadn't rushed over. It was Sebastian. The way *he* was looking at her made her feel ashamed.

"What?" she asked him, putting her hands on her hips.

"He's using you," said Sebastian.

She shook her head. She wasn't stupid. She knew her loyalty to her grandfather meant that she was making some decisions not entirely from logic, but that was okay. Sometimes you had to feel your way through things.

But she also felt icky. *Thanks, Sebastian.*

"Boy, come," ordered her grandfather. "Let's do the next part of the map." He snapped his fingers at Sebastian, who with a very audible huff followed the man to the giant table. Of course, that wasn't helping matters for Evie, Alistair being mean to Sebastian like that.

"It's not necessary yet," said Benedict from the console.

"I want to do it. I don't need your help with this," said Alistair to Benedict. "It's not like reading a map is actually that difficult. Maybe you should take a break, take a few cute pictures instead." His voice was dripping with contempt. Evie could hear it, and she understood why he was so angry. After all, they'd all voted against him. But their votes hadn't been personal, against Alistair. They had just voted their preferences. He didn't need to insult Benedict like that. Maps were hard. And taking a good picture was more difficult than most people thought, and not some "cute," easy thing to do. Not that Benedict had taken a single photograph since she'd met him.

Benedict didn't reply, just stared. Evie was positive he was angry, though he showed no sign of it. She turned to see Alistair and Sebastian bent over the map at the other side of the room. The men in black rose to form a kind of human wall between them and everyone else.

*Blip.*

*Blip.*

*Blip.*

Evie turned. She had been slightly lost in thought, but the blips brought her back to the moment. She looked at the console. The dot was blipping every second or so, still far away from the middle but moving toward them.

"Any way we can speed up our descent?" asked Benedict.

"I can try, but I can't go too much faster. Doris, can you help at all?" asked the Kid, giving her a concerned look.

"I'll do my best," she replied, and quickly ran to her hatch and slipped into whatever was below them.

The Kid reached for the lever on the right side and pushed against it carefully. There was a grinding sound, like metal against metal, and more bubbles began shooting past the window. He eased up and gave Catherine a look.

*Blip.*

"Keep trying," said Catherine.

"Is it coming right for us?" asked Evie. "Is that us in the middle?"

Catherine nodded.

"Yup," said the Kid. He cracked his knuckles and then placed his hand on the lever and pushed. This time there was no grinding sound, and he pushed a little harder. And a little harder. The grinding started once more, so he pulled back a bit. "Might be as fast as we can go," he said.

Catherine nodded. Again.

"You're doing a good job," said Benedict.

"Thanks, man," replied the Kid, but he looked very serious. The blips weren't stopping. In fact it felt like they were speeding up. "I think it's time for folks to buckle in."

"Alistair!" called out Catherine.

"We're fine!" replied Alistair. Evie tried to look over to him and Sebastian, but they were hidden behind the Mr.'s.

She looked back at Catherine, who said, "Buckle up, Evie. Take your grandfather's seat."

Evie nodded and did as she was told. She strapped in tight and then glanced behind her over her shoulder. Just past Mr. K's right arm she could see Sebastian's head bent over the map. He'd want to do up his seat belt too; he'd want to be safe.

She turned back around.

The other explorers were strapping themselves into their seats.

"If we're lucky," said the Kid, "this is nothing. This is only the instrument falsely going off after not being used for so long."

"Since when have we been lucky?" asked Benedict.

The Kid didn't reply. Evie looked at the seat next to her. The one Sebastian had sat in when they'd traveled from Portugal. She reached out and touched the arm.

"Okay, guys. Whatever it is, it's coming right for us," said the Kid loudly. He did up his seat belt, which, considering he liked to play fast and loose with safety, meant something big was coming.

Evie faced forward and stared into the dark. The blips were getting faster and faster. It was almost hard to hear them separately. They seemed to make one long note.

She was holding her breath again. She needed to breathe. Like she always told Sebastian. She hoped he was doing that too. Breathing.

There were no more blips. Just a note. Just a held note. Like an opera singer who thinks she's an actual Valkyrie.

Evie stared at the darkness. All she could see was darkness. The world to her sides melted away. She was floating in an abyss.

Suddenly in the bright headlights: a large mouth and sharp teeth. She jerked back into her chair, trying to avoid it, and watched as whatever it was swam right over them. A long body ending in a long snake-like tail, gray in the light, slinking away.

"What was that?" she asked in a panic. It was like when she'd seen the baby shark in the tank. Only this was a really big thing with big teeth, and the explorers were trapped underwater in a can.

"It's him," said Catherine softly.

"I can't believe it," said Benedict.

Evie was tossed forward then as a loud bang sounded from above her somewhere, and the entire ship shook, tossing her and the rest of the gang around in their seats. She heard stumbling behind her as the men in black fell to the floor. Sebastian! Her grandfather! She turned to look. They had both fallen onto one of the couches, a mess of arms and legs.

"Evasive action, Jason," said Catherine.

"Already on it," replied the Kid.

Evie watched as the Kid, with a hand on each lever, started pushing and pulling. She could feel the movement of the ship as they turned, the air pressure inside shifting and giving her a bit of a headache.

"No!" Her grandfather was suddenly there, right by the Kid, grabbing the lever on the right and pushing down hard.

"Stop it, Alistair!" said Catherine.

"Just keep diving. It can't follow us!" Alistair pushed harder. Evie felt herself being shoved back into her seat by what seemed like an invisible hand.

They dove and dove into the blackness.

"Stop it!" she heard herself call out. "Grandfather, please, stop!"

Alistair didn't seem to hear her. He just kept driving them deeper and deeper, faster and faster.

This time the beast didn't even attempt to swim over them. It appeared out of nowhere once again, flying up at them, it seemed, as fast as they were diving down to it. The large teeth were bared and coming right for the window. It crashed right into the glass, causing the entire submarine to spin and shift, and causing Evie to close her eyes and hold on to the armrests of her seat as hard as she could.

There was another bang from on top of the ship. And another. They whirled and shook, and Evie was feeling really sick to her stomach now. Then there was a loud cracking noise. Like something within the cabin itself had split in half.

"Hang on, everyone," yelled the Kid.

And she wasn't sure she could hold any tighter, but she did.

The air pressure in the cabin got so heavy that she thought she might pass out. She kept her eyes closed and had a sense the ship was engaged in some kind of chase, attempting to outrun the beast, going deeper and deeper and deeper . . .

And finally.

There was stillness.

And there was something in the stillness that felt even scarier than all the chaos.

Evie opened her eyes. Catherine and Benedict were still in their chairs, their hair a mess, and they appeared exhausted. She imagined she looked pretty much the same. The Kid was slumped over the console, breathing so hard that she could see his shoulders rising and falling. He eased himself up into his chair and rubbed his neck. With his other hand he pushed a couple of buttons on the dash, hit the autopilot, and fell back into his chair with a sigh of relief.

Where was her grandfather? Evie undid her seat belt and rose. It took her a moment to see him lying to the side of the console. He looked like a rag doll, in a heap, next to the window. She gasped and rushed over to him.

"Grandfather?" she asked, placing a hand carefully on his arm. When she did, he let out a moan, soft and low, and she breathed a sigh of relief.

And then. She remembered.

Sebastian.

She was on her feet in a rush, staggering toward the back of the room. Evie gasped. The men in black were in a painful-looking lump to one side, tangled up in each other's limbs, some limbs not facing entirely the correct direction. Behind them the large oak table was splintered in two, pieces of it flung this way and that.

"Sebastian!" she cried, not able to see him in the mess.

She listened closely for something, anything.

"Evie."

She heard it. She looked around hard and finally saw a leg sticking out from beneath the table. She ran over to it, yelling "Help!" as she did.

Instantly she was joined by the Kid, Catherine, and Benedict. Together they dug through the remains of the table. Finally Catherine pulled a massive section of it up, the strain of it causing her to cry out, and she threw it to the side.

There he was. Sebastian. Bruised and battered.

"Evie," he said again.

"I'm here," she replied, reaching for his hand and holding it. Only then did she notice the large table-leg-sized splinter of wood piercing him through his middle.

# ⮞ CHAPTER 48 ⮜

## In which we experience
## no pain.

Sebastian had experienced a lot of pain over the last few weeks. Sore muscles, bruised body. At one point, he seemed to recall, he'd fallen from a helicopter into a tree. But up until this moment he'd never been in the kind of pain that hurt so much that he didn't actually feel anything.

He was a little aware of what had happened. He knew the beast had attacked. He knew that he'd gone flying all over the place, that the table had broken in two, that he'd been trapped beneath it. It was a lot to be aware of, when he thought about it. But he wasn't really aware of when it was, what had happened after that, how long he'd been trapped, or much else, really.

All he'd known was that he needed Evie.

She would save him.

Like she always saved him.

She was leaning over him now, holding his hand, looking extremely worried. But he was so happy that she wasn't ignoring him that it almost made the piece of wood sticking out of his middle worth it.

Oh, hey. There was a piece of wood sticking through him.

"What do we do?" Evie was asking Catherine, who was also hovering above him.

"Nothing. We don't move him; we don't do anything," replied Catherine. "Benedict, grab those men and take their weapons. Lock them up," she ordered, pointing toward the unconscious heap of men in black in the corner. He nodded.

"I'll get Doris," said the Kid, standing instantly and disappearing from Sebastian's line of sight. "Then I'll check on Alistair."

"Doris?" asked Evie, looking at Catherine.

"She's not just good at fixing machines," replied Catherine.

"Is she a doctor?"

Catherine nodded. "She never had her own practice, quit once she was offered her first job as a physician. She didn't love working on people. It was too much for her to handle emotionally."

Sebastian found the conversation fascinating, especially as he'd always wanted to be a brain surgeon. Up until this moment he hadn't really considered that there would be humans attached to the brains. That he'd have people's lives in his hands.

"Interesting," he said softly, and then immediately flinched in pain. Okay, so talking evidently made the pain feel real. Reminded his body of the reality of the situation.

"Shhh," said Evie.

"Where is he?" He heard Doris's voice, still warm behind the matter-of-fact tone. She pushed through the others and kneeled next to Evie. "Hey, Sebastian," she said.

"Hey." He flinched again.

"Okay, okay, you don't have to talk." She eyed him. "Right. Right. Sebastian, I'm going to have a closer look. Try not to move, okay?"

He wasn't sure what to do. He wasn't supposed to talk, so he wasn't sure how he could respond to her "okay?" He hoped it was a rhetorical question and stayed silent as she carefully peeled away some of his shirt and examined his torso close-up.

Man, he was feeling sleepy. It felt kind of good. For the first time he didn't have all these worries about if he should tell Evie his secret, if he should go home, who he was as a person, what he wanted to be when he grew up, how he felt about Alistair—none of it. He felt peaceful. Ready to close his eyes and . . .

"Stay with us, Sebastian," ordered Doris.

He opened his eyelids and tried to nod, hoping she saw that he was following her instructions. If he was supposed to stay with them, then that was what he'd do. He could still do that while asleep, of course. He'd still be there. His lids began to close.

"You can't fall asleep," said Doris.

Again he opened his eyes. He *could* fall asleep, but he took her to mean he wasn't allowed to. Fine.

That would be harder to do. Fine. He'd stay awake. Fine.

Doris stood and then signaled for Catherine and Evie to follow her over away from where Sebastian could hear them. Evie really didn't want to let go of Sebastian's hand. Seeing him in such danger, it all solidified her nagging worries from before. That she shouldn't really be that angry with him, that what he had done was forgivable. But what's more, it sent her spiraling under a wave of grief. This was all her fault. Again. Well, it had always been her fault, but it was her fault now that Sebastian was like this. She had brought him into all of this. She had wanted him to be a part of all of this. Even now, even when he had said he wanted to go home, even then.

"Come on, Evie," said Catherine, placing a gentle hand on her shoulder.

"I'll be right back," Evie told Sebastian. He gave a little nod and didn't say anything, following the rules perfectly.

She stood up.

Benedict and the Kid joined the group.

"How is Alistair?" asked Doris.

"You should check on him, but . . ." Benedict looked over at Evie. Her heart sank immediately. Not him too. No, no. Not when she'd just found him. "It's hard to say."

Doris nodded. She was very serious, and Evie didn't like that at all. She wanted Doris to smile, to make everything feel okay. Like Doris was good at.

"Well, we need to turn the ship around. We need to get them medical attention right away," Doris said. "The problem is we blew one of the thruster engines. How long will it take us to get to the surface?" she asked the Kid.

"A couple of hours to get up top, and that's not including the journey to land," replied the Kid.

Doris sighed hard. She drew her hand over her mouth, thinking as she did.

A couple of hours? That seemed too long. That seemed far too long to Evie. What would happen to Sebastian, to her grandfather, during that time? She didn't want to think about it, but she had to.

She had to.

"Is there any way to fix them up now, or make something temporary to help them that will give us more time?" asked Evie.

"I mean, I can try . . . ," said Doris, her voice fading.

There was a sound from where her grandfather was lying. Evie turned to see that he was trying to push himself up.

"No, Alistair, don't!" said Catherine. They rushed to him as he collapsed back onto the floor. He started coughing. A tiny drop of blood was in the corner of his mouth.

"I have an idea," he said.

"Don't talk," said Doris.

Alistair waved her away with a weak hand in the air. "Waterfall," he said.

Evie's eyes got wide.

"Waterfall?" asked the Kid.

"Of course, the waterfall!" said Evie. "How far away is it?" She looked at Benedict.

"It's hard to say. If the beast didn't knock us too far off course, maybe around fifteen minutes. But, Alistair," Benedict said, turning to her grandfather, "we don't actually know the properties of the water. It might not do what we need it to do."

"Isn't it worth the risk? If it doesn't work, then that's half an hour added to an already long time before we can get them to safety," said Evie.

"I don't know." Benedict turned to Doris. "What do you think?"

"I think we know that it works in some ways. We've seen it heal wounds. Maybe if he drank some of the water, it would stop the internal bleeding. If we poured it on Sebastian, he'd heal up. Maybe." She didn't appear entirely certain, but she was nodding as she spoke. It seemed like she was convincing herself.

"Let's do it," said Catherine. Evie was surprised. Of all of them to want to take such a risk. Well, if Catherine was up for it, it had to be a positive sign, right? "Let's do it and stop thinking about it," Catherine continued. "We don't have the time."

"Okay," said Doris. "We'll do it."

# ➤ CHAPTER 49 ◄

## In which we tell, not show.

"What's happening?" said Sebastian as Evie returned to him. He knew he wasn't supposed to say anything, but he needed to know. He needed her to know that he needed to know.

"Shhh," said Evie, sitting next to him again. "We're going to the waterfall. We'll use it to heal you and my grandfather."

That sounded like a ridiculous idea to him. He'd never really believed in this waterfall in the first place, and now they were relying on it to make him better. He had so many more questions—like how much danger was he in, was he going to die, and what had happened to Alistair? Though maybe not in that order.

He couldn't ask any of it, though. He just had to lie there, staring at the shiny ceiling.

"I know you probably don't approve, but it's so much closer than taking you back to land and hoping . . ." She stopped.

Ah. So his life was in danger, then. Good to be aware of.

He felt so calm about it all. He certainly didn't want to die, but it was a very different feeling from when he'd been in the plane landing in South Korea. The panic he had felt then, that had been intense. Right this moment he felt almost peaceful.

He looked at Evie. She was staring at him so intensely. "I'm sorry," he whispered.

"You're not allowed to speak," she said with frustration. He nodded again. "Anyway, don't say that. I'm the one who should be sorry. I shouldn't have gotten so mad at you. You helped me find my grandfather, helped me stay safe, took huge risks for me. All you wanted was to go home and be with your parents like I wanted to be with my grandfather. And I understand the lie. I don't like it, but I get it. I was wrong. I'm really sorry."

She was so good at understanding why other people felt the ways they did. It was impressive. He hadn't had to say a word. Still, he still felt bad. He should have done more to protect her from her grandfather.

He should have volunteered to go along. Not been forced to. And he shouldn't have lied to her in the first place.

"And I'm really sorry I voted to go down farther. I'm so sorry. If it wasn't for me, you wouldn't be here. You wouldn't be . . . you wouldn't be . . ."

She was crying. How he hated seeing her cry. He knew it wasn't a horrible thing. He knew it was how she expressed herself. But it was the words with the crying that made it so awful. It wasn't her fault. He couldn't not speak. "Alistair," he wheezed.

Evie shook her head. "I know, I know. You're right about my grandfather. He seems pretty selfish. I bet that's why my parents didn't want me around him. But I still voted. I still decided, even though I could see it. I didn't want to see it. I wanted so much not to see it. And it's so hard when someone isn't *evil* evil, you know? When you can see the good in them too. When they're . . ." She couldn't finish the sentence.

"Family," he whispered.

She looked at him, tears in her eyes. She nodded.

*You're my family, Evie,* he realized. It was there, right there. Right in front of him. She was his best friend. She had a family. She had him.

"You. My. Family." It was so hard to get it out. It took every ounce of strength he had to say it.

Evie just stared at him. He was too tired to work to read the expression. Why did it take so much effort for him? He hoped she'd understood. He hoped she'd gotten it.

"We're approaching the tunnel," called out Doris.

Evie looked away from him. She was gazing across the bridge to the windows. He wanted to know what she was seeing. He wanted to see for himself.

"It's really dark, and the Kid is being careful. You can see the sides of the cave," said Evie, explaining what was going on. She clearly was a mind reader, Sebastian thought with a smile. Ow. Even the corners of his lips hurt.

"Okay, so it looks like we're driving right into a wall." She squeezed his hand tighter, which did not feel particularly good, but he didn't want her to feel bad that she was hurting him. So he didn't make a sound. And anyway, it definitely helped keep him from feeling sleepy, so that was good.

"And we're going up. We're so close to the wall that the headlights are showing every crevice on it, and you can see how we're . . . we're still going up. It's exactly like Catherine described."

And now *Evie* was describing it to *him*. This experience, evidently, would only ever be known to him through story.

"The water is rushing away from the window. We're . . . out of the water. There's darkness all around. It's hard to see anything. But I think we're here."

We're here.

Evie looked back to Sebastian. "We made it. You'll make it. It's all going to be okay. You'll see." She smiled at him.

He chose to believe her.

# ➤ CHAPTER 50 ◄

## In which we seek out a waterfall.

The first thing Evie wondered as she stepped out of the hatch was how she was able to breathe and where on earth the air was coming from. Was there a tunnel that went to the surface somewhere? There had to be. But they were in the depths of the ocean. How could a tunnel exist without getting filled up immediately with water?

Of course, the second thing she thought was, *Where is the magical waterfall?* And for some reason that thought felt far less weird than the first, so really, who was she to question what was going on?

All she knew was that it existed.

Catherine had said that Evie didn't need to come out,

but it had been Sebastian with a squeeze of the hand who'd insisted she get the chance to see this. She felt a little guilty getting to have such an experience without him, but moving him was totally not the right thing to do in this moment, so it was Evie, Catherine, Benedict, and the Kid, while Doris stayed on the submarine to keep an eye on Sebastian and her grandfather.

There was a bright beam of light that blinded her then. "Ow!" she said, holding her hand up to shield her eyes.

"Sorry, Evie!" said the Kid. "Didn't realize you were right there."

"It's okay."

"Let's climb down and get this healing water as quickly as we can," said Catherine, also turning on a flashlight. A third beam joined the first two as Benedict silently turned his on.

The cavern they were in was so huge that their lights really didn't illuminate much. Even the headlights from the submarine only lit a path into the water ahead and then fell into darkness.

"We'll walk along the top of the submarine and then swim for shore," said Catherine. "Here's hoping there still is a shore after all these years," she added.

Another hope. Another plan based on crossing one's fingers.

Here's hoping.

They did as Catherine instructed. It wasn't easy once they left the flat top near the hatch and arrived on the wet curved surface of the front of the submarine. It was slippery and her feet were unstable beneath her, but she took it one step at a time until she almost tripped and fell. She looked down as Catherine shone the flashlight at her feet. A long deep indentation ran along this part of the top of the ship.

"The beast," said Evie.

"The creature, yes," replied Catherine.

They didn't really have time to stop and marvel. They had to keep going, and by carefully watching where they placed each step, they eventually made their way to the front of the ship.

"Ready to take a dip?" asked the Kid. She couldn't see his face too well, but the way he asked it made it sound like he was grinning.

"Not really," she replied, but she sat down, following his lead. She watched in Benedict's beam of light as the Kid slid down the glass wall of windows at the front of the ship and splashed into the water. He popped back up again. This time she could see he was smiling.

"Just like last time," he said, before turning and swimming out toward the darkness, lighting his way by holding his waterproof flashlight in one hand.

"Last time?" asked Evie.

"The water is quite mild. You'd expect it to be too cold, but it's not. Not even too hot, considering that things heat up the closer you get to the center of the earth. I guess we're not that deep, though," said Catherine.

"No," replied Benedict, sitting and then sliding almost immediately after.

Another splash.

"You go next. I'll light your way," said Catherine.

Evie turned to her. "Uh, Catherine?"

"Yes?"

"I'm sorry I voted wrong," she said. It was so hard to say out loud that her stomach twisted at the thought.

"Oh, Evie," said Catherine, the beam of her flashlight falling low, highlighting Evie's shoes. "Don't feel bad. You didn't do anything wrong. You wanted to impress your grandfather, and you trusted him. We all trusted him. You have to understand, he's not evil. He, well . . ."

"He wants to do what he wants to do and not worry about anyone else. Like me," she said. She gulped a bit when she finished.

"No, not like you."

"What's the difference between us? I put Sebastian in danger by making him help me in the first place. I put him in danger again because I wanted to go on this exploration. I did all those things." She had. She'd done them. She was a bad person.

"You also told your grandfather to stop when he grabbed the steering control from the Kid. Maybe you go far, maybe you push. Who am I to judge? I push too. I made you come into the water with a shark, remember? And I certainly went too far the last time, trying to save a beast that was trying to kill us. We all make mistakes. But when we realize we made them, we don't do them again. You would never willingly put us at risk. Alistair did. Does."

Evie had never heard such passion in the animal expert's voice before. Such emotion. She wanted to believe that Catherine was right.

"Come on. Let's join them. We have to hurry," said Catherine.

Of course. Of course they did. This was not the time to talk about these things. *Another mistake, Evie. Another one.*

She sat on the cold metal and peered at the light below her. She could see the ripples in the water and also a glow coming from behind the windows of the bridge inside. *No time. Hurry up. Stop looking.* She let go, slid down the glass, and splashed into the water.

It was warm and almost comforting. She popped

back up and turned to stare at the submarine in front of her. It looked huge from this angle, like a giant whale. She could see a lot of detail inside, including Doris, who waved at her. Then Evie turned and saw light not too far off. Benedict and the Kid. They were waiting for her at the shore.

She began to swim. It was tough in her regular clothes, and they weighed her down. But the lights got bigger and brighter, and she kept moving forward until she could feel earth beneath her feet and she was able to walk the rest of the way. Catherine had caught up, and together they joined the Kid and Benedict.

They didn't say anything, just turned and started walking into the darkness. Evie trusted they knew the way, but something felt a little off. She didn't want to say it, though. She didn't want them to doubt that she was on their side now. That she was loyal to them. Now.

But, still, there was something that was making her feel not right. She couldn't put her finger on it.

"Why is it so quiet?" asked Benedict.

And that was it. That was the thing. Weren't waterfalls supposed to be noisy? Even little ones made a trickle sound. Even a faucet could be heard from a different room.

"I don't like this," said the Kid.

They kept going, but the dread was now fully over-taking Evie's body. She didn't want to feel that horrible numbness again, but, boy, she sure didn't like how this felt either.

They eventually came to a rock face.

And stopped.

It was just a wall. No water falling, not even a trickle. Evie reached out to touch it. It wasn't even damp.

The Kid swore.

This surprised Evie. She'd never heard any of the explorers swear before. It made her uncomfortable. And also really worried.

"Well," said Benedict. "Now what?"

"Now what, what?" asked Evie. But she understood. She just didn't want to understand.

"This is where the waterfall was," said Catherine.

"Are you sure?" asked Evie.

"Yes." She said it so definitively. Like she was slamming a book shut.

No, no, this wasn't the end of the story. No. "Like, maybe this isn't the right cavern. I mean, I get this might be where the waterfall is in the right cavern, but this is the wrong one. We have to go back down and find the right one." It sounded absurd as she said it. Then again this whole thing was absurd—the magic waterfall, the breathing so far underground, this whole adventure from the very start.

"No, Evie."

She hated it when Catherine said her name. It was always so final. No more words to be said. That was all. "Evie" somehow meant "It's over."

"It's not over," Evie said.

"It is, Evie."

Evie.

It is.

# ➤ CHAPTER 51 ◄

## In which a solution is needed.

There was chaos. A lot of chaos. Sebastian couldn't see most of it from where he was lying, but he could definitely hear it. They weren't even pretending to hide things from him anymore. Which he really didn't mind. He liked knowing, even if knowing was bad.

"I'll get us out of here," the Kid was saying. "The sooner we leave, the sooner we get to shore."

"No!" said Evie. "We need to keep searching for the waterfall. It can't have dried up."

"Why not?" asked Benedict. "That happens sometimes. And it's been twenty years since we've been here."

"Because . . . because we need it! Because we can't have come all this way for nothing." She sounded so sad, so desperate. Sebastian hated that he was part of the reason. He wanted to reach out to her, tell her it would be okay. Tell her that he was grateful for all of it, even the bad parts, even when he'd wanted to go home. That it all really had been worth it.

He couldn't say any of that, though. He just had to lie there. Feeling stupid.

"Evie," said Catherine, "we have to go. You know it's best for both of them. Doris will do whatever she can in the meantime, won't you?"

There was a silence.

Then Catherine said, "Good. Okay, let's get into positions."

Evidently Doris had nodded, Sebastian supposed. Well, that was good to know.

There was the sound of shuffling, and then Evie came into his line of sight. She kneeled next to him with a glass of water. "Hey, have a bit of this," she said.

Sebastian took a small sip, but it hurt to swallow. He smiled, though, pretending it didn't.

"I'm sorry. I'm so sorry," she said. He wanted her to stop apologizing already. He got it, he really did. He forgave her. But he also had never blamed her in the first place. After everything she'd been through, finding Alistair had been her only goal. Of course she was going to be influenced by him. Alistair was pretty charming, Sebastian had to admit that to himself. When Alistair wasn't being scary, of course.

"Evie."

Sebastian barely heard it, but Evie did. She turned and looked.

"It's Alistair," she said, turning back to explain to Sebastian.

There was the sound of movement in the background. "No, Alistair, don't try to get up," Sebastian could hear Doris say.

"I need to say something." That one was louder and easier to hear. Alistair started coughing, and then stopped.

"Okay, we're ready to go," said the Kid.

"No!" coughed out Alistair. "No."

"Alistair, it's over. It's done. We have to leave," said Catherine. "Everyone, take your positions."

Evie stood.

"No!" shouted Alistair again.

"We're getting you both to safety. Don't worry," said Doris.

"Listen to me!" He shouted it at them and started to cough hard again. It sounded so painful that Sebastian genuinely felt for the man. Evie got up and ran over to him with the glass of water, and Sebastian raised his head so he could watch. He didn't care how much it hurt. Evie helped her grandfather sit up and sip from the glass of water before he fell back onto the floor, his breathing strained. He raised his hand and motioned for her to come close. She leaned in. He whispered something into her ear.

Her eyes widened.

"What did he say?" asked the Kid.

Evie looked stunned, her face drained of all its color. Sebastian had never seen her that way before.

"He said 'vials.'"

"Of course!" said Doris. She reached around her neck instantly and pulled from beneath her shirt a capsule on a chain. As she did, the others did too, and all Evie could do was stare. Waterfall water!

"Does Alistair have his?" asked the Kid quickly.

Carefully Evie leaned over her grandfather. His breath was so shallow that it scared her. But before she could check, his hand came up to his throat and Alistair grabbed at a string. Evie helped him pull the vial out from beneath his vest and lift it over his head.

"Come," said Doris. She was standing by the console. "Evie, dump out the water from that glass."

Evie did as she was told
and took the empty glass
over to Doris. Each ex-
plorer carefully opened
their vial and poured
into the glass the liq-
uid they had saved
from their first adven-
ture at the waterfall.
There wasn't much. It only
filled the glass a quarter full, but it was something.
More than they'd had before.

"Guess I'm going to start being called 'the Adult,'"
said the Kid with a laugh as he looked at the glass.

"What?" asked Evie.

"I always figured that wearing the vial around my
neck all the time was what helped slow the aging process. Never knew for sure. Not until I saw these two
again," he said, nodding toward Benedict and Catherine.

Evie thought about it, how none of them had ever
looked quite old enough. It made sense. Well, not
really, but sort of.

"Come on," said Doris, making her way to Sebastian. She kneeled down next to him, and Evie was instantly on the other side. No one fought her for that

position. She wouldn't have let anyone else win it anyway.

Doris, very carefully and with an incredibly steady hand, reached for the wood piercing Sebastian. "This is going to hurt," she warned him.

He made a face that Evie was pretty sure no one else could read but her. A face that essentially said, "No kidding." She gave him a little smile and held his hand. He squeezed it hard.

Doris removed the wood so quickly that Evie was surprised it had happened at all. Just as quickly Doris reached her hand out, and Benedict placed the glass in it. She carefully tipped the water over the wound. A few drops fell. The group all watched.

The small section that she'd dripped the water onto cleared almost instantly. As if Doris had dropped water on a muddy porch and the mud had rinsed away. Evie looked at Doris and grinned. But Doris wasn't grinning back.

"What's wrong?" Evie asked.

"Alistair," replied Sebastian, wincing as he said it.

She looked at him, confused. Then up at Doris.

"He's right," said Doris. "We don't have enough, not nearly enough to help them both."

"I never thought you did."

Everyone turned to see her grandfather beside them

on his knees. How on earth he'd managed to drag himself over to them, Evie had no idea, but there he was. He was shaking, and she knew he'd collapse soon. She wasn't the only one who realized it. The Kid instantly moved to help her grandfather lie down on the floor next to them.

"I'm a fool. An old fool," he said as he reclined. "He is young, and clever." He reached out his hand, and Evie took it. No, this wasn't happening. This couldn't be happening.

"I'm so sorry," he said. "I really am."

"Please" was all Evie could say to him.

He let go of her hand and looked up at the others, taking them each in one by one. "Take care of each other. Don't lose each other again just because of me. And please, take care of Evie."

Catherine nodded. "Of course. That was never a question. We're her family."

Family. Evie gulped hard. The tears were in her eyes.

Alistair nodded. He looked one last time at his granddaughter and gave her hand a squeeze. He smiled. "My Evie."

He closed his eyes.

"No!" cried Evie. She flung herself on top of him

and held him tight. She had only just found him. Yes, he wasn't what she'd thought he would be—in fact, he was pretty terrible a lot of the time. But now, finally, when he'd lived up to all her expectations and hopes of him . . . now . . .

"Evie," said Catherine, placing a hand on Evie's shoulder.

The tears were streaming down her face and onto his tweed vest.

"Evie, he's gone."

"He can't be," she said into his chest.

"Sebastian still needs you, Evie. He needs your support," she heard Benedict say.

Slowly Evie pulled herself off her grandfather. She stared at his face, so calm, at peace. For the first time he seemed truly satisfied, as if this had all gone according to his plan. Somehow.

She wiped away tears but couldn't stop them from flowing. She turned back to Sebastian and watched as Doris carefully continued to pour the water over his wound. She watched the wound heal itself as if by magic, watched as Sebastian's breathing got more regular, as color entered his cheeks. Her own body felt filled with life as well, still heavy with grief but with a lightness too now.

"How are you feeling?" asked Doris.

Sebastian was silent for a moment. Evie held her breath. Then, finally: "That's a very complicated question."

She couldn't help herself. She was always one to indulge her feelings, but the overwhelming sensation of joy at hearing him speak made her throw herself at him and give him a huge hug.

"Evie!" said Doris. "Stop it! Just because the outside is better doesn't mean the inside is entirely well yet."

Evie let him go, but it was so hard, so very hard.

"It's good to have you back, man," said the Kid with a grin.

"It is," said Catherine.

"Yes," said Benedict. "However, even though it seems very wrong to rush right at this moment, we do need to get out of here and back up to the surface as quickly as we can."

"Right away?" asked Evie.

"No, he's right," said Sebastian, propping himself up on his elbows. "That's the most logical course of action."

Logical, yes, but difficult to do after everything that had just happened.

The other explorers seemed to agree with Benedict

and Sebastian, though, and with a bit of effort everyone was back at their stations. Evie stayed put. She didn't actually have a station, after all.

She turned to Sebastian, who was examining his torso closely, in awe. He looked up at her. She smiled. He smiled.

"How are *you* feeling?" he asked.

How was she feeling? How could anyone possibly answer such a huge question? She was so terribly sad, but also so terribly relieved. Confused, alone, and grieving, she still couldn't fully appreciate the loss. And yet she also had her teammate with her. He had called her family. Catherine had called her family. And for the first time, she realized that after all this searching and everything, she did have people who had her back. Who were loyal to her.

It was a rainbow of feelings drowning in a sea of emotion. There was only one kind of answer to that. A Sebastian answer. "That's a very complicated question," she said.

He stared at her for a moment. Then he nodded. He understood. Because if anyone understood her, it was him.

"Yeah," he said.

"Yeah."

## ➤ CHAPTER 52 ◄

## In which we experience
## a cliff-hanger.

## Just kidding.

This is a story that ends with a pig wearing a teeny hat. Or more like a story that ends with a pig in a teeny hat curled up in the lap of a boy who had always thought he knew exactly what his life was going to be and now had no idea whatsoever. And a girl sitting next to him who had finally figured out that totally by accident she'd found the family she'd been looking for all this time. Or really it's more like a story that ends with me telling you that this is a story that ends like that.

You'd think I'd be a bit better at this by now.

The point is . . .

Sebastian sat at the wrought-iron table in the tea tree house, staring down at the pig in the teeny hat in his lap as Myrtle poured him a cup of tea.

"The hat is a little off," said Evie, leaning over and straightening it.

"Thanks," said Sebastian.

"Well, your parents are certainly very interesting people," said Myrtle, picking up her teacup and taking a sip.

"Yes, they always have been interesting," replied Sebastian.

"I've never heard of punishing a child by putting him directly in the path of the very kinds of people who led him to make trouble in the first place. Cookie?" She indicated the apple and jalapeño cookies sitting on the flowery plate beside her.

"I'm good," said Sebastian.

"Me too," said Evie.

"Yes, well, I mean, they were obviously extremely angry with me," Sebastian explained, "especially because they had gotten the police involved and everything." That hadn't been fun, and Sebastian had been quite relieved not to be taken to jail for causing mischief even though he had offered to go willingly. After all, it was only right, wasting their time and everything.

But evidently that wasn't the sort of thing they put twelve-year-olds in jail for.

"The weird thing was," he continued, "despite all the fear and problems I caused, my folks were also irrationally loving at the same time, which I did not expect. Anyway, after hearing the story, they understand no one here was to blame. It was all my own fault. And they think that my learning the proper way to adventure instead of the inappropriate way is the way I need to educate myself." He was trying to appear as rational as possible, but truthfully he, too, had been stunned to learn that his parents' punishment for him was that he was to continue working for the Explorers Society. But it did make sense. Even if it really didn't feel like he was getting punished for anything. He didn't tell his parents that, of course. Because he was becoming a bit of a rebel that way.

"Obviously," said Myrtle, "we appreciate any help, and, as you know, I've always liked you, Sebastian." She glanced down at the pig. "As many here seem to."

"What about the Filipendulous Five?" asked Evie. She was shifting anxiously in her seat beside him.

"Well, that took a great deal of conversation, but

considering the great sacrifice your grandfather made, and how much they care for you, Evie, and after some conferencing with the board of directors, with West Coast operations, and with some of the international branches, we have, yes, decided—"

"To un-ban them?" asked Evie, jumping to her feet.

Myrtle smiled a tiny smile. Sebastian was impressed. He hadn't really seen the Ice Queen melt before.

"Yes," she said.

"Well, that was nice of you, to make us wait this long to tell us," said the Kid, leaning over to grab one of the cookies.

"What fun is there in life if there isn't any drama?" replied Myrtle.

Sebastian looked at the team, sitting squished side by side around the little tea table. He thought back to the puzzle box, when he'd first seen their faces. They had been strangers, people who didn't seem real. Almost like characters in a book. But they weren't that anymore. They weren't just Catherine the animal expert, Benedict the cartographer and photographer, the Kid the adrenaline junky, and Doris the engineer. They were . . . his friends.

And then there was Evie.

He'd always thought he'd known what a best friend

was with his cousin Arthur. It was someone you spent time with and did things with. But he'd never shared his innermost feelings with anyone before. He had never been so honest with anyone before. He never had trusted anyone in the same way he trusted his parents before.

Not until Evie.

"You're getting sentimental," she said just then, looking at him.

"I'm not," he said. The pig looked up and snorted at him. "I'm not!"

"It's okay. I am too." She grinned at him.[19]

"It's time," said Benedict suddenly. He stood abruptly, and Sebastian exchanged a glance with Evie. Now what?

"Time?" asked Doris.

"I'm ready." Without further explanation Benedict pulled out his chair and placed it at the far end of the platform, then took his camera from around his neck and balanced it carefully on the seat.

"He's taking a picture!" said Evie, her voice filled with excitement.

"Really, Benedict, are you?" asked Catherine.

---

[19] I am as well.

"I am," he said, leaning down and adjusting the lens. "Everyone, get close together. Get into the frame. Doris, I'm going to stand right behind you."

Doris nodded.

Sebastian leaned over to get in close.

"Everyone, smile," said Benedict, pressing a button and then walking quickly to his spot.

Sebastian stared into the lens of the camera. He felt a new sensation come over him. Not fear, not worry, not adrenaline or excitement. It was a calm feeling of being at the beginning of something new. A picture to add to the puzzle box. And *he* was in it.

"Sebastian," whispered Evie.

"Yeah?"

"I'm glad I met you."

"I'm glad I met you too."

The camera went off, and they all gave a little round of applause as Benedict rushed over to see the image. "One more time, everyone," he said.

"Sebastian," whispered Evie again.

"Yeah?"

"This time hold up the pig!"

Sebastian looked down at the pig in the teeny hat. It seemed resigned to the idea of being in the photograph.

So.

Sebastian held up the pig.

THE END[20]

---

[20] Huh. Well, look at that. It is.

# ➤ ACKNOWLEDGMENTS ◄

Ditto all the thanks in books one and two.

Plus a huge thank-you once more to Krista, Monica, my agent Jess, and everyone at Penguin Random House for their help making this series shine! Of course another big thank-you to artist Matt Rockefeller for so consistently and creatively bringing my words to life.

(And as always, thank you to Team Kress, Scott and Atticus, for the support!)

## ➤ ABOUT THE AUTHOR ≺

ADRIENNE KRESS is a writer and an actress born and raised in Toronto. She is the daughter of two high school English teachers, and credits them with inspiring her love of both writing and performing. She also has a cat named Atticus, who unfortunately despises teeny hats. She is the author of *The Explorers: The Door in the Alley, The Explorers: The Reckless Rescue,* and *The Explorers: The Quest for the Kid.* To find out more about Adrienne, visit AdrienneKress.com and follow @AdrienneKress on Twitter and Instagram.

Bruce County Public Library
1243 MacKenzie Rd.
Port Elgin, Ontario  N0H 2C6